BONE & CANE

DAVID BELBIN

12/3.

LARGE PRINT

Oxford

First published in Great Britain 2011
by
Tindal Street Press Ltd

Published in Large Print 2012 by ISIS Publishing Ltd.,
7 Centremead, Osney Mead, Oxford OX2 0ES
by arrangement with
Tindal Street Press Ltd

British Library Cataloguing in Publication Data
Belbin, David.
   Bone & Cane.
   1. Women politicians - - Fiction.
   2. Ex-convicts - - Fiction.
   3. Judicial error - - Fiction.
   4. Nottingham (England) - - Fiction.
   5. Detective and mystery stories.
   6. Large type books.
   I. Title
   823.9'2–dc23

ISBN 978–0–7531–8944–3 (hb)
ISBN 978–0–7531–8945–0 (pb)

For James and Jane Urquhart

CHAPTER
ONE

March 1997

Members of Parliament can be many things. Campaigners. Law makers. Media personalities. Even detectives, of a rather public kind. One thing MPs can't be is shit-faced in public, especially in their own constituency. In the House, it was okay to let your hair down. When you were guest of honour at a very public party, it wasn't wise to be one drink away from legless. Sarah was well aware of this. But tonight she had a right to celebrate.

"Another?" The stocky man with the shaved head and fat neck had already planted two slobbery kisses on her lips. Sarah was determined to avoid a third.

"I'm going to take a pause," she shouted. "I've drunk enough already."

Ed had been inside for several years, so he wouldn't be used to heavy social drinking. Yet he didn't look drunk, not as drunk as Sarah felt.

The PA blasted out "Free Nelson Mandela".

"Want a word," he yelled over the music. "Come outside for a minute."

Ed had been given two life sentences for a double murder. The first victim was a police officer, Terry

Shanks, who Ed had a grudge against. The second victim was the police officer's young wife, Liv. She had probably been raped before she was murdered, but Ed had not been charged with that.

Sarah, campaigning in a by-election that she wasn't expected to win, had made all sorts of promises to the voters. One of them was that, if elected, she would raise Ed's case in the House of Commons. She'd kept her promise, even helped found the campaign group that organized tonight's celebration. The more she found out about Ed's case, the more dodgy the conviction had looked, but his first application for appeal was turned down. This despite the only forensic connecting Ed to the scene — a hair on the carpet — being highly questionable.

Last year, Sarah had agreed to visit Clark in Nottingham Prison. She'd not been in a prison before, so arranged for the governor to show her round.

"You're the first politician we've had for a while," he told her. "We get the occasional judge or magistrate, but mainly it's out of sight, out of mind."

Afterwards, the smell stayed with her for hours: stale, cooked cabbage, probably masking the stench of sweat and urine. She couldn't forget the wretched clothes of the men on the lifer's wing: cheap, worn-out rags that a charity shop would reject. Everything about the place made her question the justice system. It was so hopeless, so hateful. She expected prison to have taken its toll on Clark, but when they met, he was all smiles.

"You had a wander round then?"

"Just a short one."

2

"I could tell by look on your face. It's grim. But you learn to get by."

Ed was far more cheerful than ninety per cent of the people who attended her MP's surgeries. There was no swagger about him. He even took care to look at her face rather than her chest. He had fair hair then, which made him appear younger, softer.

"I've made lots of mistakes in my life, but a double murder weren't one of them," he told her. "Terry Shanks were one of theirs, so the police needed a result. I was the obvious suspect. But you'd have to be bloody stupid to kill the guy who put you inside only a couple of weeks after they released you."

Sarah agreed that you would. Ed didn't come across in the least stupid. Inside, he told her, he'd taken A levels in Sociology, Economics and Law, got good grades. He planned to start an Open University degree course.

"You've got to do something to take your mind off life inside. The time I did before was enough to make me go straight. I'd never risk them sending me back, no matter how much I wanted revenge. Anyway, I weren't bothered about getting back at Terry Shanks. He were only doing his job."

Sarah believed Ed. The more she looked into the case, the more she thought that Clark's conviction was a classic miscarriage of justice. Strong emotions had overwhelmed both judge and jury, resulting in a flawed verdict.

That visit to Nottingham Prison was a turning point in Sarah's new parliamentary career. She had found an area that she wanted to focus on. She joined the Howard League for Penal Reform, began reading up on prisons, wrote to newspapers and the Director of Public Prosecutions, highlighted inconsistencies in the evidence that convicted Clark. The group she'd set up circulated a petition, organized a letter-writing campaign. At last, Ed was given leave to appeal. Yesterday lunchtime, Ed Clark's conviction had been quashed.

Sarah followed the freed man out of the ballroom. In the corridor, he squeezed her arse. Sarah didn't complain. Today, of all days, Ed could be excused for behaving badly. Sarah was aware that Ed fancied her. Some level of desire was the background hum to most of her relationships with straight men and she had become adept at avoiding unwanted advances. Her signals were only mixed if she intended them to be.

Once they were outside, the October breeze sobered her a little. There were other people on the balcony beyond the ballroom, but none within listening distance. Without warning, Ed gripped Sarah's left thigh with his large right hand. He leant into her right ear.

"You and me are going to celebrate in my room. Tonight."

"That's very flattering," Sarah began, then realized the line wasn't strong enough to deflect an ex-con the day after he'd got out. This evening, Ed's prison humility had been replaced by a brute arrogance.

"There are a dozen women in there who'd go upstairs with me the moment I clicked my fingers. You're the only one I want."

4

His hand moved another inch up her thigh. It didn't pinch. Nor did it faze her: alcohol helped that way. She might have found the firmness of Ed's grasp exciting had it come from a man she fancied.

"I'm sorry, Ed. I have a boyfriend."

"I don't give a shit," Ed whispered, hand stretching to the panty line. "You want me too. I know what makes you tick. When you visited me inside, I could see you thinking, *I hope he's innocent, because I really want to fuck him.*"

"You've got it wrong. I helped you because you're one of my constituents, nothing more. Now I have to go."

She pulled away.

"My room's number seven, when you change your mind."

Ed wasn't a bad bloke. He was a randy, working class lad with a home-made tattoo on one arm and a hard-on for his local MP. Sarah empathised. When you'd served four and a half years for a crime you didn't commit, you were desperate to get your end away. But she'd never succumbed to doling out a sympathy shag, not even with men she fancied. Not even when pissed.

Tonight, Ed had handled rejection well, all things considered. She'd had to fight off more assertive approaches from half a dozen of her fellow MPs. But now it was time to leave. Sarah hurried past several couples and found herself in the corridor behind the back of the over-lit ballroom. She'd noticed a public phone booth somewhere round here.

Not this corridor. One of these days, she would get herself a mobile phone. She took a turn at the end, noting that the fleur-de-lys pattern in the pale purple carpet was starting to move about. That was what came of letting people buy you doubles. There the booth was, next to Reception, where Ed Clark was getting his key from the desk. Sarah ducked into the phone booth, out of sight.

Dan answered on the tenth ring.

"Tell me you haven't had a drink."

"I haven't had a drink. Sounds like you have, though."

"Is it that obvious? Look, I could really stand being rescued. If you turn up, we could make a graceful exit. And I'd owe you one."

"Did you remember to have anything to eat?"

"Finger food."

"And you wonder why you're drunk. Where are you?" She named the hotel. "Twenty minutes. But don't make me hang around. I was about to turn in."

Sarah stepped out of the booth and tried to work out the quickest route back to the ballroom. Maybe she should freshen up first. Had she passed a bathroom? There was bound to be one by Reception. Sarah looked down the hall to make sure Ed had gone.

"Sarah!"

Ed was coming out of his room, key in hand. Before she could head him off, he was upon her, an arm hooking beneath her elbow, as if to hold her up, then locking around her waist.

"Glad I found you, duck. I knew you'd change your mind. Sorry about before. I shouldn't have tried it on in public like that."

He steered Sarah towards his room. The door hung open. She'd made a real pig's ear of this. They were within earshot of Reception. News of any incident would be all over the party in minutes. Would it be easier to go into Ed's ground floor room, sort it out there? Ed pushed her inside and the decision became irrelevant. Number seven. She'd have noticed it when walking past if she hadn't been so slaughtered.

"Don't close the door."

He ignored her. At least he didn't lock it. There was a glazed look in his eyes that hadn't been there minutes earlier. Sarah realized he'd taken something. There, on the dressing table, was a tell-tale white trail.

"I was ringing my boyfriend. He's coming to collect me. I'm sorry, Ed. I thought I made myself clear."

"We'd best be quick, then."

He let go of her, had his hand on the buckle of his jeans. Now was the time to act. Still, Sarah hesitated. She was due to make two public appearances with Ed in the next week. He unzipped his flies.

"Ed, it's not going to happen. I've got to go."

He grabbed her by both buttocks and pulled her towards him. This was getting out of hand. Sarah wished she hadn't worn a dress. He was a sweaty animal, his erection digging into her waist.

"Ed, that's enough."

He knocked her to the floor. Before she could react further, he clicked shut the lock on the hotel door and began to pull down his jeans. He got one leg off and she tried to get up, but he put a foot on her stomach, pressing her back down. In a moment of clarity, Sarah saw that she would have only one chance to fend him off. He lifted his foot in order to finish pulling off his jeans. She moaned and turned onto her left side.

He gave a growl of arousal and began to lower himself onto her. Sarah pulled back her right leg.

"Stop!" she said again.

Ed held himself up with his left arm. With his right he tried to push Sarah onto her back. This was it. Sarah let her shoulder fall. He thought she was succumbing. Then, instead of rolling onto her back, she thrust her right knee into his groin.

Ed yelled and rolled off her, cursing. Sarah got to her feet. Her best green dress was ripped, she realized. Time to unlock the door. What did you do? Press? No, turn. Or maybe that thing on the side? Too late. Ed grabbed her ankles, pulling her down. Sarah lost balance and slipped. She landed hard on the matt green carpet. Her face was next to his. His eyes had watered from the pain, but he was grinning. How long before he recovered sufficiently to start again?

"I'll scream," she told him. "Someone will come. You don't want that."

It was the stuff he'd taken, she told herself: coke, speed, some shitty street drug . . . With one hand he held her down, scratching her thigh with the other as he ripped her knickers down her legs. For a moment, he stared at her pubic hair. Next, he bunched her knickers in his right hand and held them to his nose.

"Frightened cunt," he whispered in her ear. "Lovely."

Then he let go. It was as if that was all he'd wanted. Sarah stood quickly, put on her shoes. Ed sat up, legs apart, still in pain. This time, she remembered how to open the door — press in the switch on the side, turn the knob to the left. Ed began to speak softly.

"I did it, you know. Killed him and fucked her. She enjoyed it, I can tell you. Same way you'd enjoy it if you let yourself. Ashamed how much she enjoyed it, with hubby dead in the corner. Begged me to kill her too. So I did."

The smile on his face was smug, rather than demented. Sarah couldn't read him well enough to know if he was telling the truth.

"I'm going to pretend none of this happened," she said, in her MP's voice, like that put her in control. "But I don't want to see you again. The rest of the week, the media stuff, don't show up. Call in ill or I'll have you arrested for assault."

He lifted her knickers to his nose and sniffed them again. Sarah hurried down the corridor, out through Reception, into the chilly car park. She stood in the cool and collected herself. Then she hurried back in, used the bathroom and returned to the ballroom for her bag. She told the chair of the Campaign Committee that, sorry, she was exhausted and had to leave: no fuss please. There were no comments about the small rip in the side of her dress.

Ten minutes or so passed before Dan found her, waiting in the car park, holding her dress down over her cold bum. He didn't notice that she was shivering, but kissed her on the cheek.

"Quick getaway for once, huh?"

She nodded. During the drive home, Sarah only managed a couple of words, but if Dan made anything of this, he took it as drunken tiredness. They didn't talk as much as they used to, weren't as interested in each other's lives as partners ought to be. That was one of the reasons why, only a few days ago, they had tentatively agreed to split up. Neither of them could be bothered to try.

As soon as they got in, Sarah showered. In bed, when Sarah didn't respond to his caress, Dan turned over. Within minutes, he was snoring. Sarah lay awake, thinking about Ed Clark's confession to double murder. She tried to convince herself that he was only winding her up.

CHAPTER
TWO

Sarah sat in the plush Pugin Rooms, one of the House of Commons' less busy watering holes, uncertain whether she'd chosen the right outfit. She wore a Planet navy suit, aligned with a pale cream Ghost blouse. Lately the party had taken on a fashion consultant who advised women members on what to wear. Sarah tried to follow that advice, in the Commons at least, although a lot of the suggestions made her look like an 1980s bonds trader without the shoulder pads. She avoided heels, opting for plain Clarks flats with a decent sole. When you did as much walking as she did, you couldn't deny the need for sensible shoes.

"You've changed your hair. It looks great," Donald said, by way of a greeting. Donald was Labour's Chief Whip, a dapper Scot.

"Thank you," Sarah said, though she hadn't changed the style in two years. Her long, brown hair was a pain to manage. She had grown it to impress selection conferences with her femininity and she did like the way it framed her face. Having thick hair also hid her rather pointy ears, a family trait that reminded older members who her grandfather was. Sir Hugh Bone had been in Wilson's 1960s Labour cabinet. She'd soon tired of comments about the resemblance.

"Thanks for joining me." Donald summoned a waiter with much the same casual authority as he'd summoned Sarah to meet him. She knew what he wanted. Sarah was the party's new spokesperson on miscarriages of justice. The evening before, she'd been on *Newsnight* accusing the Tories of wanting to abolish trial by jury. She'd gone off on one and added a line on the spread of HIV in British prisons, going a step beyond party policy. She'd expected to be admonished, but not so urgently. With an election on the way, party discipline was moving into overdrive. She listened politely to her dressing down.

"I made it clear that I was venturing a personal opinion, not policy," she responded when the Chief Whip was done.

"Needle exchanges in prisons, no matter how sensible, sound bad to the public," Donald told her. "We can't be soft on drugs."

"In that case, the party has to support handing out condoms on demand," Sarah argued.

"The Prison Officers Association wouldn't even consider that," Donald said. "There are all sorts of uses for condoms. But there's no point in getting into these operational issues until we're in government. And government is what I want to talk to you about."

Their tea arrived. Sarah lifted the lid off the pot, gave the tea bags a stir, then let it rest a minute before pouring.

"You did well with that miscarriage of justice, must have done you a power of good in your constituency. Hasn't hurt you nationally, either, though the guy doesn't sound like a saint."

"He isn't," Sarah said, trying to keep the weekend's party at the back of her mind. "But I think he'll keep his nose clean, not embarrass us."

"That's good. You're doing some media with him, I'm told."

"Nothing controversial, I promise."

In fact, after what happened last Saturday, she had pulled out of her joint TV appearance with Ed. It was only local TV, anyway. Sarah splashed a dash of milk into her bone china cup, then poured the tea.

"I'm sure that will be useful exposure in the run up to an election but — let's be frank — not useful enough. That's why I wanted to see you." Donald tested the temperature of his tea. "We'd like you in the government, Sarah. You're exactly the kind of person Tony wants to represent New Labour. But he can only appoint you if you're still an MP. Even our most optimistic polls show you falling short of re-election."

"I know." It had taken a big by-election swing for Sarah to get elected, two years ago. Nottingham West was normally a safe Conservative seat. Sarah stood at a time when the Tories were at only twenty-five per cent in the opinion polls and got in with a majority of five thousand. But by-election victories always reverted to the original holders. It was one of the ineluctable rules of British elections. Support for the government party would need to drop to below thirty per cent for Sarah to stand a chance this time.

"Am I missing something here? Do you not want to continue?"

"I want to continue. But Nottingham's my home, as well as my constituency. I can't let people down. After the general election, I'll look for another seat. A by-election, maybe . . ."

"And lose your chance? What will you do in the meantime? Work as a lobbyist while Johnnies-come-lately get the start you should have had? Wise up, Sarah. There won't be any by-elections, not in Labour seats. Everybody who's ill or needs pensioning off will make a sudden exit in the next few days. It's already started. Soon it'll be a flood. If you want a move, I'll hold you a place. But I need to know now."

Sarah sipped her tea. She was being offered the chance to behave like a Tory. Lots of their top players were being extricated from marginal constituencies and given safe seats to contest in the forthcoming election. For example, Barrett Jones, a member of the Tory cabinet, was standing against her. His old seat had become marginal after boundary changes, so he was deserting it. But Sarah wasn't a deserter.

"I appreciate the offer, Donald, I really do. However, if you're going to press me for an instant decision, it'd have to be a no. Can I have the weekend to think it over?"

Donald nodded. "I can't promise, but we'd try and get you a Yorkshire or Derbyshire seat. Local roots help calm the locals when there isn't time for a full selection contest. Talk to me on Monday."

He left Sarah alone with her strong tea. If the party had her parachuted into a new constituency at the last minute, could she live with that? A Yorkshire seat. It was very tempting, if it could be handled adroitly. But she already had a fallback plan. Her family came from Chesterfield, where Tony Benn had hinted that he meant to stand down at the next election but one. As a local girl, she'd stand a good chance there.

That said, selection processes were never a sure thing. In Nottingham West she'd had to defeat a former council leader, an ex-MP and two favourites of the hard left when she was selected to fight a by-election that was meant to be unwinnable.

Any minute now, the division bell would sound. Sarah finished her tea and tried to remember where the nearest Ladies was. This place wasn't designed for women — you always had to plan a pee. The Junior Trade Minister walked in. Sarah gave Jasper March the smallest nod.

"Have you got a moment, Sarah?" She sat on a select committee with Jasper, one of the less obnoxious Tories.

"Thirty seconds."

"Could you spare me a couple of hours if I stood you dinner? Something I need to talk over. You choose the restaurant."

Good food was a weakness of Sarah's that she rarely had time to indulge. An MP's salary meant she could afford to eat well, but few Labour colleagues shared her tastes and Dan wasn't much of a gourmet. Sarah didn't like to dine alone. She checked her diary.

"I can do Quaglino's after the vote on Tuesday."

"Brilliant."

This use of *brilliant* as a synonym for "really good" was unexpected in a Tory minister, even a youngish one. Sarah wondered what he wanted.

While she waited for her question to come up, Sarah tried not to think about how different her life would be if she had a safe seat. Her turn came at 3.27p.m. This was going out live on the BBC. She had brushed back her long, brown hair and hoped that her blue tailored suit made her look slim. She gave the number of her question. The PM referred her back to his earlier answer. Then Sarah rose again.

"Will the Prime Minister show his concern about the spread of HIV and Hepatitis B in Her Majesty's Prisons by allowing prison governors to sanction the free distribution of condoms to all inmates who require them?"

There were boos and animal-like jeers from the government benches. The PM blathered about understanding her concerns, but not wishing to do anything that might encourage drug taking.

"The honourable gentleman seems to have misunderstood. I am not advocating needle exchanges in prisons, although there are strong arguments in favour of such action. I am suggesting urgent measures to reduce the tragic and costly spread of HIV through anal sex between prisoners."

16

At the mention of anal sex, the PM's eyes glazed over.

"I have no such plans at this time."

The Chief Whip joined Sarah as she left the chamber.

"I can see tomorrow's tabloid headlines: *New Labour Backs Gay Sex Orgies in Prisons.* Very helpful."

He was playing at being angry. Or so she hoped.

"Remember," Donald said. "I need a decision by Monday."

Sarah took the 16.29 from St Pancras.

"How does Ed Clark feel now he's out?" asked Brian Hicks. Brian, formerly the crime correspondent for the *Nottingham Evening Post,* was now their political editor. He was a small, fifty something, roly-poly man with a dry wit and a constant thirst.

"Haven't you asked him?" Sarah was surprised Clark hadn't given Brian an interview. The paper had covered her campaign sympathetically.

"I would, but he's gone to Tunisia for a break. Paid for by the *Mirror,* who he's sold his story to. When his compensation comes through, he should be a wealthy man. Half a million, he's told his mates."

"Money can't replace five lost years of freedom."

"Don't get sentimental on me," Brian said. "Ed Clark was always a scrote. Half a million pounds is untold riches for someone like him."

"Ed did A levels in prison. He's intelligent enough to use the money well."

"If you say so," Brian replied. "I presume now it's established that Clark didn't do it, you'll be campaigning for the police to find the real killer."

"That's for the police, not me."

"Off the record, the police are saying they're not looking for anyone else. You know what that means, don't you?"

"I really can't comment, Brian, on or off the record. I'm sorry."

"Either they're still convinced Ed did it, or they blame the wife."

Brian left the train at Leicester. He was heading for Derbyshire, where he and his wife had a weekend cottage. But his question wouldn't go away. A police officer and his wife were dead. They had two children and wider families, all of whom deserved answers. Ed Clark *was* a scrote, a minor villain who'd picked up a handful of burglary and violence convictions over the years. The first four had resulted in non-custodial sentences. The day after Ed was released from a six-month sentence for his fifth offence, Terry Shanks, the policeman who'd put him in prison, had been murdered. His wife, Liv, who had recently had sex, was found dead beside their bed. Both victims had been shot. Terry had also been bashed in the head, almost certainly before the shooting. The bodies were discovered when a neighbour brought the Shanks' children home from primary school because their mother had failed to collect them.

There had been no direct evidence that Liv Shanks was raped. She had some vaginal tearing, a couple of bruises, and traces of a lubricant used on Durex. If Ed had raped Liv Shanks, he'd worn a condom. Some of Ed's defenders suggested that Terry Shanks, the other murder victim, had raped his own wife and was also responsible for the bruises. Forensics showed that Terry had had sex within the previous twenty-four hours. In this theory, Liv knocked him out with a heavy blow to the head, then shot both him and herself with the unregistered gun Terry had recently bought for protection. According to the defence at Ed's appeal, only a dodgy copper would keep such a gun. Liv, in the defence's version, had killed Terry as retribution for marital rape, then killed herself rather than let the children know their mother had killed their father.

Forensics was not as exact a science as the TV shows suggested. Sarah didn't have a theory as to who had killed the husband and wife. She only knew that the evidence against Clark, her constituent, was incredibly flimsy. DNA testing was in its infancy when the murders took place, but it was established that a used condom found in the bedroom bin contained Terry Shanks' sperm. The prosecution had motivation, a disputed hair on the carpet and a dodgy witness — a neighbour who claimed she saw Clark leave the house half an hour before the bodies were found. In court, the defence drew out several inconsistencies in her testimony.

When Sarah first heard about the case, early in her by-election campaign, she figured that the imprisoned man was probably guilty. Ed Clark, a taxi driver, had a poor alibi. His girlfriend at the time worked as a prostitute on the Woodborough Road. She claimed Ed was watching out for her, but she had been with clients on and off that day. The Shanks lived less than two miles away, in Mapperley. Ed could have been there and back in half an hour.

By taking on Ed's case, she turned a few friends into enemies. Some were police officers who had been colleagues during her brief stint in the force, ten years before. Privately, other officers told Sarah that they shared her doubts. The new evidence that swung the appeal was proof that the murder weapon, far from belonging to Ed, had been in Terry Shanks' possession for several months before the murders.

If Ed didn't do it, what had really happened? Sarah never did make up her mind. She didn't think that Liv Shanks had killed her husband, then herself. There was no motive for that. A burglary gone wrong? Nothing had been taken. After Ed's drunken boasts, Sarah had even less idea what to think. She only knew that the evidence against him was wafer-thin. The Law Lords agreed and he had won his appeal. Therefore Ed deserved to go free.

The appeal wouldn't have happened but for Sarah. Most of the campaign's supporters believed in her far more than they did in the alleged victim of injustice. If Ed committed new crimes, people would hold Sarah responsible. And rightly so.

CHAPTER
THREE

Quaglino's was half empty, which suited Sarah fine.
She told Jasper March about Donald Dewar's offer of
the week before.

"He gave me until yesterday. I thought of discussing
it with my agent. The local party probably would have
let me go, wished me well, all that. But they wouldn't
have meant it and I'd have hated myself for ever. So I
called him and said that I was staying in Nottingham
West."

"You did the right thing," Jasper March told Sarah,
then drained his espresso. "I can see the decision's
starting to eat away at you. Don't let it. Once you show
the whips you'll put ambition over everything else,
they've got you."

"That's reassuring," Sarah said.

They were on after-dinner brandies. March, ten years
her senior, was an old fashioned Tory with old-
fashioned good looks: square jaw, jet black hair, not too
much tummy. Their conversation had been absorbing
enough for the food to be of secondary importance.
They'd had two bottles of Madiran: a complex,
tannin-rich wine that complemented the game they'd
eaten. Jasper had drunk more than her, but only a little.

Sarah was pissed enough to be relaxed. Pissed enough to fancy him a little, even though he was too smooth to be her type. She'd been surprised when he asked her to dinner.

Jasper hadn't given the slightest hint of flirtation all evening, so she was probably safe from making a drunken fool of herself. She could count the number of men she'd slept with after drinking too much on the fingers of one hand. All three she regretted. Jasper was a barrister, she reminded herself, searching for something to talk about.

"Do you still practise?"

"No need to practise. I'm pretty good at it by now."

She forced a smile. Jasper had made it clear to her that his marriage was over, that he would divorce after the election regardless of whether he held his seat. So maybe he was flirting, in a cack-handed way.

"I meant the law."

"Not since I joined the government. But I'll keep my hand in — when — I mean *if* — we get shown the door. Politics isn't the be-all-and-end-all. Why do you ask?"

"Oh, nothing." A waiter returned with Jasper's credit card. "Why did you ask . . . me out to dinner, I mean," Sarah said, as the minister helped her on with her coat. "I got the impression you had a specific thing you wanted to discuss with me."

"I did have an excuse worked out," Jasper said, with a rehearsed chuckle. "Do you know, I can't for the life of me remember what it was."

It didn't matter how pissed she was, or how long it had been since she had had a shag, Sarah would not sleep with Jasper tonight. But she decided not to rule out the possibility of sleeping with him in the future. When he put an arm around her waist as they were leaving the restaurant, she didn't remove it. She didn't quite reciprocate either, only leant into him enough to let him see that his attentions weren't entirely unwelcome. Then the flashbulbs started going off.

Twenty minutes later, when she got back to her one-bedroom retreat in Parliament View, she rang Dan.

"I thought I ought to warn you, there'll be some press sniffing around tomorrow. They might even try to get to you at work."

She explained what had happened with Jasper March.

"You don't waste much time, do you? I only moved out yesterday."

"He said he wanted advice, not a date. Or a beard for the tabloids."

"They won't get to me, but thanks for the warning. You ought to tell Winston."

Winston was Sarah's electoral agent. She poured herself a pint of water before getting into bed. It was a double bed, though Dan had rarely come over from Nottingham to share it with her. His social-work job kept him there in the week and often left him drained at the weekends. They had been together for two years and could easily have drifted on for another two. Until one of them met somebody who really excited them.

But Sarah was too busy to meet new people and Dan quite enjoyed having an MP as his partner. He didn't seem to mind theirs being a weekend-only relationship. Nor did he object vociferously when Sarah suggested that he move out. Indeed, he'd managed the whole thing in less than a month.

"At least they called you 'a rising star'," Steve Carter told Sarah, six days later. Steve Carter was the closest friend Sarah had on the Labour benches. They were having a late lunch in Sarah's favourite small Italian restaurant, at a table well away from the window. The purpose of the lunch was to discuss damage limitation after the Jasper March story had been splashed all over the Tory tabloids. Sarah often acted as a soundboard for Steve and he, less often, did the same for her. "And the serious Sundays didn't touch it," he went on. "They could tell that the story was a crock."

"The *Mail On Sunday* had a nasty paragraph," Sarah said. She had glanced at the papers on Sunday but not really taken them in.

"People who vote for you don't read the *Mail On Sunday*."

"If I had some of their readers, I might have a chance of winning. 'How did they know we were going to be there?' I asked him. 'Somebody at the restaurant must have called them,' he said. No fucking way. You should have seen him grab me as we went through the door — he knew they were outside. What I don't know is why he needed to do it."

"His divorce is about to hit the papers," Steve said. "He's doing what we do every time we announce a watered-down policy — *getting his betrayal in first.*"

"You mean he'd rather be exposed as an adulterer than a cuckold?"

"My guess is he's hardly a cuckold. It was always a marriage of convenience, but she's fallen for someone else."

"You mean. Oh shit, I mean, I knew about . . ." Sarah named the three most prominent gay Tory MPs, "but March . . ."

"I'm pretty sure that's it. He escaped my gaydar for a while. But here's how I guessed: during my first few weeks here, he was quite friendly. When I came out, he became perceptibly cooler. He's too slick to be a homophobe. *Ergo* . . ."

"He didn't want to be gay by association. Fuck me."

"You're asking the wrong man, sweetie."

Steve had got in at the last election, after nine years working for the Low Pay Unit. He had come out shortly after being elected, and survived a lot of stick in his constituency as a consequence. Shortly after Steve came out, the former party leader, John Smith, showing his tolerance, made him an education spokesman. More recently, Tony Blair had made Steve shadow second in Transport. As Steve's career prospered, the local prejudice had quietened down.

"Excuse me." Sarah looked round to see that she and Steve weren't the only MPs in the restaurant. "I just wanted to say, treat it like water off a duck's back. It's the only way." The speaker was Gill Temperley, a Home

Office minister who had prospered under the current Prime Minister. "Gossip's the engine oil of politics," she went on. "If you can, best to be flattered by it, to use it."

"Like Jasper used me?" Sarah asked.

"I'm sure you'll find a way to use him back." Gill gave her a wink which was almost dirty before gliding out of the room, followed at a discreet distance by a tall young man with a mop of blonde hair.

"Didn't know you two were friendly," Steve said when they'd gone.

"That's the first time we've spoken."

"A Compassionate Conservative. I thought they were a media myth."

Sarah tried to work out how to phrase a delicate question. Steve was better at collecting gossip than she was. Pushing fifty, Gill was attractive, but not overwhelmingly so. In Parliament, as Sarah had found, a reasonable figure and a pretty face made any woman into an object of lust. Men had to have someone to fantasize about during long debates. She lowered her voice.

"Do you think the dirt on her is true?"

Gill was reputed to have an open marriage. Her husband was a Euro MP who spent weekdays in Brussels. Gill certainly had a different, always handsome, male "researcher" every year, but that proved little.

"Oh yes."

"But the papers leave her alone."

"Tories are better at managing these things than we are. Gill's discreet. Both her and her hubby are friendly with the papers' owners. And they're rich enough to sue. A paper that wanted to get her would need its story spot on, fully backed up."

"Whereas I can't afford to sue anyone," Sarah pointed out.

"There was nothing in any of the papers for you to sue over. Litigation only benefits lawyers. Anyway, I'm telling you, babe, if the punters think you're fucking a handsome bastard it isn't going to hurt you one little bit."

CHAPTER
FOUR

Sarah's fortnightly surgeries rotated around every ward in the constituency. The second surgery of the second month was in Stoneywood Library. Most of the cases she took on could be handled by a Citizens' Advice Bureau but an MP carried more weight with the agencies concerned, usually branches of the Home Office or Social Security. This Saturday, her last visitor was a member of the Shanks family, the dead police officer's younger sister, Polly Bolton. The poor cow had adopted the murdered couple's children.

Sarah had seen to it that Polly was the last appointment. They could go on as long as necessary. However, she was already running half an hour late.

"I'm so sorry," she told Polly. "But I can stay as long as it takes."

"I can't." Sarah's age, with hard, grey eyes, Polly looked nearer forty. For all that, her platinum blonde hair was professionally done and her steely, over made-up face formed a striking carapace, beneath which beauty might lurk. "I go on shift in half an hour," she continued. "I've a taxi coming in ten minutes."

"I do apologize."

"Doesn't matter. What I have to say won't take long. That Ed Clark was all over the paper yesterday, going on about justice and the compensation he has coming. What I want to know is, where's justice for my brother, rotting in his grave? Where's justice for our Liv?"

"I share your concern," Sarah said, wishing she could explain how true this was. She talked about police systems, about due legal process. Polly interrupted.

"Police talk to me. Terry was one of theirs. They say they'll reopen the case but there's no point, because they know who did it: Ed Clark. They say if Ed Clark puts a single foot wrong, they'll have him back inside, but they have to be careful or it'll look like victimization. Far as I can see, you and his lawyers are the only people who think Ed Clark's innocent. So tell me, who do you think did it?"

"I don't know," Sarah said. "Whatever officers who aren't connected to the case are telling you, the investigation *is* ongoing. Believe me, nobody will rest until they find out who killed your brother and sister-in-law. We all want to see that monster brought to justice."

Polly stood abruptly and went to the library window.

"My taxi's here."

"Let me walk you out."

"If you have to."

Sarah tried to make conversation as they walked, asking about the Shanks children, but the sister wasn't having it.

"That slimy Tory MP," she said, apropos of nothing. "How could you?"

Sarah gave the answer she'd given a hundred times in the last three weeks. "It was a dinner about work. The paper made up the rest."

"Pull the other one. What kind of woman are you, standing up for murderers and adulterers?"

Sarah didn't reply, transfixed by the sight of the guy getting out of Polly's taxi. It couldn't be who she thought it was.

Polly, not expecting a reply from Sarah, left the building, went straight up to the driver. The cabby stubbed out the cigarette he'd just lit. From this distance, the taxi driver was a dead ringer for Sarah's first love, Nick Cane, aged by the twelve years since she'd seen him last.

When Sarah got in from the surgery, she tried to restore her spirits with a long bath. She opened the half bottle of champagne she kept on standby in the fridge. But drink didn't help. When she wasn't on a guilt trip about what Ed Clark might do now that he was out, she was thinking about the man driving the taxi.

She'd got off with Nick after a Labour Club meeting during their second year at uni. He was the best-looking bloke she'd ever been out with. The smartest, too. That evening, he'd actually come to resign from the party. Which dispute was it that alienated him? She didn't recall. He hadn't wanted to let his membership lapse. He'd wanted to tear up his card at a meeting. But when he'd got there, Sarah was the only other person who'd turned up. So they talked.

She'd seen him around before. He had a strong chin with a small dimple in the centre, warm eyes and dark, thick hair. Nick wasn't what she thought of as her type — she'd been drawn to more earnest men until she discovered how quickly they bored her. Nick liked a drink and a smoke, but he had a serious side and was more pragmatic than her. That first night they talked about Sarah running for the union presidency. The time might be right for a real socialist, Nick reckoned. Last year, the election had been won by a joke candidate who, when he became president, turned into a bureaucrat.

Nick helped Sarah to write her manifesto, advised her to grow her hair before having any photos taken. "Blokes will vote for a woman they fancy. And they fancy women with long hair more than women with short hair. Proven fact." She was twenty years old and it was her first election. He introduced her to dope, which she'd been sniffy about. The "comrades" saw it as a decadent bourgeois habit. It relaxed her.

The union presidency was her first election victory. By then, she was living in a shared house with Nick. She won by a ten per cent margin over the Anarchist candidate. That summer, she and Nick hitched around Europe together. They visited her father, who was living in Spain. She took him to meet her paternal grandfather, Sir Hugh. Well into his seventies, he had retired from Parliament, but was still on top form. He entertained them with stories of suppressed scandals from the Wilson years, when he had been a cabinet minister. Grandad also had scathing anecdotes about the turncoats who had recently defected from Labour to form the Social Democrats. The SDP went on to split the anti-Tory vote, letting the bastards back in by a landslide at the next general election, in 1983.

By then, Sarah was in her final year, after the interruption of a year spent as Union President. Nick was doing teacher training. She knocked herself out to get a first, while Nick found his course much more demanding than his degree had been. Nevertheless, the two of them made time to work for Labour in the general election. They were in love with the struggle against Thatcher, as well as each other.

That year, they considered getting married, but decided against. Marriage was a "bourgeois institution". Nick was less convinced of this argument than her.

"We might change our mind when we want kids," he said. Sarah thought it best not to mention that she had no intention of ever having children.

But she couldn't hide her decision to join the police. They talked it over endlessly. Not rows, as such. Nick knew where she was coming from, understood that she wanted to make a difference, but he thought she was making a big mistake. Turned out he was right, but it had taken Sarah three years to work it out. You didn't join the police because you were interested in justice. That was why you went into politics. You joined the police because you were interested in keeping order. Back then, she thought Nick was being naïve, that he was prejudiced against the police because of his fondness for soft drugs. But she thought that they were solid.

Nick started his first teaching job and she left for police training in Henley. He rented a flat and she visited most weekends. At first, Nick was overwhelmed by his job. He liked to get smashed out of his face on Friday and Saturday nights to make up for the fifteen-hour days he worked the rest of the week. Sarah had little patience for this behaviour. Nick showed little interest in her new career.

They had niggling arguments rather than big rows. For instance, he never came to her police accommodation. Then he did, once. That awful weekend, when they were both drunk on bad wine, she tried to get a rise out of him by saying she was tempted to see someone else. He replied that he was, too. Unlike her, he seemed to have someone particular in mind.

"Maybe you should go for it," he said.

"You'd like us to have an open relationship, would you?" she asked. Open marriages were still fashionable at the time. Lefties who wanted to screw around came up with ideological reasons to do so. There was a terrible meanness in the air: another facet of Thatcherism.

"I don't know what I'd like us to have," he mumbled.

"Me neither."

"Why don't we see how it goes?"

"Okay, I guess."

And that was it. They fucked up a great thing by casually giving each other permission to screw around. Sarah shagged a sergeant on her training course. Nick had a brief affair with Sarah's best friend in Nottingham, Louise. This came out in a phone conversation, the memory of which Sarah had since done her best to suppress. As soon as they told each other, each knew that it was over, but they never formally split up. They just stopped calling. Louise stopped calling too, so Sarah no longer had any reason to visit Nottingham.

He did write to her, later that year, when Grandad died. It was a warm letter, but with no news, no suggestion of a meeting, no return address. He'd probably have written when her father died too, but that didn't get into the papers. Anyway, he'd used Mum's address, and she'd moved by then. He wouldn't know where to find her.

The last time she saw Nick was the following year, the summer of 1985, when she was a fast track probationer. Sarah was on duty at a march in support of the miners' strike. It was in Leicester. Nick was there, with the Nottingham contingent, a pretty Asian girl by his side. Sarah saw him, but prayed he hadn't seen her.

When Sarah was putting herself forward for selection, she was asked about her view of the strike. She'd been out of the force for years, doing different short term contract jobs, mostly in London, looking for a seat to stand in. Having been the president of the local university student union didn't hinder her, but her university dates didn't overlap the strike. Nobody at the selection conference brought up the police connection and neither did Sarah. She used phrases like "tactically

34

outmanoeuvred" and "the fatal failure to hold a democratic ballot" and got by.

The strike was less popular in Nottingham than elsewhere (most of the scab miners were from nearby pits) and, anyway, this was meant to be a safe Tory seat. But Sarah had been on the wrong side of a picket line, and knew what it felt like to be a class enemy. Nick's father was a miner, long dead of emphysema. If Nick had seen her that day, he would never have forgiven her.

She later learnt that Nick was working as an English teacher at an inner city secondary school. Louise, when they reconnected, a couple of years later, told her that she and Nick had only seen each other for a few weeks. She'd apologised for messing up their friendship but she'd always had a thing for Nick and had to take her chance. Sarah understood that the prospect of a lasting romance always overrode friendship. But she was sorry she'd given Louise the opportunity. Last Louise heard, Nick was living with the Asian girl Sarah had seen at the march. They got a lot of hassle. The girl's brothers had twice beaten Nick up. That wouldn't put him off. Nick always liked a challenge. And he was smart, at least as smart as she was. Sarah wouldn't be surprised if he was a deputy head by now, with an Asian wife, lots of kids. Nick had no strong ties to Nottingham she knew of, not unless you counted the footballer brother he had never got on with. So he could be anywhere.

We all make mistakes when we're young. You have one great, fulfilling relationship and, if that runs into trouble, naturally you assume that another, even better one is waiting round the corner. Staying with Nick was the great *what if* of Sarah's life. Her longest relationship since then had been with Dan. They'd enjoyed plenty of good moments, but the whole was a pale facsimile of what she'd had with Nick.

Louise moved to the US in 1988. She invited Sarah to her wedding, but Sarah couldn't go and they'd since lost touch. Sarah had never been very good with female friendships. Most of her friends were in the party. Nick would have stopped that happening, if she'd stayed with him. On nights when she got drunk alone, played old records, became a bit teary, Sarah was still convinced that Nick was the love of her life. He'd left a hole that she filled with work, work, work.

If by some chance the driver she'd just seen was Nick, what was he doing driving a taxi? Sarah got out of the bath and checked the phone book. No Nick Cane. There was a Joseph Cane, who had two numbers, one of which was for Cane Cars. She remembered Nick's younger brother and used to keep an eye on his football career, though she had left the city by the time he came here to play for Notts County.

People's lives fell apart. An MP who did casework was more aware of that than most. Sarah was tempted to ring Joe's number, ask to be put in touch with Nick. But if Nick had been in Nottingham all this time, he must know she was a local MP. He could have contacted her at any point during the last two years. Which meant he didn't want to.

* ★ ★

On Thursday, Brian Hicks from the *Evening Post* showed up in Sarah's first-class carriage from St Pancras. He sat down next to her, stale aftershave mingling with the sweat and booze odours of an afternoon spent picking up gossip in Annie's Bar. This was the one House of Commons watering hole where journalists and MPs were able to meet on equal terms. Brian spent a lot of time there. It was too blokey for Sarah.

Tired, she forced a smile. "Good to see you, Brian."

"Ed's back from holiday. Fancy doing that joint interview with him?"

Sarah shook her head. "It's old news now."

"Human interest stories don't date. And you pulled out of the one we had scheduled last month. You owe me this."

Sarah kept her tight, professional face on. Brian would know that there was something she wasn't telling him. "I owe you one, Brian, but it's not going to be this one. An election's about to be called."

"At which you'll lose your seat. Any publicity will help."

"Anything short of an unprecedented landslide won't help. Leave it, will you?"

A steward came down the carriage with coffee. Time to change topic. Sarah considered asking Brian whether he knew anything about Cane Cars. But Brian was a gossip by trade and she didn't want to alert him to her sudden interest in an old university boyfriend.

"Got any plans for what you'll do after the election?" Brian asked.

"I expect I'll take a holiday," Sarah said.

"Your Dan can get the time off?"

"He's not *my* Dan any more," Sarah said.

"Sorry to hear that," Brian said, and the look he gave her was sincere. "That wasn't connected to the Jasper March incident, I hope."

"No, we split before that. He moved out ten days ago. You know how it is, relationship not going anywhere."

"I've had a marriage like that for twenty years. Never thought of moving out though."

Sarah gave him a weak smile. She had never met Brian's wife, who spent most of her time in their Derbyshire "weekend" cottage, but suspected that the marriage was a good one. They had no kids, so why would they stay together otherwise? Sarah had an unfashionably idealistic notion of marriage. Some people stuck together out of fear of being alone, but she would never settle for less than love, for less than she'd once had with Nick.

CHAPTER
FIVE

March 1997

In prison you spend all your time waiting for the future to begin. Leaving prison wasn't like *when I fall in love* or *when I have kids* or *after Labour wins the next election*. This future was going to happen. On a set day, you would be released. Until then, you could legitimately put your life on hold.

Nick had done four years, seven months and eighteen days of an eight year stretch. Five years ago, he'd been pasty-faced and flabby, a packet-a-day smoker, with several joints on top of that. Now he was well built, down to ten slender rollies a day and hadn't touched draw since a random drugs test cost him three months' remission.

His brother was waiting for him at the gates in a yellow taxi with *Cane Cars* on the side. Nick got into the passenger seat.

"You look well fit, my friend."

Nick smiled sheepishly and reached out his arm. The brothers were six years apart, far enough for the two of them not to have been close growing up, near enough for the gap not to matter now. When he went inside, Nick thought he had many friendships far stronger than that with his younger brother. But Joe was the one who kept visiting, who offered him a place to stay on the out. Most of his friends had slipped out of touch by the second year.

The two men hugged awkwardly over the handbrake.

"Caroline's cooking something special for you," Joe said, enthusiastically. Joe's wife wouldn't want him in the house, Nick knew, and who could blame her? But it was only for a few weeks, until he got a place of his own, one his probation officer would have to approve.

"How's the teaching going?" Nick asked.

"She'll be glad to get out for a while," Joe said.

"Get out?" Nick asked. "You mean the Easter holidays?"

Joe didn't reply. They turned off the ring road.

"This is where we live now," Joe said. They entered a hillside estate of 1920s semis with big back gardens. Nick knew his brother had moved while he was inside, but hadn't realized his new home was so close to the prison where he had begun his sentence.

"Nice place," Nick said, as Joe parked the car.

"Still needs painting on the outside," his brother told him. "You should see what we've done inside, though. Come on."

The house looked like the early eighties had never ended: stripped pine, original Adams tiles on the floor, framed prints, big patchwork cushions, a cheese plant, a rubber plant and pastel colours on the walls.

"It's great," he told Joe.

"That's mostly down to Caroline. She'll be home in half an hour. Want a beer? We've got champagne in, but I thought we'd wait until . . ."

"I haven't had a drink in five years. Best take it easy to begin with."

"Your liver'll be in better shape than mine." Joe put the kettle on before getting out his gear to roll a spliff.

Nick stood at the window. Massive Magritte clouds rolled across the sky. A young mother was wheeling a pram on the opposite side of the street. Cars passed. Ordinary life going on. Sweet.

"Here. Let's have one of these before she gets in."

Joe passed the joint so that Nick could start it, then poured the tea. Nick hadn't had a smoke in so long, he almost refused. He liked having a clear head. But he didn't want to offend Joe. And what was Nick keeping his head clear *for*? The joint flared into life, giving off a pungent odour. Nick got the buzz before the first draw had left his lungs, a heavy, sweet high. Then the acrid smoke made him cough.

"Skunk," Joe told him. "The stuff kept getting stronger while you were away."

Getting stoned was easier than making conversation. Joe put on a Radiohead album and the two men sank into it: doomy stuff, full of self-pity — it reminded Nick of the prog rock he listened to at fourteen. He was glad when Caroline came in and Joe took the album off.

Nick had always fancied Caroline, with her thick, brown hair and intelligent eyes. Today, however, his sister-in-law looked exhausted. She was only thirty, but had four fine lines beneath each eye. Her stomach was bloated.

"Open a window, can't you?"

Joe did as he was told. Nick hugged his pretty sister-in-law with the hennaed hair and ripened boobs. He kissed her on the cheek.

"You're looking really good, Nick. A different man."

"This is a surprise," Nick said, pointing at her belly.

"We wanted to wait until you were out before saying anything."

"Congratulations. I'm sorry I missed the wedding."

"You had to miss a lot of things. Has Joe shown you around?"

While Joe made more tea, Caroline took him on the house-and-garden tour, finishing with the newly decorated box room that would be Nick's base until he found better. Nick enjoyed Caroline's pride in the house. It might be done up more to her taste than Joe's, but she worked hard for that privilege.

"When does your maternity leave start?" Nick asked, solicitously.

"From the weekend, effectively. I'm not going back after Easter."

Nick would have to get a place of his own pretty soon then, but didn't say so: never make a promise you can't be sure of keeping, that was one of the maxims he'd adopted inside.

"You know, I really appreciate . . ."

Caroline gave him a plucky, this-is-what-I-do smile, which humbled him.

"I'm not feeling very articulate," he mumbled.

42

"You're Joe's brother," she said, putting a gentle hand on his upper arm. "And you're stoned. There's no need to be grateful all the time. But don't go getting Joe into any trouble, okay?"

"Okay," Nick said.

The following afternoon, Nick decided to look at his stuff. A combination of legal bills and negative equity had cost him his flat in the Park. With it went his white goods and other fixtures and fittings. When Joe visited in prison, Nick had told him to throw away whatever he saw fit to lose. Joe only had a flat at the time, so the best storage available was a friend's lock-up. Some of Nick's things were still in that garage, on the edge of some allotments, but Joe had moved the more valuable stuff here when he and Caroline bought the house.

The loft was accessed by a pull-down metal ladder. It covered the full width of the detached house. Nick found his hi-fi tucked into the eaves, wrapped in plastic sheeting: Quad record deck, Mission speakers, NAD amplifier and an early AIWA CD player. Behind them, covered in bubble wrap, was a sweet piece of equipment: his FM/AM tuner — an elegant wooden box with a huge dial that Sony made in the mid-sixties. Andrew Saint had given it to him when he upgraded his in the late 1980s. Underneath the tuner was Nick's scratched up, matt black AIWA double cassette deck. He'd used this to make endless copies and compilations, what Joe called "mix tapes". Where were his boxes of cassettes? He hoped Joe hadn't thrown them out. Nick used to have several hundred vinyl LPs. They would have been too heavy to lug up here but should still be in Joe's friend's garage.

Here were his CDs. A small selection. He'd only upgraded to CD a few months before being arrested. *Nevermind* by Nirvana. Led Zeppelin's third and fourth albums. He'd forgotten he'd bought that new Joni Mitchell, couldn't remember a thing about it. *Pod* by the Breeders. Those Van Morrisons he'd picked up because he'd never owned them on vinyl. Sarah took hers away when she moved out. And there was the Beatles box set, shaped like a writing bureau. He'd bought that out of his homegrown money, along with those Atlantic soul CDs. When Nick was inside, Joe offered to bring in some with a CD Walkman, but HMP didn't allow CDs. The silver discs, so easy to crack, made good weapons. In prison, the cassette was still king. Nick had given his small ghetto blaster to his cellmate, Baz, when they let him out.

Nick's SLR camera was there, too, tucked into a box which also held old T-shirts and jeans that, since he'd dropped a waist size inside, would no longer fit him. Most of the T-shirts had politically related slogans: *People's March for Jobs, Think Global, Act Local, Bushwhacked!* There were more clothes, but Nick's chest had expanded while his gut declined. Oxfam for them.

Then there were the boxes of books. The English teaching ones were a waste of space. Nick would never be allowed back into the profession. He should have told Joe to dump the politics, too. The densely packed paperbacks ranged from Tony Benn's diaries to the complete speeches of Lenin. He'd bought half this stuff to keep up with Sarah, but soon found that she had even less patience with political theory than he did. They were idealists, not ideologues. Saving the world was a possibility when they were in their twenties. At thirty-five, Nick had to concentrate on saving himself. He had to put prison behind him and think about his time there as little as possible. Most of all, he needed to find work, any kind of work.

Box after box of books. Why did people collect them when they could visit a library? He could have used some of these inside. Outside, who had the time to read whole books once, never mind a second time? Nick looked in each box anyway. There was his collection of Giles Annuals, most of which used to belong to his father. Two Posy Simmonds books that were his mother's. At least Mum and Dad had both died before he was sent down. He had been spared that shame. Paperbacks of *Batman: The Dark Knight Returns* and *Watchmen*: his, though he was surprised Joe hadn't nicked them. Graphic novels made ideal late night, stoned reading.

There were lots more comics, stored in individual plastic bags, some of them maybe worth a few quid. *Dr Strange. The Silver Surfer.* In the big house, Nick used comics to teach reading. *The Beano* and football comics, anything he could find. Half of the men he met were illiterate. They liked the pictures and could be teased into deciphering the words. Nick wrote letters for people, too, but that was a sadder job. When you were inside for years, relationships on the outside faded away. The guys he wrote letters for tried to hang on to relationships that were tenuous before they went down. No chance. Inside, it was hard enough to keep a marriage going.

Friends had fizzled out on Nick, too. There was one former teaching colleague who wrote to him, but she never visited. Two mates did come regularly early on, but not after he was moved from Nottingham prison. Only his brother came then. He'd learned that family counted for more as you got older. Only family had no choice but to stick by you.

What else was up here? Rock posters of dubious historical interest, a framed Picasso print and a few photographs in clip frames: Sarah, Nazia, his parents, Joe on the pitch at Meadow Lane. Last of all, an ancient sheet music case in cracked brown leather, filled with letters and postcards. Nick dipped into the letters, most of them from the 1980s. Nazia's strained yet poetic syntax, Sarah's cramped handwriting, every page full of events and ideas. There were postcards from each of his parents. His mother, in a letter written just before her death, talked about how much she missed his father. He put the letter down quickly, before he welled up, then closed the case. It held too many missing people.

"Joe?" a voice came from below.

"No, Nick. You shouldn't be climbing that."

Caroline clambered up the narrow ladder to the attic. "I'm not an invalid. We thought you were out. How long have you been up here?"

Nick looked at his watch. It was gone ten. "Hours."

"Joe went out to drive for a while. I saved you some dinner."

"That's good of you, thanks."

"I fell asleep after dinner and thought you must be Joe, come back."

"It's okay for me to be up here, isn't it?"

"Of course it is. Sifting through memories?"

"Something like that," Nick replied, wondering if she knew what was in the music case in front of him. Had Caroline been through these intimate things? Maybe she had a right to, since they were in her house.

"You know, I am kind of hungry," he said.

"Come down and I'll put the lasagne in the microwave," she told him. "I could do with some company. There might even be a glass of Valpolicella left in the bottle."

CHAPTER
SIX

In TV shows, when the criminal gets out of prison, he walks into a pub or bar where everybody knows him. There are cheers, pats on the back, followed by wild, boozy celebrations. He's bought drinks all evening, and goes home with a woman who's been keeping her bed warm just for him. Maybe it did happen that way for some ex-cons, the ones who belonged to gangs or extended criminal families. Nick had always worked alone. He spent his first few nights of freedom drinking with his brother, schlepping into the garden for a spliff every so often. Tonight, midweek, Caroline was away visiting family and Joe was working until ten. Nick had nowhere to go before then.

In the old days, Nick divided his drinking time between the Limelight, which was the bar attached to Nottingham Playhouse, the Peacock, opposite Radio Nottingham, and Walton's Hotel at the top of the Park. The crowd at the Limelight had changed and he could no longer afford Walton's. That left the Peacock, with its mix of political activists and mature students fresh from their evening classes at the Workers' Educational Association. Nick got there early.

When Nick was sent down, you could still order a drink in the lounge at the Peacock by pressing a button on the wall. He tried it now, but the bell behind the bar didn't ring. Chris Woods and Des Amos were at the far end of the lounge. He'd been to parties at their house and was always bumping into them at demonstrations. Both glanced round when he came in but neither made a move to greet him. Nick headed towards them, then bottled it and went through to the public bar. This always used to be populated by students from Trent Poly, or Trent University, as it had become just after he was sent down.

In the near corner was Trev Wilcox, a Politics lecturer who Nick had worked with on an anti-cuts campaign in the mid-eighties. Two tables away from him was Pete Tolland, a former stalwart of Notts for nuclear disarmament, and a Labour party branch chairman the last time that Nick had seen him. Nick bought a pint and gravitated towards Trev, whose flat hair was a little shorter than before, burst blood vessels starting to sully his nose. He was with a couple of thirtyish women.

"Hi, Trev, what's happening?"

Nick clocked the sideways glance that preceded Trev's cheery, "Nick, good to see you!" and was followed by a short pause, after which Trev should have introduced him to his friends.

Instead, he said: "Actually, we're in the middle of . . . so if you'd excuse . . ."

"Sure," Nick said. "Good to see you."

He moved on quickly, pretending to be oblivious to the muttering that followed this dismissal. He'd have to get used to being cut. But he'd thought Trev was a mate. Pete, at least, was sitting alone, wearing new, narrow glasses, otherwise unchanged, thin as a whippet and hair jet black. Nick smiled at him as he walked over. Pete stared right through him, then looked down into his drink.

Nick froze. He'd been blanked by several people, slight acquaintances, mostly, since coming out of prison, but this wasn't an I'm-pretending-I-didn't-see-you blanking or an I've-forgotten-who-you-are Alzheimer's impression. This was an I-wouldn't-be-seen-dead-talking-to-you, in your face insult. Pete had been to Nick's house, smoked his dope, played pool with him after meetings. Now Pete was being joined by a shrewish woman with a stud in her nose, clearly his new partner. Nick's imagination lip-read their conversation.

Who was that?

An ex-con I used to know before he went bent, probably trying to scrounge a pint.

In a corner, chatting up a short-haired woman half his age, was Tony Bax, who Nick used to play football with on Saturday afternoons. Tony was a city councillor, last Nick knew. He'd fought Nottingham West back in 1987. No chance of becoming the MP. Nick had worked his arse off for him anyway. Tony couldn't blank him, would give him the bear hug that would validate Nick's existence to the rest of the pub. But Tony was having an intense conversation. Nick hesitated. Five years was five years. Time dissolved everything. Nick's pride couldn't risk his being blanked again. He left the pub, knowing he wouldn't go back.

Nick had promised to join Joe before last orders. Maybe they'd go clubbing, Joe said. Nick didn't feel like dancing, trying to pull. But family was family, so he looked for Joe in the crowded Golden Fleece. His brother was with a couple of mates, one pint in front of him, another waiting. Joe saw Nick arrive and spoke gently to the guys he was with, who left at once. They would be football hangers-on. Plenty of people remembered Joe with affection from when he was a talented midfielder for County.

"Here, get this down you," Joe said.

The small white tablet could have been an aspirin.

"What is it?"

"A dove."

Nick borrowed Joe's pint to wash the pill down.

"I thought we'd go to Rock City, for old time's sake."

"Why not?" Nick said.

Rock City was a big venue. Nick had been to more gigs there than he could count. The first time was when he was a student. New Order's second ever gig. They came on at eleven and played for just forty mesmerising minutes. Then there was R.E.M., with fewer than a hundred people in the audience. The Smiths, early on. Elvis Costello and the Attractions, with The Pogues supporting. Maybe fifty shows since. It would probably be full of students. Nick would feel his age. But at least he wouldn't meet anyone he knew.

As they walked down the hill, Joe got out a spliff.

"Better have this now, before the E kicks in."

Nick watched him light it. "Isn't that a bit . . ."

"Don't worry. Everyone's dead relaxed about it these days. All the cops care about are violent drunks, you know?"

He handed the joint to Nick just as they were passing the Peacock.

"Nick?" It was Tony Bax, coming out of the pub. Up close, Tony had aged. There was grey in his beard. A paunch showed through his jacket.

"Nick, good to see you!" Tony threw his arms around Nick. "How are you?"

"Surviving," Nick said, stupidly self conscious about the joint in his hand. Tony had never been a doper.

"What was it like?" Tony asked, in a sympathetic voice.

"I won't be going back again in a hurry."

Tony focused pointedly on what was in Nick's right hand.

"Then I wouldn't smoke that a hundred yards from the central police station. You're on parole, aren't you?"

"Yeah," Nick admitted. Tony was right. Having the joint was stupid. But the E was starting to kick in and this conversation felt uncomfortable. He tried to say something diplomatic. "I . . . eh . . ."

"Sorry," Tony said, "Didn't mean to be rude. I'm sure you know what you're doing. Look, I've got to catch the last bus, but if there's anything I can do, I'm still in the book, all right? Don't be a stranger."

He hurried up the hill to catch the Arnold bus.

"Who was that old fart?" Joe asked, as Nick returned the joint.

Nick didn't reply.

The skunk might be stronger than it was five years before, but the Es weren't. After they'd got past the queue, checked their coats and bought a drink, Nick took an extra half. Then he and Joe had a snort of speed in the bogs. When the drugs were working properly, he hit the dance floor. He found that E'ed up he liked to dance to the techno numbers best, because it didn't matter if you knew them, they rocked, whereas the guitar songs sounded stodgy and retro. The last gig he'd been to here was Nirvana, in 1991, just as they were breaking big, and rock didn't seem to have moved on since then. Tonight, when "Smells Like Teen Spirit" came on, he felt the old throw-yourself-around-the-room exhilaration, the E, the speed and booze combining to give him a surge of wild energy.

Nick loved drugs: dope, speed, ecstasy, magic mushrooms and, later, when he had the brass, coke. He drew the line at smack: getting a habit was too big a risk. And acid. It wasn't a fun drug. Acid took you deep inside yourself, deeper than he cared to go. He liked a drink with the drugs, too. People said you shouldn't mix booze and E: they counteracted each other. He'd never seen it himself. More was more.

Joe was dancing closer and closer to a student in a tight camisole and leather jeans. Nick's brother had taken off his round glasses and his wedding ring. Caroline had started her maternity leave and gone to visit her mother for a couple of days. Was Joe faithful to his wife? He used to be a philanderer, running three or four women at the same time. Caroline knew all this, had been aware that he wasn't monogamous when she first went out with him. She went along with it for a while, then chucked him.

That was a first. Joe didn't like being chucked. He thought it was a negotiation, but Caroline cut him out of her life. He left it a while, then asked her out. When Caroline didn't come running back, he offered to stop seeing other women. Caroline let him know that she was seeing other guys. She made him beg, then got him back on exactly her terms. A few months later came the injury that ended Joe's career. Caroline stuck with him and helped him set up the taxi firm. They married not long after Nick was sent down, but had waited four years to become parents.

Weird, your kid brother becoming a father before you. Nick used to think the world was too bad a place to bring children into, but prison had taught him that his old world was a damn good place, compared to most. What did Joe think? Nick and Joe didn't have those kind of conversations. Joe had never come to Nick for advice.

Joe had left school and Sheffield at sixteen. Five years later he was at Notts County, the country's oldest football club. Even though they'd ended up in the same city, he and Nick kept their distance. By the time Nick got his first teaching job, Joe was in the first team. He'd always been the successful one of the two of them, and let Nick know it. Then his career went tits up. Scratch Joe deep enough and he'd bleed a reservoir of resentment. Still, County were in the Second Division this year and Joe was thirty. If he'd stayed in the game, his playing days would be numbered.

The girl dancing with Joe would have been five when Nick started teaching, twelve when he finished. He thought about the last woman he'd slept with. During that final drug-fucked fling between his arrest and his conviction, Nick had found himself in bed with a former pupil. He'd picked her up in a club, didn't even recognise her, and she hadn't let on. In his bed the next morning, she'd repeated her name, said she'd had a big thing for him when she was in Year 8. Nick found that he could picture her, a dumpy girl with a bad haircut and crippling self-consciousness. Looking at her graceful, naked, adult body, he had pictured the twelve-year-old girl within and felt very old.

"Why did you leave teaching anyway?" she asked, as she dressed. "I've got a friend still in the sixth form. She said you just stopped turning up one day."

"I'd had enough," he told her. "Burnt out."

"I'm glad that's all it was," she said, making him ashamed. "You know, there are stories going round, but I never believe gossip."

Whatever the girl had seen in him, she'd exorcised it in that one night. When he phoned the number she'd given him, hoping for an encore, Nick found that it didn't exist.

Both brothers found women to dance alongside, but neither pulled. It had taken Nick until he was thirty to develop the confidence required to pull at nightclubs — only for him to find that one-night stands were rarely exciting enough to justify the effort involved. He and Joe left Rock City at quarter to two, just before it closed. Cane Cars were fully booked, so they queued to take a black cab home.

This evening had confirmed what Nick had been expecting. His old world was no longer there for him. He was tainted, discredited, an embarrassment to all concerned. The only way to live with that kind of humiliation was to drop out of sight. Under the terms of his probation, he couldn't leave the city, not unless he got a job elsewhere. His probation officer said there wasn't much chance of him finding a job anywhere. Not soon, anyway.

That left the black economy or, if he was lucky, the grey one. Maybe now was the time to ask Joe a favour. Once they were back in the house and Joe was skinning up, Nick decided to chance it.

"You're always short of drivers after closing time," he said.

"Yeah, the buggers can pick and choose. Some of them won't even do evenings."

"What are the chances of me doing some driving for you? Sharing a cab."

Joe gave him a lazy grin. "Are you tapping your little brother up for a job?"

"What does it sound like?"

"Oh, man . . ." Joe took a hit on the joint. He smoked half an inch of the spliff before speaking again. "We can't employ ex-cons. That's the law. I'd lose my license."

"If I wore a pair of clear glasses, I could pass as you."

Joe laughed at this, but Nick could tell it made him uncomfortable.

56

"I don't see you as a taxi driver," Joe said, after passing Nick the joint.

"I can't think what else I could do at the moment."

"You'd need to find somebody willing to share their cab with you. Generally, if two drivers share the same car, I charge them one and a half times the normal fee, seeing as they can't both be working peak times. But the council would never license you, so it'd have to be off the books."

"You must have other drivers who moonlight, fiddle their papers," Nick argued. "I'd be careful not to land you in it. If I got caught out, I'd say I nicked your ID, did a private deal." He got up and poured them both a Jack Daniels from the bottle he'd bought with his first dole cheque. "Night cap."

Joe grinned. "S'good to have you back, mate." He paused and grimaced, as though making a difficult decision. "Tell you what, I'll see Bob when he's next on. He doesn't like to work long hours, and, if you made it worth his while, he might be up for some extra cash."

CHAPTER
SEVEN

On Monday, Nick turned in at the cab office just before three, hungover. He had been drinking with Joe for the second night running. After all those years off the booze, Nick wasn't used to it. His brother had been at the office since nine, and showed no sign of wear. He was chatting to the daytime switch operator, Nasreen, a Pakistani in her early twenties.

"Nas, this is my brother, Nick," Joe said. "He might be doing a little work here on the q.t."

"Like that guy who . . .?"

"Right." Joe didn't let her finish. "No questions asked, but I want you to look after him."

"My pleasure," Nas said, flashing Nick a flirtatious smile.

Nick gave her a sheepish grin. He wasn't used to Asian women coming on to him so unabashedly, but maybe there had been some rapid changes in their sexual mores while he'd been away. Nas wore western clothes that showed off her figure: well-cut jeans and a sweater tight enough for him to imagine the contours of her small breasts. She was Nick's type. Except for the wedding ring. Nas might flirt like a western woman, but Asian women didn't play away.

Nas answered the phone and Joe called Nick over to him.

"Bob's not been in yet."

Nick picked up that day's evening paper and turned to the story of some guy who'd got out on appeal after being cleared of a double murder. Then Bob arrived. He had a big paunch and facial hair sprouting in every direction. A clump here, a twisty bit there, a moustache that extended over his lips and began to curl upwards, the whole thing a salt and pepper combination with occasional bursts of brown. Beneath the beard, he could be any age from forty to sixty. Joe introduced them, explained what he wanted. They agreed a price.

"I tend to knock off a bit later than this," Bob said, "after the school runs. Say I meet you here most days, between three and four. You drive me home. The car's yours until you drop it off outside mine that night. Deal?"

Nick would spend his first hour every day driving for no pay then get caught in rush hour. But he was unlikely to get a better offer.

"Deal."

Nick's insurance position was dodgy. They talked it over with Joe. He promised Bob he'd see him right if there was any kind of trouble. Bob, in turn, offered to leave Nick the flick knife he kept beneath his seat for awkward customers. Nick told him that carrying a weapon was too big a risk. He'd rely on the brawn he'd picked up in prison. He would carry a pair of round, metal rimmed glasses, like Joe's, only with plain lenses. The two men looked enough alike to convince anyone checking the ID. Despite many years living in the same city, he and Joe had never had mutual friends.

The next afternoon, Nick got in early and had a go at chatting up Nas. Wouldn't hurt to get in some practice at talking to a woman other than his sister-in-law. Whatever flirtation he'd picked up yesterday wasn't there when it was just the two of them on their own. It had been a long while, but didn't that usually work the other way round?

He picked up the only paper on the small, stained table by the door. When he saw which one it was, he nearly put the thing down again. The *Sun* held little Nick would describe as news, and this copy was, anyway, several days old. The headline was NEW LABOUR TOTTY TO MARCH. Nick glanced at the large, colour photo on the front page. The woman wearing evening dress was disturbingly familiar. He didn't know who Jasper March was, but the Labour MP looked like a glammed up version of his ex, Sarah. He turned inside for the full story and his heart sank. The heading was: *Sexy Sarah Gives Top Tory a Boner.*

When asked about his relationship with sexy Sarah, March said "no comment". Bone swore at photographers, but our picture tells its own story. Sarah wouldn't be the first female MP to have the hots for the Tory heart-throb, who is separated from his wife. But she is the first from the Labour benches. What will Tony say when he finds out?

Nick had to read the story twice before he took it in. Sarah had become an MP. In Nottingham. When Joe arrived, he showed the paper to him.

"Did you know about this?"

"I don't follow politics. Didn't even vote last time. Here's Bob."

Nick nodded at Bob before going on. "This is my Sarah, the one I went out with for two years. And she's an MP just down the road?"

"I thought she joined the police," Joe said. "Isn't that why you dumped her?"

"She's my MP," Bob interrupted. "Got in at a by-election two years ago. Nice lass. She came to the door. I voted for her. Won't last though. Nottingham West has always been Tory. I'm a Tory myself, but I fancied a change."

"Fancied her you mean," Joe said. "As for not telling you, Nick, I never knew your Sarah's surname. And, let's face it, she was mousy in those days, little glasses, didn't show off her chest. Whereas here ... I'm surprised you recognised her."

Sarah used to dress down. Political women did in the 1980s. Nick was always encouraging her to grow her hair, with limited success. In the photo in the *Sun* it was long and wavy, perfectly styled. Nick felt a surge of he-didn't-know-what: some kind of reverse jealousy the Germans would have a word for. Sarah had finally become the woman he had always known she had the potential to become. That didn't surprise him. What did surprise him was that she was fucking a Tory frontbencher.

Nick did a school run followed by calls to Carlton and Top Valley, on the edge of the city, to and from the Meadows, then Hyson Green, which had Nottingham's biggest black and Asian population. Evening came quickly. Nick was tempted to pick up one of the punters coming out of the pubs, but only licensed city cabs were allowed to pick up on the street and in the taxi ranks. They paid for the privilege. An unlicensed driver would get a fine if the police spotted him. A beating, if he cut up a licensed cabbie who'd had a bad day. Even so, everybody did it, especially on quiet nights like this. But Nick was keeping his nose clean.

One good thing about working nights, there wasn't time for heavy drinking. Nick would have to cut down on the dope, too. He wasn't a kid any more and he was on probation. From now on, he would only take calculated risks and the fewer of those, the better. He wasn't going back.

He kept a low profile around the taxi office. Anybody, at any time, could grass him up: to the dole or the probation. He'd been grassed up once already. He'd refused to believe that at the time, putting his arrest down to a combination of bad luck and good police work. Inside, he'd learnt that the idea of police investigatory work was a nonsense: the drugs squad relied on grasses and confessions like every other detective. And Nick hadn't been stupid enough to confess.

The will for revenge eats at the soul: that was another maxim he'd made up for himself inside. Let it go. But this was a hard one to stick to. Nick wanted to know who'd put him inside. Revenge might've been their motive, too. Best not to keep that wheel turning. He'd like to be sure, though, so he could put it behind him. There was a modern cliché saying success was the best form of revenge. Nick ought to devote himself to becoming a success. That wasn't going to happen when he was driving a crappy cab for his brother.

At one in the morning he stopped for diesel. He always left more in the car than when he borrowed it, but if he'd had a bad night, the fuel, on top of the car hire, might mean him working for only a couple of quid an hour. Tonight he'd worked long hours, though, done pretty well. He got out of the car. At night you had to pay at the front of the petrol station, through a small gap in the window — another change while he'd been inside. The cashier's voice through the grille was disembodied.

"Hey, don't I know you?"

Nick looked up.

"Mr Cane, right?"

"Right."

"You were my English teacher — like, ten years ago."

"Sure, I recognise you — Neville?"

"Nigel. What are you doing driving a cab? Couldn't hack teaching no more?"

"It's a long story."

"You were a good teacher. Got me a C. Only C I got."

"Thanks, Nigel. I'd better go. Got a pick up."

There was somebody behind him waiting to pay. Nick took his change.

"All right. G'night Mr C, g'luck."

"Same to you."

And what happened to Nigel, Nick wondered, that he was working as a night cashier at a petrol station when he was twenty-five? He'd not been a dim kid, just unsuited to school.

At two, there was a call to Mapperley Road. A working girl was finishing for the night and wanted to go to Aspley. Most of the older prostitutes lived a long way from their beat. That way, their neighbours wouldn't know what they got up to. This woman was Nick's age, nearly past it in sex worker terms.

"Mind if I smoke?"

"You'll have to open a window," Nick said, apologetically. "It's not my cab."

"Thanks, duck."

She didn't speak again, making her Nick's favourite kind of customer. He knew where he was going, could relax while listening to Radio One. He'd missed hearing new music while he was inside. Late nights, Radio One played dance, Indie stuff or techno, which was pretty new to him. He'd picked up the difference between techno and drum'n'bass. If it sounded like it had been programmed by a computer, it was techno. The best record was called "Born Slippy", by a band called Underworld. When that came on, Nick was inclined to turn the radio up, though the punters sometimes complained. They wanted Radio Trent or Gem AM, bland commercial pop pap. Tonight, though, when Nick put a couple of notches on the volume for something trippy by Orbital, the woman in the back said, "Yeah, louder."

They got to her place and she leant forward, her tits hanging out and having the intended effect.

"Do you want to come inside for a few minutes?" she proposed. "Party?"

"Sorry," Nick said. "I don't pay for it."

"Maybe you wouldn't have to. I've got some beer, a smoke. If you could just run the babysitter home first."

"The journey cost six quid, duck. Sorry. I'm tempted, but I've got a living to earn."

Best not to offend anyone unless you had no choice. This was the new, sorted Nick (*sorted* was one of the words that had taken on new meaning while he was away). He hadn't had sex in five years, but the first time wasn't going to be with a pro. He hadn't fallen that far.

"All right. Another time. Here's a tenner. The sitter will be out in a minute. She's only five minutes away. You can keep the change, all right?"

"Thanks."

The sitter took her time. Probably fallen asleep. He nearly sounded his horn, but figured that would draw attention to the working girl's late hours, so he got out of the car to see, locking it, because you couldn't be too careful. The other drivers all had stories about times they'd been robbed, the tricks that had been played on them in the most unlikely places.

The girl came to the door in shorts and a vest. She looked about thirteen. The bloke with her was at least twenty, a wiry, sour-faced youth with matted hair, a ring through the nose and jeans more torn than together.

"Sorry about the wait," the woman called.

"Where are you going to, love?" Nick asked the girl. She told him. "And can you take my friend, too?"

"I've only been paid to take you home."

"He'll pay."

They got in the back, sat separate as strangers. Through the rear view mirror, Nick saw the guy rolling up. The girl's place was two minutes away. She got out and ran to the door. Her boyfriend didn't say goodnight.

"Where to?" Nick asked.

"City."

"Any particular bit?"

"I'll tell you when we get there," he said, putting the roll-up in his mouth.

"Sorry," Nick told him. "You can't smoke in here."

"Yeah, but someone has, han't they? I can smell it. Tell you what, I won't tell if you don't," the guy told him, lighting up.

Sometimes a cabbie was like a teacher. Discipline had to be instantaneous and consistent, otherwise you lost control. Nick slammed on the brakes.

"Either the fag goes out or you do. Rules."

Nick didn't look in the rear view but he could feel the guy staring at him with hatred, or something like. Then he heard the door open.

"All right. It's out."

"The ride into town'll be four quid. Let's have it now."

While you were in control, use it. This was an ordinary saloon. There was no way for Nick to lock the doors to prevent the guy doing a runner at the end of the ride if he chose to.

"You're joking."

"It's the rules."

"Who makes the rules?"

"I do."

"Sod that," the youth said. "I'll pay you when we get there."

He didn't have the money. Nick could sense it. He could smell the street on the guy, too. Even if he had the money, he wouldn't pay if he could help it.

"Get out," he said, turning so that the crusty couldn't jump him.

"Make me."

Nick reached beneath the seat with his right hand. The guy went into one of his pockets, probably had a knife. Nick darted forward with his left, pinched the guy's bollocks so hard that tears ran down his face. A trick he'd had to learn inside.

"Stop, stop!"

Nick let go.

"You're a fucking maniac," the pipsqueak said, opening the door.

"S'right, but at least I don't have to get my rocks off fucking thirteen-year-olds," Nick shouted as the guy hobbled along the side of the ringroad, leaving the door open. Nick accelerated so that the door caught the jerk on the side before slamming shut. What chance for the girl he'd been screwing? Nick had few scruples where sex was concerned, but he'd never knowingly had an underage girl.

Stop moralising, Nick told himself. For all he knew, it might have been the girl who did the seducing. Nick used to be professionally responsible for girls her age, otherwise he might feel differently. Was he really concerned about the girl's welfare? No, what it came down to was that girls under sixteen didn't turn him on. He needed to put all the old liberal, seeing both sides of the story crap behind him. Ethics were a luxury he couldn't afford. He should take whatever was on offer, but keep to the law, even when he didn't agree with it. Without law there was chaos: *tough on the causes of crime*, he'd heard that one inside. He wondered what Sarah made of all that. Sarah, who had been on his mind all day. Sarah, who had never been far from his mind for the last fifteen years. Sarah, with her Tory-boy lover.

CHAPTER
EIGHT

The call-out took Nick to a library in one of the city's biggest council estates. He was early and got out of the cab for a smoke. A sign on the library door announced that this morning there was a surgery with Sarah Bone, MP. The photo was a bad one. Sarah wore a forced smile and big hair that didn't suit her. The red jacket she was wearing matched her lipstick. Red might be the party colour but it made her face look ghostly-pale. He wanted to see what the real Sarah looked like, but before he could summon up the nerve to go inside, a woman came out: bottle blonde, ample chested and hard faced — one hundred per cent Nottingham.

"Waiting for me?"

"Polly Bolton?" Nick stubbed out his rollie and opened the cab's back door. "Meeting your MP?"

"Recognised her, did you?" She sounded bitter about something.

"Saw her in the paper a while back. She was dating some Tory."

"They were having a work meeting, she says."

"In that dress?" Nick glanced in the mirror, checking out the woman's breasts again.

"If I went out in a dress like that, I'd be looking to pull."

"If I saw you out in a dress like that, I'd be first to make a move."

The woman laughed. "You flatter all your punters, do you?"

"No, love. Only the ones I fancy."

In Sheffield, where Nick came from, *love* was the equivalent of *duck* in Nottingham, a friendly endearment. In Nottingham, his home since university, he used it more sparingly. He parked outside Tesco. Polly leant forward to pay and flashed him a smile that was more than friendly.

"Can you pick me up just after ten? By that door?"

"Sure."

"It'll be you, will it?"

"I was planning on finishing around then, so I'll make it my last stop."

He watched her hurry into the supermarket and wondered why he'd volunteered that last piece of conversation. No, he knew. She might be a little older than him and her hair colour came out of a bottle, but Polly Bolton was still handsome. Maybe Sarah, after all these years, had done him an unintended favour. She owed him one.

Six hours later, in New Basford, Polly's babysitter left, taking a toddler and a sleeping baby with her. Polly and Nick went straight to the bedroom. They kissed and undressed in the dark, then had at each other. After five years without a woman, Nick was desperate for a coupling of any kind and Polly's need seemed as urgent as his. Their bodies were raw meat. Their encounter felt more like wrestling than an act of love. For both of them it ended too quickly.

"Will I see you again?" Polly turned the light on. Her naked body was fuller than he'd expected, yet softer, more youthful. He'd forgotten how much better some women looked with their clothes off.

"Try and keep me away."

"You can stay if you want." The words teasing rather than tender.

"If I didn't have to return the car, I would."

"Best excuse I've heard in ages."

"Hear a lot of excuses, do you?" He pulled his trousers back on.

She wasn't embarrassed. "How easy do you think I find it to meet a decent bloke when I have four kids to look after? You're the first I've been with in a long while." The neighbour who had been looking after the kids was also a single parent, she said. They took it in turns to babysit so that they could each work the few hours they were allowed before it cut into their benefits. Some nights, therefore, she had six kids to see to.

"How old are they?" he asked.

"Oldest is in her first year at secondary school. Youngest is seven. The oldest two aren't mine. They're my brother's, who died."

"Oh." Nick thought it best not to ask what happened to their mother. "Have you been single long?" he asked.

"I split up with Phil nearly six years ago. We were married four years. I were twenty when we wed. Too young."

Nick was surprised to find that Polly was five years younger than him. But looking after four kids would take it out of you.

"How long have the older two been with you?"

"About five years now. It was rough at first. Both their parents were killed on the same day. But they're good kids. They cope."

"How did they die?"

"Murder. It's a nasty story. I'd rather not tell it."

"Sure."

Nick didn't need to ask why Polly's husband left. Two extra kids, probably still traumatised, constantly reminding you of a tragedy. He kissed Polly lightly on the lips. "You were my first in a long time, too."

"Do you really finish at ten?"

"No, I often work until three at weekends. That's when you make the money."

"You can come late if you want."

"I really do have to return the car."

"I don't mean tonight. You can come late at night, any time. I sleep badly. Just ring me first."

He understood what she was offering. "We can go out. It doesn't have to be just . . ."

"I don't do relationships, duck. I know you're holding something back and I don't care. If you're married, living with someone, it's no skin off my nose. I'm after the same as you're after, something to look

72

forward to at the end of a day. Now, go quietly. I don't want you waking the kids."

Polly was only half alive, he decided as he drove back into the city. Whoever took her brother and sister-in-law's lives took a large part of hers too. Most of the time, he only felt half alive himself. But not tonight.

The arrangement was that he dropped the cab off at the owner's house and one of the lads was there to pick him up, dropping him off at his brother's on the way to their next job. Sometimes the driver charged him a little, sometimes he got a freebie. Nick did another hour's driving before knocking it on the head. He parked the car outside Bob's, slipping the keys through the door. His taxi showed up when he was coming back down the path. Nick got in the front seat, as was expected. The driver looked familiar, but not from the cab office.

"Don't I know you?" he said, as they drove back into the city.

"Don't think so," the driver said, keeping his eyes on the road, driving at a steady thirty, his shaved head glinting when a police car swept by in the opposite direction. "I'm sharing a car, like you."

"Right." The guy might have convictions, too, so it didn't do to ask many questions. Nick directed him to Joe and Caroline's. When they stopped, he tried to pay.

"Forget it. You'll do the same for me one time."

"Appreciated. I'm Nick." Nick offered his hand. The guy turned to him for the first time. His grip was rock hard.

"I'm Ed."

73

CHAPTER
NINE

At the Commons it was easy to avoid people you wanted to avoid, especially when they were in another party. A problem only arose when you sat on a committee with them. Jasper March was on the Justice Select Committee, so Sarah had to share the same semicircle of leather upholstered chairs as him once a month. When Sarah took the spare seat, to Jasper's right, the MP forced a smile. He wrote "sorry" on his top committee paper.

"You should be," Sarah wrote back.

"Lunch to apologise?" March wrote beneath her reply. This schoolboyish note passing was open to all sorts of misinterpretation, but the damage was already done. The Commons, a hotbed of gossip, now had them conducting an affair since the previous summer, when they had sneaked a long weekend in San Tropez — at least that was what Steve Carter had heard from somebody at Transport.

When Sarah didn't reply at once, Jasper added to the note: "Somewhere quiet but expensive?"

Sarah ticked the word "lunch" but crossed out the other four words, replacing them with: "My office, tomorrow at one. Bring sandwiches."

Jasper ticked the word "one" and wrote underneath, "but come to mine. Much better view. And I have a fridge."

Next day, at the appointed hour, Jasper poured Sarah a glass of Chablis. "You'll like this. Recent vintage but from the old vines. Lots of character."

He was right. Sarah sipped her wine and took a crayfish salad sandwich from a pile Jasper had acquired at Pret A Manger.

"I'm sorry that the *just good friends* line didn't take with the press."

"No, you're not," Sarah told him. "You should be grateful I didn't tell them the one thing that would've convinced them their story was crap. That you're gay."

"Are you saying that because I didn't make a pass?"

"Don't flatter yourself I wanted one. If you'd told me what you were up to, I would have understood. I might even have said yes. Having the press jump out at me, then letting me work it out for myself, that wasn't very clever."

"A couple of tabloids were sniffing around my marriage," Jasper admitted. "I panicked."

"Why? I can't believe your wife's going to tell them the truth."

"She won't if I settle things to her liking."

"She must have known what you were like when she married you."

"She knew, but . . ." March had already finished his glass of Chablis. He poured himself another. "I used to be more . . . ambivalent than I am now. Melissa hoped

75

my sexuality would develop in one direction but, as things turned out, it went in the other."

Sarah wanted to talk about Barrett Jones and Ed Clark, not Jasper's delusions of bisexuality. "There's a delicate matter I need to share with someone. Can I trust your discretion?"

"Sure."

Sarah poured herself a second glass of wine and told Jasper March about Ed Clark's confession.

"What do you think?" she concluded. "Is there any way I can find out the truth?"

"Let it go," March said. "There's no percentage in publicizing Clark's guilt, for you, or him. That was a very effective campaign you organised, but it sounds like the police have his number. He'll be convicted of something else in due course. Or clear off abroad when his compensation comes through, if he has any sense."

"Compensation could take years. And the police have to be extra careful with him. So neither answer's any comfort to the woman who's bringing up his victims' kids."

"You can't tell her anything that will bring their parents back. Some people you can't help. You must have discovered that by now."

He had given the answer she was expecting. "I had, but sometimes I need reminding."

"I still owe you one," Jasper said, as she got up to go. "Sorry I couldn't help much with that last thing. If there's ever anything else . . ."

"I won't be here long enough to call in that debt. Unless, that is, you've got any dirt on Barrett Jones which might help my campaign."

"Ah yes, I can see how you'd be upset about having a minister like Barrett parachuted in to oppose you. Nobody likes a carpetbagger, do they?"

Jasper chuckled and held the door open for her. Sarah wondered whether the seed she'd just sown had landed on fertile ground.

Billboards in Nottingham boasted that British Rail could take you to London in ninety minutes, but the train Nick was on took two hours, as it always had done. St Pancras hadn't changed either: a grim, gothic pile that stank of tar and burnt oil. Nick walked into Bloomsbury. There were still plenty of cheap hotels around Great Russell Street. If he needed to stay over, a basic room was thirty quid a night. An overnight stop would give Caroline and Joe a break. Caroline, he'd begun to sense, was fed up of his constant presence. She probably wasn't happy about him driving a cab for Joe, either, but was too tactful to tell him so.

Nick was here on the scrounge. He needed to find money for the deposit on a flat, and didn't want to go begging to his younger brother. A phone call might suffice but in person was better and, anyhow, Nick couldn't get Andrew's new number. He'd rung round a few old friends and acquaintances the day before, people he hadn't spoken to since he'd been convicted. The conversations weren't comfortable.

"Nick Cane? Been a long time . . . Didn't . . .? I can understand you not wanting to talk about it. Haven't seen Andy in five years I'm afraid. No, I don't know who might know. Probably ex-directory. He's gone up in the world. Wouldn't surprise me if he's permanently in New York now."

"Andy Saint? He still has his place in London, I think. Last I heard of him was in the financial pages, land development, that sort of thing."

None of the people Nick had spoken to suggested meeting or catching up. Middle-class criminals were rarely caught. The bad smell that came off Nick might attach to them. But as far as everyone knew, Andrew's home address hadn't changed. Nick could find him. A letter wouldn't do. It might be opened by somebody else. Also, Nick didn't want to give Andrew time to think. The Saint owed him and that should be that. How much he owed was open for discussion.

Nick took the tube to Notting Hill. When Andrew bought this place, it was dirt cheap. The house was a white-walled, six-bedroom wreck that had been squatted in throughout the seventies, abandoned and boarded up in the early eighties and finally sold for a song just before the property boom got under way. Andrew's place was freshly painted in Sherwood green. The windows looked new. Smart paving tiles had been laid at the front where there used to be scrub and weeds. A Merc was parked in the drive. It was in the same league as the other vehicles on the street. Most were big cars with child seats and plenty of leg room in the back for the teenagers they dropped off at Holland Park School.

The bell used to be two bits of wire you pushed together. At least then you could hear it ring. The new one made no noise. There was an intercom. A round aperture high in the porch might be a security camera. Nick wasn't expecting Andrew to be at home. He may have to wait hours before he returned. Would Andrew have been expecting him to show up at some point? If Nick hadn't failed that drugs test, he could have been out three months ago. But people on the outside were liable to forget that prisoners could earn remission of part of their sentence for good behaviour. Andrew might think that Nick was still serving his full time.

The footsteps Nick heard would be a housekeeper. Nick would ask when the boss would be home and refuse to leave his name. He was ready to hang around for a couple of days if that was what it took.

But, to Nick's surprise, the figure who half opened the door was Andrew — a smarter, less portly Andrew than when Nick had last seen him. His glasses were mildly tinted. Nick thought he saw momentary confusion. Then a warm smile spread across his old friend's face.

"Nick! You're back with us. Come in, come in."

They hugged.

"I'd have rung first but you've changed your number," Nick said.

"No need, no need. It's great to see you."

Nick followed Andy into the kitchen. The house was an odd mix of shabby and swish. Old floor tiles, new kitchen units. A cork notice board displayed only a couple of takeaway menus and a taxi card.

"Sorry, mate. I should have stayed in touch when you were inside, but life got insanely busy. Things are so much more complicated when you go legit."

Nick smiled. "Completely legit?"

"Completely. For years now."

Nick had suspected as much from Andy's pruning of old friends. He wondered how long it would be before Andy tried to get rid of him.

"That's good to hear, Andy."

"No one's called me Andy for years. We're grown-ups now. That's the time of life we were given full names for."

"Okay, *Andrew*, as long as you don't start calling me Nicholas."

"Remember what they used to call the two of us?"

Nick laughed. *Saint Nick*. There'd been a time at university when they were inseparable. Mates would talk about going to see Saint Nick, meaning the two of them. "Long time ago," he said.

"Starting to feel like that. Is it too early in the day for a drink? Have you heard the news?"

"What news?" Nick asked.

"Major's finally called the election. May the first. The last possible date. Wine? Beer? Something stronger?"

Andrew had one of those huge, American fridges you saw in sitcoms. If you were to take out the shelves, it would be big enough for its owner to stand up in. He got out two bottles of Budvar.

"Sarah's an MP now," Nick told him. "In Nottingham."

"Yeah, she got in at a by-election. Unlikely to survive, though. Safe Tory seat, as I recall. Not been to see her, have you?"

"No," Nick said. "I've thought about it."

Andrew poured Nick's beer for him. "Wouldn't if I were you. Last thing she needs is the press finding out she used to live with . . . you know."

"That had occurred to me."

They went into the living room to talk. The room had a new, polished wooden floor and a gold shagpile rug. It was dominated by a huge TV with a wide screen.

"Never seen one like that before," Nick said.

"Latest thing." Andrew turned it on. "Fantastic for movies."

The politicians being interviewed on some satellite news channel looked bloated, stretched. A Liberal candidate was protesting that, while Labour was likely to win, it would be a hollow victory. "They've watered down so many of their promises that expectations are low. As far as their activists are concerned, Labour's already betrayed all its principles. Anything good they do will seem like a bonus. But what's the point of winning if all you have to offer is a cleaner version of business as usual?"

"Do you think they'll stay clean?" Andrew asked, turning the set off with a swollen remote.

"Power corrupts," Nick replied, falling easily into what felt like an old conversation. "But it corrupts some more than it does others."

"Tell me about it. You'd be amazed at the number of backhanders I have to pay in London: permits, planning permission, this and that license, mostly going to Labour councillors or the twerps they employ. It's all graft."

Nick wondered if Andrew intended a warning. He didn't like hitting his friend up for money. But the only alternative was to ask for a job. That would be more uncomfortable for both of them. Family was different. Having your younger brother for a boss might be humiliating, but it was an acceptable temporary solution. Joe was helping him out, not ordering him around. Whereas Andrew was a natural boss, always had been, even back when they both despised bosses. It wouldn't work.

"How did you deal with prison?" Andrew asked. "As bad as they say?"

"At first. Then you go into a kind of limbo, pace yourself. It's the only way to get through."

Few people asked about life inside. That was the point of prison. It was elsewhere, a place civilized people needn't think about. But Andrew didn't flinch from the tough questions.

"No beatings, attempted buggery, the stuff you hear about?"

"There's a lot of bullying, but I'm big enough to make people think twice and I kept myself fit. A few lads came on to me. You learn to say 'no', firm but polite."

"You're heavier, in a good way."

"Mostly muscle," Nick said, dismissively. "Plenty of time to work out inside. It stops you thinking too much."

Andrew's voice became more serious.

"It could have been me in there, some of the tricks I used to get up to. I don't think any the worse of you for it. Sorry I didn't stay in touch."

"You and all the rest," Nick told him. "I kept your name out of it anyhow."

"Appreciated," Andrew said, stroking his beard the way he did when he had something to think about. "Mind, I really was out of it by then."

"Pull the other one," Nick said. "You gave me the contacts."

"And left you to it," Andrew told him.

"You took a cut," Nick reminded him, gently.

Andrew gave a faint smile. "Nothing traceable."

"Sounds like you have a flexible definition of *legit*."

Both men allowed themselves a wide smile, the grin of old friends who understood each other.

"What do you need, Nick? You know you only have to ask."

"Money," Nick replied.

"How much?"

"As much as you can afford to give me."

CHAPTER
TEN

The Commons had no system for boxing up and returning an MP's possessions when they lost their seat. Sarah locked the door of her office for the last time as an opposition MP. She'd have to return before the next parliament to clear out her room.

"Sarah?" It was Gill Temperley. The minister's light-haired, blue-eyed young researcher stood a respectful few yards behind. "I wanted to wish you luck. There are too few of us here and you've made such a strong start."

"Thanks. It'll be a tough one, but you never know."

Gill smiled gamely at this show of bravado, then swept off. Her years as a minister were over, but she'd had a good run. There would be many more women in the Commons when Labour won the election. Labour had instituted women-only shortlists for candidate selection meetings to ensure that. A legal challenge had stopped the policy, but not before dozens of female candidates had been installed. There would be plenty of women to take Sarah's place.

"Ah, I caught you." Jasper March intercepted Sarah in the lobby and handed her a brown envelope. "I don't know where you got this," he said. "I suspect it was dug up by some diligent reporter on your local paper. Make sure he gets all the credit."

"Or she," Sarah said. "Thanks for . . . whatever it is."

"We're even," Jasper said. "Or maybe when you've used that, you'll owe me. But I won't call in the favour until you're in government."

He leant forward and placed his hand on Sarah's back, then made the affectionate rubbing gesture that was currently prevalent in London but had yet to penetrate Nottingham. The gesture was a kind of polite, implied hug, both too subtle and too shallow to catch on north of Watford.

Tories wishing me luck, Sarah thought. *What does that mean?* She wanted to open the envelope straight away but to do so would mean returning to her office for privacy and she was already late. She placed the envelope beneath the *New Statesman* in her briefcase. So many MPs were leaving the building that she had to wait ten minutes for a cab to St Pancras, where she was just in time for the 17.04.

Sarah took a seat in first class but couldn't open the envelope. There were too many other MPs around. David. Alan. John. Graham. Tony. She tried to work out what juicy morsel might puncture Barrett's balloon. Extra-marital affairs were two a penny. Domestic violence, maybe. Or bribery. Another cash-for-questions scandal would be hard for a Tory to live down. Better, some straightforward, old-fashioned kind of corruption.

The train was delayed. Sarah thought about taking the envelope to the loo, opening it there. But you couldn't flush the loo while a train was in the station. Her going there would look strange. Outside the carriage, a familiar figure hurried by, clutching one of those large, cheap, pre-booked tickets. This time, Sarah was sure it was him. Nick. No different at this distance from the way he looked twelve years before. His hair was the same length, not short enough to be fashionable now, not long enough to be fashionable then. Even his leather jacket was the sort of thing he wore when she knew him. And he was getting on this train. To talk to him, all she had to do was walk down a few carriages.

Dan had been gone for a month now. She missed him, but only a little. Not the way she had missed Nick, for years and years. Nick would never have let her get away with not telling him about Ed Clark's assault. He would have noticed her change of mood, wormed it out of her.

The train started to move. Sarah sat stock still for several minutes. The PA system announced that the buffet car was open. There was a trolley service in first class that most passengers used. Her presence in second class might strike some as strange, if they knew MPs could travel first class for free, but she set off anyway. None of the seats Sarah passed had the reservation slips sticking out of the top. Nick would be in one of the reserved seats. It wasn't enough that the railway made you travel on particular trains in order to get a cheap ticket. They also made you sit with all the other cheap ticket holders.

86

There was a large queue at the counter in the buffet car. She stood in it for a few moments in case Nick might come by. But he didn't. Now she was faced with the choice of returning to her seat or walking through the remaining four or five carriages, looking for him. She would be recognised. Constituents might try to draw her into conversation. Even were she to join Nick, find a free seat next to him, there was every chance that somebody would eavesdrop on what was bound to be a delicate conversation. No, she decided. She would leave it for now. After the election, when she was a free woman, then she would find him.

The train got in at quarter past six, twenty minutes late. Nick watched as the suits hurried to get to the front of the taxi queue. Andrew had given him a couple of grand, in cash. Enough to be going on with, not enough to flash on cabs or a hotel in London. He'd felt uncomfortable in London. Nottingham was home. And he'd soon be out from under Joe and Caroline's hair. Provided he could sort out a couple of references to convince the letting agency, Nick now had the deposit for a small flat on Alfreton Road. Probation would wonder how he got a decent place without a job, but Nick had a couple of lies prepared for them, too.

After eating, he drove for a couple of hours, then stopped off in New Basford. The kids were in bed and, soon, so were he and Polly. They could hear arguing in the next room.

"Do they do this often?" he asked Polly, when she came up for air.

"One can't sleep, so they wake up the other, who's bad tempered. Then they start to fight. They only do it if they think I'm asleep. I'd go in there, except I sometimes bring one of them back to this room and . . ."

"It's okay." It wasn't okay. The only way he could focus on sex was by making it more intense.

"Turn over, would you?"

She did as he asked. He entered Polly from behind, one hand propping up his body so that he didn't crush her.

"Harder!" She panted, and grabbed his spare hand, guiding it to her clit. The rougher he was, the more she seemed to like it. Polly had to bite the pillow to keep from making a noise. Both came quickly.

In the next room, the bickering seemed to be over.

"Think they heard anything?" he whispered as they lay together in the dark.

"I don't care any more," she said.

"How long ago did you say it was?" he asked, because if he didn't ask soon, it would sound like he wasn't interested. "The murder?"

"It was five years ago today."

Ouch.

"What happened?" he asked, when she'd been silent for a while.

"Their dad, my brother Terry, he was in the police. This bloke Terry put away got out. Soon as he got out, he took his revenge. At least, that's what the court said at the time. This bloke, Ed Clark, got out on appeal.

That's what I was seeing the MP about, the time you picked me up."

"And Ed Clark was found guilty of killing them both?"

She spoke quietly, on the edge of tears. "Shot them. Raped her first, the prosecution said, but the evidence was always slim. Look, I don't . . ."

"Sorry, I didn't mean to . . ." There were no words, so he held her tight. "How much do the kids know?"

"They were too young to really understand. But one day . . ." She began to cry. He kissed away her tears. Then he made love to her again.

"I needed that," she said afterwards. "Stay the night if you want."

He kissed her tenderly on the side of her lips. "Too complicated, love. I'll be off soon."

She kissed him back. "I like it when you call me *love*. Go on then, get back to your wife."

He ignored the taunt. Easiest to let her think there was a wife.

He left ten minutes later and drove for a while. When he got back, Caroline was up, drinking cocoa in the living room. She had been sleeping badly for a couple of weeks now.

"Long night?" she asked. "Make much?"

"Enough to get by. I should be out of your hair soon. Seeing a flat tomorrow. Then I can make a bit of space in the attic and give you the spare room back."

Caroline gave him a tired smile. "I like having you here some of the time, Nick. But now that I'm on leave . . . Joe and I want this baby all to ourselves when it comes. I'm sure you understand."

"I do. I need my own space too. I'm going to go outside for a quick smoke before I turn in. Helps me sleep."

"I'll join you."

He found the joint he'd left half finished two nights before. The three-inch tube was dry and flared when he lit it, illuminating the night. A half moon hid behind metallic grey clouds. He took care to blow the smoke away from Caroline.

"When you came out," she said, "I thought you'd go on an enormous binge and take Joe with you. But you soon calmed down."

"I know what I was like before. I'm not going to make those mistakes again."

"We're all condemned to repeat our mistakes, aren't we?"

Nick didn't answer.

After Sarah had opened the envelope, there hadn't been time to see Brian Hicks from the *Evening Post*. She'd had a long session with the Nottingham West party executive to plan the local strategy. The meeting made clear that, for Sarah to have a real chance, she needed to give herself an extra edge. Jasper March had already provided it. She couldn't tell the exec members that. Not tonight. Probably not ever.

She wasn't able to catch up with Brian until midnight. Two hours ago. The contents of Jasper March's brown envelope lay spread across Sarah's kitchen table.

"Quite a start to the campaign." Brian Hicks drained his third glass of malt. He was over the limit, but that was his problem, not Sarah's.

"You aren't going to tell me where you got this, are you?"

"Not likely. Am I wrong to use it?"

"Good God, no. Though better that it doesn't seem to come from you. Let me try another tack: where do you suggest I say I got the story?"

"I thought journalists protected their sources."

"Only when the source has something to hide."

Brian picked up his laptop. He had the story almost written, thanks to Sarah's assistance, but it wouldn't appear for another day. The final edition of the paper went to bed at eight in the morning. Brian needed to pass Legal and get a quote from Barrett Jones. He would talk to Jones at the last possible moment, not giving away how much he already knew. By then, he also hoped to have spoken to the girl's father.

"Are we even now?" Sarah asked.

"Oh yes. But you stand to make a lot more out of this than I do."

"I've given myself half a chance, that's all."

"I always thought you were ruthless, when it came down to it. I like that in a woman."

Sarah smiled, and sidestepped the kiss she could tell Brian was about to plant on her.

"Looks like I'll be keeping you up all night, Brian," she said, giving him a friendly wink.

"A man can dream," he said, then saw himself out.

CHAPTER
ELEVEN

Cane Cars' Sherwood waiting room was for drivers and walk-in punters alike. Nick read the *Mirror*'s sports pages. He'd followed football before he went inside. Since getting out he'd struggled to reconnect with the game. When Joe was playing, Nick often went to see him at Meadow Lane, but these days Joe kept his distance from the club.

"A'right, kid?"

Nick nodded at the bald-headed driver who'd just walked in.

"Don't come in here much, do you?"

Nick avoided the cab office when he didn't have a reason to be there: he didn't want the other drivers to connect him to Joe. Only Bob and the switch operators knew. This guy had given him a lift back to Joe's one night but, as far as Nick knew, had not made the connection between the brothers, even though they looked similar. Maybe he didn't know Joe. This afternoon, Nick was waiting for Joe to return and give him a lift to the flat-letting agency, where he would collect a set of keys.

"I've seen you, anni? Inside."

"Sorry, I don't recognise you."

"I was in wi' the lifers. Got out on appeal."

The lifers had their own separate block at Nottingham prison. There'd been no reason for Nick to associate with the men there.

"Been out long?"

"A few weeks. Look . . ."

"Don't worry," the guy interrupted, mouth twisted into a wry smile, "I won't mention it round here. Paid your debt, haven't you?"

"S'right." It wasn't as simple as that. Your crimes followed you around. "How long did you do, before the appeal?"

"Five year. Thought I were screwed until I got the local MP on my side."

"You must have had a good case, for an MP to take it up."

"Not bad. Sarah Bone, she's called. Knew I had her hooked once she came to see me. Wanted a feel of my bone, she did. Couldn't wait to get me out and have her wicked way wi' me."

Nick winced. Inside, he'd developed a nose for sexual braggadocio. He'd been pretty enough to get advances. Chat-ups were often preceded by sexual boasting. The idea was to demonstrate that the suitor was straight on the out, that whatever the pair of them got up to inside was done out of necessity. It didn't stop them being men. Nick looked at the shaved head, square jaw, slightly piggy eyes. The driver looked like a bouncer, maybe an ex-soldier. There were lots like him inside, which was why Nick hadn't recognised him. Sarah wouldn't touch a guy like Ed in a million years.

"Still seeing her, are you?" he asked, keeping the cynicism out of his voice.

"When the mood takes. Not serious, like."

Nick had never liked discussing sex with blokes. He'd left that stuff behind as a teenager. Once you started doing it, there was no need to talk about it. This guy was a tosser, yet Nick couldn't leave it alone.

"Good looking, is she, this MP?"

Ed grinned, and got a leaflet out of his pocket. There was Sarah, smiling as she shook hands with the leader of the opposition. She wore a trouser suit that did nothing for her, but Nick liked her hair. It looked more natural than in the *Sun* photo.

"Nice," he said.

"Goes like a rocket," Ed told him. "What were you in for?"

"Drugs. You?"

"Murder. A policeman, and his wife."

Nick stiffened. "Ed, wasn't it?"

"Aye, and you're Nick. I never forget a face."

Another driver came in, threw a set of keys at Ed.

"Ta." Ed got up to go, grinned at Nick. "See you around."

Ed was sharing a cab, like him. Nick was about to ask the other driver how he knew him. Then his brother came in, accompanied by Nas.

"You want to watch out, arriving together," Nick told Joe. "People talk."

Nas glared at Nick. Joe gave him one of his more bashful grins. Nick was only joking. Even Joe wouldn't

94

be mad enough to fool around with a married Pakistani woman. Would he?

"Want me to help you move?" his brother asked.

"That's the plan. But, before we go, did you see that guy with the shaved head, left as you were arriving?"

"Ed Clark? Yeah, I know about him. Sharing with Mike Dawes, paying a reduced tariff. You got a problem with him?"

"I'll explain in the car."

All Tuesday, the phone rang. Sarah was so busy fielding calls, she had to miss most of the canvassing, joining Winston at the Elm Park old people's home at quarter past four.

"Well?" He was checking the signatures on postal voting forms.

"Tories are meeting this evening. Barrett's nomination papers aren't in, so they could substitute another candidate."

"Pity the *Post* didn't hold on to the story for another couple of days."

"They'd've had trouble with electoral law if they had. As it is, the Tories have to back Jones or sack him. He isn't denying it, so they can't claim dirty tricks."

"Story must have come from the father," Winston said. "Angry sod must have waited until the moment of maximum damage before taking his revenge."

Sarah mirrored his knowing smile. "I hope they manage to keep the daughter's name out of it. Think Jones will do the decent thing?"

"It'd be the first time."

Sarah did the round of the old folks. A handful of them seemed to know who she was. Not one mentioned the story in that day's paper, although it had been out since midday. Maybe the story had no legs. There'd been so many corruption stories, what was one more?

Then, as they were leaving, the paperboy arrived. Of course, no evening papers were delivered until school was over.

"Better than a dozen leaflets, that," Winston said, watching the lad heave a bag full of *City Finals* into the reception area. "We're in with a chance."

Sarah closed the door behind her. "Here comes trouble," she told Winston.

The Merc pulling up outside the home had shaded windows, one of which was half open. This was the first time Sarah had seen her Tory opponent in the constituency. She'd brushed by Barrett a couple of times in the Commons, but they had never spoken, not even to acknowledge that they were about to fight each other. Now there was no avoiding it.

"Hello, Barrett."

"Sarah." Her main opponent wore a three-piece suit, with shiny black shoes. His shirt lapels were too wide, but seemed in keeping with the unfashionable sideburns he had chosen as his trademark. Hard to imagine him in a torrid tryst with a fourteen-year-old. Fifty was a long way from thirty-five, she realized. It was the distance between nursery school and university, between Jones and her.

"You're wasting your time in there," Sarah told him. "And the evening papers have just arrived."

"Maybe I can beat them to the door," Jones said, with a suave, unruffled smile. "Get my side of the story in first."

"Your side being?"

"A misunderstanding combined with an exaggeration. Nothing to get excited about. It'll be forgotten by the weekend."

Jones tried to get into the building but the door was locked, as such doors always were. While his agent buzzed the manager, the minister stared at the ground. He looked tired, run down. Sarah didn't feel sorry for him. He had come to her patch, looking for a soft landing. The least he deserved was a good fight.

In politics, your whole life was up for grabs. In 1995, when her Tory predecessor died suddenly, forcing a by-election with no Labour candidate in place, the shortlist for Nottingham West's Labour candidate was drawn up by a Labour Party national executive subcommittee. Sarah came clean with them. She'd smoked a little dope at university and had once had a brief affair with a married man. These were the only things she could think of that might be used against her. They weren't enough to disqualify her as a candidate, though if she'd told them who the married man was, the committee might have been more concerned. He was still in the Shadow Cabinet.

Tony Bax, who'd fought the seat before, was excluded from the shortlist, being seen as too left-wing. Sarah was the nearest to a local candidate on the shortlist. She was selected on the first ballot.

★　★　★

The flat was on Alfreton Road, at the top of a hill overlooking the city centre. This road was the city's main artery to the M1. It was a noisy area, but the windows were double glazed. The flat was on the first floor, above the storeroom of the locksmith that owned the building. The road itself was run down, with a quarter of the shops empty. Alfreton Road had always been shabby, whether the economy was poor or prospering. Nick had lived near here when he first started teaching, liked it. You could walk into the city centre in ten minutes.

Once they had everything inside, Nick told Joe what he knew about Ed Clark. Joe listened, said he'd think about it, then changed the subject.

"Think this still works?"

Nick's hi-fi had been in Joe's attic since he was sent down. Time was, the first thing he'd do on moving into a new place was set up the stereo. Nick looked at his CD player. The machine was state of the art six years ago but now appeared bulky, with far more buttons than was currently fashionable. Nick couldn't remember how much money he'd paid for it. A fortune, in cash. He never put much money in the bank, in case there were questions about where it came from.

Caroline was due in five weeks. Once they had everything inside, Joe hurried home to her. Nick moved boxes around, unpacked his meagre supply of kitchen equipment, turned on the fridge. He needed some stuff to fill it: milk, a pizza maybe, a couple of beers for when he got in tonight. He'd been scrounging off Joe and

Caroline for so long, he'd forgotten what it was to provide for himself. The two grand Andrew had given him wouldn't go far, and there would be no more, Nick suspected.

"Gotta keep moving on, Nick. It's the only way to do business," were Andrew's farewell words, after handing over what amounted to little more than his walking round money. "Move on to where?" Nick failed to ask. Despite the distance between them, the first call he made on his new phone was to Andrew. Nobody home. He left his new address and number on his old friend's machine.

The Co-op on Alfreton Road had closed down, leaving Nick to try a minimart on the opposite side of the street. It sold newspapers. Before Nick went away, only newsagents sold newspapers. He saw the *Evening Post* and was intrigued by the headline. THE MINISTER, THE HOLIDAY AND THE UNDER-AGE GIRL. It wasn't the usual sort of *Post* headline. Beneath it was a photo of Sarah's opponent, Barrett Jones, the paunchy minister for whatever was being privatised this week. Alongside was one of Sarah. "Distressing if true," she was reported as saying.

Nick bought a copy. Barrett Jones was alleged to have had sex with an unnamed fourteen-year-old girl, the daughter of friends he was on holiday with in Southwold. The Minister was thirty-five and between marriages at the time. He now had a daughter aged thirteen and a nine-year-old son with his second wife. The underage girl and her family weren't named. It seemed the father had made strong protestations when, only a few months after the affair, Jones became an MP.

If she'd been fifteen and looked older, Jones might get away with it. But Jones knew the parents. That made it worse. What kind of man went on holiday with a couple and their kids, unless he had an unhealthy interest in the wife or daughter?

Maybe Sarah had a chance in this election after all. Nick would like to help her. He used to enjoy working on the elections. They'd canvassed together in 1983, even though it was just before her finals and he'd had loads of teacher training work to do. They'd worked hard for the Labour candidate in Nottingham South, Ken Coates, a veteran left-winger whom they admired hugely. The canvas returns were promising. Ken seemed to have a good chance, but lost by several thousand votes. That election campaign, when Labour was nearly overtaken by an alliance between the SDP and the Liberals, was the last time the two of them had been really happy together. It was the last time that Nick had been really happy, full stop.

Winston drove Sarah to the campaign headquarters, a three-bedroom council house on the outer edge of one of the constituency's better estates. The canvas team were watching *East Midlands Today* on BBC1. Barrett Jones was the lead item.

"The MP insists that the story has been hugely exaggerated and will answer the charges at a special meeting of his constituency party tonight."

100

"Like hell he will," one of the canvassers said. "According to the main news, the girl's already hired Max Clifford to sell her story to the papers."

"Splendid," Winston said. "Nothing like a tasty tabloid interview to keep the story bubbling away for days."

The local news report concluded with the chairman of the local Tories.

"We'll see what he has to say," John Pike told the reporter, tight-faced.

"Wanted a go at the seat himself," Winston said. "Maybe he can still get one."

"Come on," Sarah told the others. "Let's get out on the knocker."

Much of the canvassing this time was being done on the phone, but voters still liked to know you'd been seen on their street. Tonight, most of the ones who wanted to talk wanted to talk about Jones.

"I wasn't going to vote for him anyway, but now I know he's a kiddy-fiddler, he'd better stay away from our estate," said one of the fancy-front-door-to-show-she'd-bought-her-own-council-house brigade.

According to the dossier that Jasper had given to Sarah, when the Conservative party investigated the allegations made by the girl's father, they discovered that no report had ever been made to the police. The girl, who had been studying for O levels, did not want to make a statement. The father had been warned of the dangers of libel and told that if somebody wanted to nominate him for an OBE for his charity work, the application would be approved. The girl's name wasn't in the letter Sarah had given Brian Hicks, but the father's was. Brian had found him easily enough. The OBE had been relegated to an MBE without a by-your-leave. His daughter's seduction still rankled and the father had been happy to confirm the story as long as her name was left out of it.

Sarah rang the journalist when she got in at eleven. There was nothing on the evening news about the Tory party meeting.

"It's just broken up," Brian told her. "They didn't reach a decision. Word is, Barrett denies sleeping with the girl but the tabloids are having a bidding war over a kiss and tell, so the constituency can't stand by him until it sees what she says."

"But nomination papers have to be in by Friday."

"Exactly. So they're meeting on Thursday night to decide whether to select a new candidate. Central office want to take over the process but John Pike put his foot down. I've got to go. Cheers."

Sarah poured herself a brandy. The flat was cool, but not cool enough to justify turning the heating on. She went upstairs for a sweater, warming the brandy glass in the palm of her hand. She thought about ringing Dan, inviting him over for a drink. It was late enough for him to be pretty sure what she really wanted.

She and Dan had been fine until he moved in with her, upsetting the equilibrium of what had been a casual, low-maintenance relationship. They were not quite in love with each other and didn't want quite the same things, not in the long run. Dan, for instance, wanted children. She didn't. Bed was fine, but, after two years, bed wasn't enough. Tonight, though, bed was all she cared about. They hadn't even had a farewell fuck. The thing with Ed Clark had put her off that.

Sarah checked her watch. Dan would already be asleep, most likely. If she put in a booty call, there was a distinct possibility that he'd say no, in which case, her pride would never let her call him again. So, instead, she got the vibrator out of her underwear drawer.

For Sarah, masturbation was always about memory. There'd been a big evening party at her grandad's, the last one he'd had and the first that, not quite sixteen, she'd been invited to. She'd bought a push-up bra and was experimenting with hard contact lenses and hard liquor at the time. There were no boys her age so she'd flirted with a married man. Around midnight, she'd found herself in the bathroom, being felt up by this handsome, inebriated Scot twice her age. She'd gone further with him than she had with the boys who'd taken an interest in her. She might have gone all the way. Only, when he'd said, "I'll bet we could find an empty room upstairs", she replied foolishly, "My room's got a lock on it." Her randy Scot swiftly ascertained that he had a hand down the knickers of his host's granddaughter and hurried back to his wife.

Sarah replayed this scene, as she had many times before, with one crucial dialogue change. In the attic bedroom, her sexual initiation was brief but satisfying. When the fantasy was over, though, she felt emptier than before. In real life, just after this failed seduction, acne set in. The hard contact lenses hurt her eyes. They kept falling out and, in the end, had to be discarded.

Male interest shrivelled and, partly in retaliation, Sarah adopted a hard feminist line. Short skirts were out. It was four years until Nick arrived and she found out how good sex could be. Better than it had been since.

"You want to hang on to that one," Grandad said, after meeting Nick, not long before he died. "He'll go a long way."

CHAPTER
TWELVE

"You're letting him stay?"

"The only convictions on his record are so old they don't count against him. The city council say he can have a license. I've said I'll give him his knowledge test next week."

"What about the customers, when they recognise him?"

"All they'll remember is that he got off. But you know how it is, most people don't even look at their taxi driver."

"His victims' kids still live round here!"

"Nick, he's innocent. What's your problem?"

Nick couldn't explain, not without letting on about Polly. He didn't want Joe to know about her. His brother would let it slip to Caroline, then Caroline might invite Polly round and Polly might think there was more to their relationship than there was.

"Ed got off, Joe. Doesn't mean he's innocent."

"Whatever. He's a good driver. I don't take people on because I like them. I take people on because they're reliable and they make me money."

"He could lose you money, too."

"I'll take that risk. I met the bloke. He seems okay. A lot of people reckon he deserves a decent shake."

Nick gave up. Nobody likes their big brother telling them what to do. Ed might fail the test. If not, Nick would have to warn Polly not to use Cane Cars. Joe had lots of drivers but, one day, Polly was bound to draw Ed.

"Time I was getting back for dinner."

When Joe had gone, Nick picked up the tabloid on the table and folded the paper back to the front page: "NOTHING SLEAZY ABOUT MY TRYST WITH TORY" SAYS UNDERAGE GIRL. According to the daughter, now nearly thirty and hanging onto her anonymity, her father had inflated the incident with Barrett Jones out of all proportion.

There were several crucial differences between this story and the one Nick had read three days before. Jones wasn't a friend of the girl's family. He happened to be staying in the next holiday cottage. The family had taken pity on him because he'd just split up with his wife, who was meant to be there with him. The girl insisted she had come on to Jones, not vice versa. He had not taken full advantage of the situation.

"I would have slept with him if he asked me," she said. "I prefer older men, always have. My current boyfriend's forty-six."

Absorbed by the story, Nick didn't look up when he heard the door open and close. "Things got physical," the article went on. The paper used innuendo to describe how the teenager had masturbated Jones beneath a towel on the beach. Later in the day, she had offered her virginity to him. He demurred and gave her oral sex instead, saying it was safer and he was very good at it. Her father, unknown to her, had a second key to their hiding place. He'd found the minister-to-be going down on his fourteen-year-old daughter on the floor of the family's quaint old beach hut.

"I'm not sure Barrett knew how old I was before, but he found out then."

Nick laughed out loud. He became aware of the other driver looking over his shoulder.

"Silly slut," said Ed Clark. "She thinks she's doing him a favour, telling the world he let her wank him off when he could have fucked her. That's not a man."

"Hardly a vote-winner," Nick said, carefully.

"I reckon my Sarah's gonna get back in now."

"Follow elections closely, do you?" Nick asked, trying not to let a sardonic note slide into his voice.

"Only this one. Personal interest, like. You're same as me, aren't you?"

This threw Nick. Ed wasn't talking about prison. "How so?"

"Shouldn't be driving. Doing it on the side. No choice."

"No choice," Nick agreed. Was there an implicit threat? *Be sweet to me or I'll shop you to the taxi authorities or Probation.*

"Blokes like you and me, we ought to stick together."

"Right," Nick said, though his crime hardly equated with rape and murder.

"There's a club a few of us go to when it gets quiet. The Ad Lib."

Nick remembered a club with that name. He'd seen bands there in the 1980s. Ed told him where the place was. Not the same.

"There's women, if you need one. They're all pros, like. But they go there to relax, too."

"I might come along later," Nick said. He ought to stay friendly with the other drivers. Suppose Polly was wrong about Ed? The only thing Nick had against Ed was his claim to have screwed Sarah. It was bollocks, but it didn't make him a murderer. If Sarah believed Ed, then, regardless of whether she fancied or fucked him, maybe Nick ought to believe him too. At least give him the benefit of the doubt, for now.

Bob announced himself with a chummy "Ay up". Nick had to drive him home before starting his shift.

"Might see you down there, then," Nick told Ed as he left.

On the drive to Bob's, Nick passed a trade union office he hadn't noticed before. It had a big new sign in the window: SARAH BONE MP, CAMPAIGN HEADQUARTERS, surrounded by red and yellow NEW LABOUR — SARAH BONE posters. Nick decided to go in later, see if they wanted help.

This election, the party insisted that all candidates be reachable by mobile phone. Sarah kept forgetting to turn hers on. It rang as she was driving to the campaign HQ, distracting her to the extent that she nearly hit the car in front. She pulled over at a bus stop. She had only given out the number to a handful of people: her staff, her agent and Brian Hicks. Important calls only, she'd said.

"They've booted Jones out," Brian told Sarah.

"For making a fool of himself or claiming to be good at cunnilingus?"

"They're having an emergency selection meeting later tonight."

"Won't Central Office impose somebody?"

"The Tories aren't Stalinists like your lot. Local parties have complete autonomy. They'll choose a local candidate."

"Jeremy Atkinson?" Sarah said. He was the businessman she'd beaten in the by-election.

"I doubt it. They don't like losers. Got anything for me?"

"A quote? How about: *It doesn't matter who their candidate is, New Labour won't let this seat go back to the Tories.*"

"Perfect. Catch you later."

In any canvas, there were a handful of people the MP ought to see in person. Not party members. They were either ignored or gently nagged to put up a poster. Sarah needed to see community leaders. She also had to visit vociferous voters with outstanding grievances, to reassure them that their case was still being looked at. Even when it wasn't true, like in her first call tonight. Best to get it over with. Sarah rang the doorbell of Polly Bolton's council house.

"Mum!" A seven-year-old in a Batman T-shirt yelled. "Visitor."

Sarah was led through the crowded hall, past the blaring telly in the front room, into the kitchen-diner. The dinner table had been folded up to make room for an exercise cycle. Polly, in a baggy T-shirt and sweat pants, was pedalling away. She glanced up expectantly, the look of a woman hoping to see a lover. Finding Sarah instead, her face fell.

"You've got a nerve."

"I'm canvassing for votes," Sarah apologised. "I felt I ought to call on you, see if there's anything . . ."

"I'm Labour, always have been," Polly interrupted. "You vote for the party, not the person."

Her legs kept moving, straining against the pedals. This was, Sarah remembered from her cycling days, the least efficient way to use energy for movement, but maybe it worked best for the figure.

"Is there anything I can help sort out for you while I'm here?"

Sarah meant benefits or legal fees, but didn't need to spell this out.

"I get what I'm entitled to," Polly replied. "No more, no less. People say Ed Clark's back living round here again. You'll probably get his vote, too."

"I don't want it," Sarah said. "I . . ." There was nothing she could say without revealing what Ed had said to her. And Polly was the last person she could tell.

"Still seeing that Tory MP?" Polly asked.

"I was never . . . I'm not seeing anybody. No time to meet men. You?"

"I don't have time to meet men, but I found one anyway."

110

"Worth getting into shape for?" Sarah said, regretting the intimacy of her words as soon as they came out of her mouth.

"He's worth two of you." Polly gave her a cold, judgmental look. "It's true," she added. "You could stand to lose a few pounds."

"I'm too busy to exercise."

"Lose this election and you'll have all the time in the world."

"If I get back in, and you need help, you know where to find me."

Polly's wheels began to turn more quickly. Sarah saw herself out. From the hall, she glanced into the front room, where four primary school-aged kids stared at *The Simpsons*. She'd had an easy escape, but felt bad about it. Sarah had come into this job to help people like Polly, not make their lives worse.

CHAPTER
THIRTEEN

Nick was getting the hang of the city. He knew most of the shortcuts, where the road works were and which streets to avoid because they had the new speed bumps. He knew most of the new buildings around what used to be called the Boots Traffic Island, on the railway station side of the city. The Boots building had just been demolished and was to be replaced by a new BBC broadcasting centre. A magistrates' court was being built round the corner.

Nick could even find his way round hell-holes like the Maynard Estate, where he dropped off his first call. Bob had to go to a parents' evening, hence his early start tonight. There was a fair bit of work at this time, so it would be mad for Nick to go and leaflet for Labour, losing himself forty-odd quid in the process. Maybe he would call in on Polly. Her eyes had lit up when he told her he might be able to pop in for an hour mid-evening. "You'd better watch out," she'd said. "The neighbours might notice and think you're a real boyfriend."

Nick still let her think he was married. Polly never pushed him. He wasn't ashamed of having been in prison. What he had done was against the law. It turned out to be a stupid risk. But not a bad deed, like murder. Not even wrong, by Nick's code. Polly might accept that part of his past if he told her. Only she had no time for drugs and her brother had been a copper, so chances were she wouldn't. When push came to shove, things were the way Nick wanted them. No way could he take on four kids. He didn't like the idea of four kids of his own, never mind someone else's.

At twenty, Nick thought by the age he was now, thirty-five, he'd have met the right woman and started a family. Instead, he didn't even have a proper job. Probation were on at him to apply for an opening as a warehouseman at Arnold Asda. He'd been to a couple of teaching agencies about doing private tuition. But he'd had to come clean about where he'd been for the last five years. After that, they lost interest.

This week he'd put a card in a shop window on the Alfreton Road, HELP WITH GCSES AND A-LEVELS, at a price undercutting the standard rates for English tuition. There were plenty of Asian families with money, anxious to push their kids on to university. At Nick's prices, they were unlikely to press him for watertight references. His card made it clear he would provide home tuition. There would be no worries about leaving him alone with their daughters. He'd had one query so far. It was the sort of career Nick could declare to Probation and the dole while driving on the side. He'd enjoyed teaching, once upon a time. In prison, he'd enjoyed helping a few blokes with their reading and writing. Once, he would have objected to parents buying an advantage for their children by paying for a private tutor. Now he saw this was the way of the world, their main alternative to the private schools only the wealthy could afford. Until you abolished all privilege in education, you couldn't blame people for buying the best for their kids.

Polly was newly showered when he let himself in, drying her hair.

"Someone came round just after seven," she said. "There I was, cycling away, sweating like a pig, but I said 'come in' anyway. Thought it was you. Know who it turned out to be? That bloody MP, Sarah Bone. Wanted me to vote for her."

Sarah seemed to be following him around, yet they hadn't met. Suppose she had found him here, with Polly?

"Did you tell her where to go?"

"She only stayed a couple of minutes. Asked if I had a boyfriend. Can you believe the cheek?"

"What did you say?" Nick asked.

"I told her I did and asked if she was still seeing that Tory."

"And is she?"

"She said she was too busy to meet men. I said I was too, but it didn't stop me finding you."

She put down the hairdryer and kissed him, her robe falling open. Polly's tummy was flatter than when they'd first slept together, nearly two months before. She was losing weight for him.

"How long have you got?" she asked.

"I need to be back on the road when the closing time calls start."

"Plenty of time, then."

He kissed her and put his hand between her legs.

"Wait." She pushed the table in front of the door so one of the kids couldn't barge in. Nick took off his shirt. Polly spread her dressing gown across the floor, then unzipped him and took him in her mouth. After a while, he went down on her. Nick found himself pretending he was in a beach hut, going down on a knowing fourteen-year-old, an athletic girl who slowly transmogrified into Sarah.

When he and Sarah first made love, they barely knew what they were doing and had to experiment, make up a language to talk about it. Those baby words came back to him now, killing the fantasy. Polly didn't taste or smell or sound like Sarah. When she pulled his head up and he entered her, she sensed that he wasn't fully with her, and became less responsive.

Nick worked harder to please her, first on the floor, then bent over the table. He wanted to want this. He had five years of missing sex to make up for. He should be present in the moment, not fantasising about something that, in real life, wouldn't turn him on. Inside, fantasy was a necessary habit, but he was out now, free. Unless it really was like the long-term lads said. You never got the old feeling of freedom back. The only freedom you got was to carry your own cage wherever you went, weighing you down at every step.

After they'd finished, he lay beside her. Not cuddling, but close. Time passed. They were woken by a child at the door.

"Go back upstairs. I'll bring you some water in a minute."

While Polly was gone, Nick made them both a cup of tea. At half past ten, he got up to go.

"I can get a babysitter if you want to make a proper night of it."

"I'd like that," Nick said, "only I've got to earn as much as I can right now. Getting a place of my own."

Her smile seemed to speak of patience. Polly never asked questions, only chewed over whatever he told her. He wished he hadn't said that about getting a place. Polly might think he was on the verge of leaving his wife, because of her.

Dan rolled off and removed the rubber he'd worn without asking.

"We should do this more often," he said, when he came back from the bathroom. Sarah didn't reply. She didn't want to make love with him ever again. He had been attentive enough and she didn't mind condoms. Only, now it was over, she felt crap. Worse than she sometimes felt after using the vibrator. Much worse than she had before accepting her ex's invitation to inspect his new flat. But Dan, it seemed, couldn't tell the difference between the empty sex they'd just had and what it used to be like. Which was really depressing. He pushed his luck.

"Can we do this every time I canvas for you or was tonight a one-off?"

"A one-off," she replied, then added, to let him down easy, "otherwise we'll forget we split up."

116

"Shame," Dan said. "I thought we could be fuck buddies."

"*Fuck buddies?*"

He explained the term to her. Sex as a friendly transaction between temporarily single people who had firmly ruled out having a relationship.

"I don't think so," Sarah said. "I need the bathroom. Can you call me a taxi?"

"Are you seeing anyone?" Dan asked, when she was dressing, with her back to him.

"I wouldn't have come round here if I was. You?"

"There's a woman at work. It's messy. She lives with someone, wants to leave, but this place isn't big enough for two and it's still early days between us. She isn't sure how good a bet I am."

"She's right to be cautious, if you're cheating on her already."

Dan looked affronted. "I'm not sleeping with her. We've talked and kissed, that's all. Taking it slowly. She says I'm still not over you."

"Doing this won't help, then."

"No, it has. I mean . . . you were right to finish it. We weren't going anywhere. I might even tell Clare what happened."

"Including the 'fuck buddies' bit?" Sarah asked.

"Glad to see you're as sardonic as ever." Dan gave her a wry smile. Outside, a taxi sounded its horn.

"That was quick."

"I told them it was for *Sarah Bone, MP*."

Dan signalled to the driver while Sarah finished dressing.

"Now that we're finished, will you tell me something?" she asked.

"Anything."

"Were you faithful to me, all the time I spent in London?"

Dan hesitated. "Not entirely. You?"

"Not entirely," Sarah lied. "I'm glad we've got that out of our systems. Let's be buddies, but without the *fuck* bit. Okay?"

He saw her out to her taxi. Sarah was sorry it had come so quickly. She wanted details of Dan's infidelities. Had he slept with anyone she knew? How often had he strayed? As soon as she was inside, the taxi set off towards the Park. It was a Cane Cars taxi, Sarah noticed, and, for the first time, looked up to see the driver, just in case it was Nick.

It wasn't. Nor was the driver the person in the ID photograph hanging from the sun guard.

"Let me out," she told Ed Clark. "This is not a good idea."

"Just doing my job," he told her. "I'm taking you home. We don't have to talk if you don't want to." He pulled up at some lights.

"I want to get out," she said. When he didn't react, she tried the door. It was locked.

"We get a lot of runners," he told her. "It's a standard precaution."

"Ed, I don't want to ride with you. I don't want you to know where I live."

"I already know where you live," he told her. "I'll prove it to you."

They sped up. Had Dan given the firm her address? Taxis didn't normally ask for a precise address on the phone.

"Why do you know where I live?" Sarah asked.

"I'm interested in you. You know that. You're interested in me, too. Otherwise you'd still be living with that Dan guy, wouldn't you?"

"Stop!" Sarah said. "I want to get out, now!"

"We're nearly there," Ed told her. "I was kidding, in that hotel, last month. I didn't like getting knocked back, so I had a go. Childish, I know, but it was a stressful day and I'd had too much to drink. I'm sorry."

"Apology accepted," Sarah said, as he turned off Derby Road into the Park with its wide, unlit avenues. "I can walk from here."

"No, you can't. It's dangerous."

Ed didn't ask directions, but pulled up right outside her flat. It was two o'clock. None of the flats in her building had any lights on. He still didn't unlock the door.

"What do I owe you?" Sarah asked.

"Nothing. Are you going to invite me in for a drink?"

Nick wasn't sure what he was doing in the club. He liked to chill after driving for several hours, but he could do that at home. He didn't need company. Especially when the music was so loud you had to shout over it. Ed Clark wasn't here, but several street girls were. All looked dog rough. Two had the sallow, used-up demeanour of junkies. Most of the girls sat together in the corner opposite the entrance, talking

119

loudly, laughing, showing no interest in the men who hung around the bar, watching.

A Motown tune rattled the speakers. Finish this pint, Nick thought, and I'll be gone. His desire for the evening was spent and he'd never, anyway, slept with a professional. The idea didn't appeal to him. He watched the girls laughing, gossiping, smoking like chimneys. He had an inch of his pint left and was about to down it when somebody tapped him on the shoulder.

"Another?" Without waiting for an answer, Ed ordered Nick a strong lager.

"Meant to finish earlier but I had a special job," Ed said when he returned with their drinks.

"Yeah?" Nick downed his old drink, trying to look mildly interested.

"My Sarah. She called my cab, asked for me special, took me back to hers for a good seeing to."

"Surprised you didn't stay the night," Nick said, careful not to let it sound like an insult. Ed grinned.

"Nah, I'm her bit of rough. She don't want a gorilla like me around in the morning, when her fancy mates show up. She likes a good shafting last thing, full length at both ends."

Nick, to hide his distaste, began drinking his new pint too quickly. He knew that Ed was lying, but couldn't stop himself picturing the sex he described. Nick had good sex with Polly. He'd soon learnt that she liked things a little rough and only came when he took her from behind. With Sarah, sex was always romantic: exciting, but not dirty the way it was with Polly. It was

120

part of being in love, a state that had only happened to Nick twice. With Polly, it was something else. Passion, yes. But also a release, a means of expression, even a kind of revenge.

The booze had gone to his head. He blurted out what was on his mind. "Did Sarah Bone really think you were innocent? Or did she get you out of nick simply because she wanted to screw you?"

"A question I often ask myself," Ed said, with a smug grin.

"Because," Nick leant forward, speaking into Ed's ear on the side of his head that was away from the bar, "I reckon you did it, but had a good brief who got you off on appeal. And I'll bet she thinks the same."

"S'right," Ed said, grinning from ear to ear. "That's exactly what she thinks."

The next question was the clincher: *And is she right?* but Nick didn't ask it. Let Ed tell him in his own good time. One of the two junkie girls, seventeen at most, was giving Ed the eye. He raised his glass to her.

"Not had enough?" Nick couldn't resist asking.

"Sarah isn't the only one who likes a bit of rough. Catch you later."

Ed downed his drink and headed out. He must be one of those people who found it hard to distinguish between lies and the truth. Whatever came out of their mouth was the truth and God help you if you disagreed with them. A sociopath, near enough. If Ed were to confess to killing Polly's brother and sister-in-law, Nick wouldn't know whether to believe him.

What was Ed doing here, in this seedy dive, at half three in the morning? Nick left his drink unfinished on the bar. Outside, in the alley, he could see Ed's bald pate, gleaming in the moonlight, as he did to the girl what he claimed to have just done to Sarah.

"Not so hard," the girl was saying. "It really hurts."

"That's because it's meant to, duck."

CHAPTER
FOURTEEN

Sarah slept fitfully and didn't check her messages until ten. She called her agent. Winston was trying to set up a public debate between her, the Liberal Democrat and the new Tory candidate. The Tories had selected Jeremy Atkinson, the candidate she had seen off in the by-election. She had wiped the floor with him during all three public debates then. Now that he was the favourite to win the seat, Jeremy wasn't so keen, but Winston thought her opponent could be strong-armed into doing it.

"Barrett Jones suggested the debate in the first place, so Atkinson will find it hard to refuse, even though he hasn't got the public-speaking skills you have."

"My public-speaking skills don't feel so sharp this morning," Sarah confessed.

"International Community Centre, Tuesday week."

"Evening? Okay, I suppose."

"And I fielded a call from a bloke claiming to be an old friend of yours, wanted you to give him a ring. Name of Nick Cane. Know him?"

Sarah reached for a pen. "Used to. Give me his number. I'll call him."

She called Nick as soon as Winston rang off, her heart leaping. Nick's phone rang and rang. No machine. Sarah hung up. Where was Nick living, she wondered? Was he a partner in his brother's cab firm? There was probably more money in that than teaching. Neither teaching nor cab work was the career she'd expected Nick to end up in. She'd seen him as a journalist or a campaigner of some kind. He might have become a politician, if he hadn't been so keen on getting stoned all the time. She'd liked a smoke herself, but not several, every night. Nick used to get so spaced out, she felt lonely when she was in the same room as him.

The phone rang again and, because she was distracted, Sarah picked it up herself instead of screening with the machine.

"Sarah Bone."

"Sarah, long time no see." The voice was only vaguely familiar.

"I'm sorry. This is . . .?"

"It's Andrew . . . Andy Saint."

Jasmina was fifteen but looked older. Her father let her wear jeans at home when most Sikh families insisted on traditional dress. Working in the family newsagents had made her comfortable dealing with white adults. When she and Nick were alone, she got straight down to business.

"Can you write it for me?"

"I'm afraid not," Nick told her. "This is coursework. It counts as part of your GCSE result."

124

"I hate Shakespeare and my parents pay you to help me."

"That's as may be, Jasmina, but . . ." The girl's mother was in the next room. He could call her in, explain the situation and make sure that this didn't come up again. But suppose mother backed daughter? He'd lose twenty quid an hour and Nick couldn't afford that. He only had one other pupil. So he prevaricated.

"The thing is, if you get caught using essays written by somebody else, it's not just English Lit. you'll fail. They'll assume you cheated in all your coursework."

"You just don't want to do it," Jasmina complained. "The other girls with private tutors say they tell them what to write. Otherwise what's the point? I get normal teaching at school."

"I can teach you how to structure an essay. That's better than telling you what to write. Look, let's go through this."

Nick ended up staying over an extra twenty minutes, more or less writing Jasmina's first paragraph and planning the rest of the essay for her. At least the result would look like Jasmina's work. Her English teacher should recognise the improvement, but also the mistakes.

Mr Sahor thanked him at the door and paid him in cash. Nick insisted on giving him a receipt.

"It's not necessary. I do not need to know whether you declare it or not."

"I appreciate that, but I want to make an honest living," Nick said. "Please tell your friends about me."

"I will, I will. In fact I have a cousin whose son is struggling with . . ."

This could build up, Nick thought, as he wrote down the number. An hour or two every evening would never pay as well as full-time teaching but, combined with the late-night driving, it might keep him going.

"There's my taxi," he said. "See you next week."

Bob was picking him up here so that Nick could drive him home.

"Knocking off a Paki, are we?" Bob slid over to let Nick take the wheel.

"I'm hiring myself out as a stud," Nick said. "Know where I can get a cheap answering machine? I don't want to miss calls from horny housewives."

Bob chortled. "If you're serious, I might be able to fix you up with one." He didn't quiz Nick any further about why he was where he was. Probably thought Nick shared Joe's taste for a risky Asian bit on the side.

Nick had another reason not to miss calls. On an impulse, he'd rung the number on Sarah's leaflets. Better, he'd thought, to arrange a meeting than bump into her on the campaign. That would be awkward, given how close they'd once been. He'd meant to leave contacting her until after the election, then Ed's bragging got to him. But Sarah would have already rung by now if she was going to. Nick guessed she'd heard that he'd been inside. No way would she call him after hearing that, especially just before an election. She'd be better off hanging out with Ed Clark.

Sarah had suggested the restaurant. He was already there when she arrived.

"Andy!"

126

He stood up to greet her, planted a kiss on her left cheek.

"It's Andrew now. I got fed up with having a kid's name."

"Andrew, then." They exchanged a half serious hug.

Andrew Saint had changed little in the thirteen years since Sarah last saw him. His hair was thinning slightly. The once messy beard was neatly trimmed, with no hint of grey. He was a little paunchier maybe, but not much. Andy had always been on the stocky side. He had always been an inch or two shorter than her, too, but was now the same height. She assumed lifts in his shoes.

"I'm impressed you've come to Nottingham to see me," she told him, as they sat side-by-side in the bar of the Lace Market Hotel. "I was looking you up on the web. Your name pops up all over the place, but not in the East Midlands, as far as I could tell."

"It's good to have an excuse to come back," Andrew told her. "I don't think I've been in the city since 1991. Were you here then?"

"No, I was in London. I only moved back after the by-election."

"Did having been union president help with getting the nomination?"

"A little. But I fought an unwinnable seat in 1992. I paid my dues."

"They say Nottingham West can't be won this time." Andrew pointed this out in a tone that was rather too droll for Sarah's liking.

"Thanks for the vote of confidence."

"You're confident? I'm sorry, I didn't mean . . ."

"No, I'm sorry for snapping at you," Sarah said, quietly. "The chances aren't good. But during the campaign, you have to rev yourself up, convince yourself that you have a fighting chance."

"Have you thought about what you'll do if you lose?"

"Take a holiday. Then go back to London, get a job."

"Anything lined up?"

"It'd look awful if I was touting for jobs. That's what Tories do when they're about to lose. We're about to gain power, unless something goes massively wrong in the next thirteen days."

"Which makes you a valuable commodity, with very good contacts."

"I suppose." Sarah began to see where this was leading. The waiter came with their glasses of Moët et Chandon. Andrew leant forward.

"If the worst does happen, I'd like you to come and work for me."

"As what?"

"Lobbyist, public relations, policy adviser . . . name your own title. I can take you on full-time, part-time or as a freelance consultant."

"Why do you need me? Don't tell me it's a favour for a friend."

Andrew replied with his Cheshire cat grin. "We aren't real friends, not yet anyway. Never were. We had a mutual friend, that was all."

"Do you ever see Nick?"

"Not since . . ." Andrew thought. "I don't know when. You?"

"I haven't spoken to him in twelve years." Something stopped her telling Andrew that he'd tried to phone her. "I think he might be in Nottingham though. I saw someone who looked like him, driving a cab."

"He could be helping out his brother. Doesn't Joe have a cab firm?"

"How do you know that?" Sarah asked.

"I hear things. Will you consider working for me?"

"I will," Sarah said. "But you haven't really answered my question. As what? What aspects of your business do you need help with?"

"I have emerging interests. Stuff I can't tell you about until you've signed a job contract and a confidentiality agreement. I don't mean to insult you. That's the way business is these days."

"I see," Sarah said. "For the sake of argument, if I agreed to work for you, say, three days a week, what kind of deal are we talking about?"

Andrew told her. It was far more than her MP's salary.

"There'd be fringe benefits, too. A very large expense account."

"You must be doing well," Sarah told him.

"I'm doing extremely well," Andrew said, and there was a lascivious edge to his smile that made Sarah wonder whether this job offer wasn't just an attempt to get into her knickers. Andy had tried it on fifteen years ago, even though he was supposed to be a big mate of Nick's. She'd made it clear then that she didn't fancy him. But Andrew was rich now, and Sarah was still single. Hardly surprising if he assumed she'd lowered her standards.

She ate duck and Andrew had veal. While they ate, they gossiped, neither of them dwelling on the past. Andrew told her stories about people he'd worked with in New York, dropping famous and familiar names in a casual but well-rehearsed manner, making it very clear that he'd stepped up in the world. Sarah fed him some juicy morsels of political tittle-tattle. They parted on a warm note.

"I'll think about it very seriously," she said, before agreeing to have lunch with him the week after the election.

CHAPTER
FIFTEEN

There were still mornings when Nick woke and was surprised not to find himself inside. Late night working had cured him of waking early, but he doubted he'd ever get rid of the prison dreams. Today, he didn't hear the doorbell ring, but did hear the voice shouting his name. He thought it was a cellmate and he had overslept. Then he remembered where he was.

"Hold on!" Nick pulled on a sweatshirt and tracksuit bottoms before opening the door. He expected a meter reader, but found a familiar face.

"Are you going to invite me in or just stand there like a dummy?"

Nick had given his old friend the new address, but never expected him to visit. Andrew stood at the window while Nick put the kettle on.

"Alfreton Road," Andrew said with a sigh. "We used to come here for pizza when we were flush. What was the place called? Gino's?"

"Reno's," Nick said. "Next door to the Red Lion."

"That was it." He looked round the sparsely furnished flat. "I paid for this, did I?"

"In a manner of speaking."

"Sorry I didn't have more when you called. I brought you the rest."

Andrew pulled a brown envelope from the inside pocket of his Armani jacket.

"Thanks, Andy." Nick used the old name uncomfortably. He opened the envelope. There was around three grand in it.

"It's starting-up-somewhere-else money," Andrew said. "You can't hang around here for ever, not when everyone knows you've been inside."

"Where else do I go?" Nick asked. "Are you offering me a job?"

"I would if I could," Andrew said. "But it's a delicate time. I need to be whiter than white. I can't take on ex-cons."

"So what do you suggest?" Nick tried to keep sarcasm out of his voice. His friend had given him five grand, after all. "Maybe I should move to Wales, set up another hydroponics operation."

"That game's moved on while you were away. A lot of dangerous, greedy bastards are in on it. You might find it's more trouble than it's worth."

"I wasn't serious," Nick said. "I've got form. I have to stick around here, report to probation, keep my nose clean. But the money'll help."

"I'm glad to hear it, but I'd still move if I were you. You can't make a new start in a place where you've got so much history. What are you working as, a cab driver?"

"Where did you hear that?" Nick asked.

"I hear lots."

"I've done a bit for Joe. But I'm trying to set up a private tuition business. Schoolkids wanting help with GCSEs, that kind of thing."

"Not much money there. You ought to get yourself a nice cushy job in some boarding school. Most of those places don't do criminal record checks. If you're stuck for references, I know people who know people."

"Thanks," Nick said, then changed the subject. "Have you seen the posters for Sarah all over the place? How weird is that?"

"I hadn't noticed," Andrew said. "You haven't got in touch, have you? That's the last thing she needs."

"You told me that last time we met."

Andrew didn't reply. Nick handed him a mug of tea. "Sugar?"

"Stopped taking that a long time ago."

Nick needed to do something to break the ice.

"Excuse me a mo." He went outside. The Golden Virginia tin where he kept his kit was stashed behind a loose brick above the fire escape.

"Fancy a smoke?" he asked on his return.

"Haven't touched the stuff for ages," Andrew explained. "And you shouldn't have it around the place. Get done for possession and they'll put you back inside."

"Maybe. But it helps me to keep sane."

Nick began to roll himself a single skin spliff.

"Not driving today?" Andrew asked.

"Only in the evening. I work a lot of nights. Like it that way." Nick lit up. "Remember when Trevor

Blackwell got lifted for looking like the Canning Circus rapist and the police went back, searched the house?"

Andrew chuckled. "They told him they weren't interested in the dope plants he had growing at the top of the stairs outside his room. Your dope plants."

"Minute they'd gone, he helped me clear them out. Five minutes later, the drug squad shows up."

Andrew laughed. "The dogs went crazy, but couldn't find anything. I still remember the look on their faces."

"That was Sarah," Nick said.

"Who drove the plants away? Shit, of course it was. I'd forgotten about that. You'd only just started seeing her."

"She'd borrowed her mum's car to bring her stuff up to Nottingham. When she took it back, her mum wanted to know how she'd got earth into every crevice of the upholstery."

Andrew laughed. "Maybe I will have some of that."

Nick handed the spliff to him. Andrew took several hits.

"S'nice," he said, handing back the nub-end.

"What really brings you to Nottingham?" Nick asked.

"The university want to give me an honorary doctorate for my contributions to society," Andrew said.

Nick laughed. "Seriously?"

"Seriously? A little business, that's all. I wanted to see you, make sure you were okay. But now I need to be off."

"Want me to call you a cab?"

"Only ten minutes' walk to Slab Square from here. I can use the exercise." Andrew put on his jacket, then paused at the door. "We didn't discuss this last time, but it's been playing on my mind. Have you any idea who grassed you up?"

Nick shook his head. "The police claim they got a lucky break. Better to believe that than the alternative."

"I suppose," Andrew said, "but if you've got enemies, it's best to find out who they are. Then you can watch your back if you need to."

"Thanks for the advice," Nick said. "And the money. It's appreciated."

Andrew took his leave. When he'd gone, Nick lay on his bed, glad Andrew had come, and not just because of the money. Only two people knew about the growing operation in the caves below his flat. Nick had shown Joe the caves as soon as he discovered them. Andrew had advised Nick on security, and given him contacts to help sell the stuff. Nick insisted on giving him a cut. Andy was in the States when Nick was arrested. Nick had never seriously thought that Andy had betrayed him. But it was nice to be sure. Andrew didn't need to bring the money. He didn't need to ask that awkward question. He gained no advantage from Nick's arrest. It was time to stop doubting him. Time to leave Nottingham, too? Andrew had a point. There wasn't much for him here. The phone rang and he answered it.

"Nick, hi. I'm returning your call. It's Sarah."

His voice on the other end of the phone was higher than she remembered. He sounded nervous, as though she'd caught him unawares.

"Sarah? Um, thanks for calling. It's been . . ."

"An age. How long have you been back in Nottingham?"

"Just a few weeks." She waited for him to fill in what he'd been doing, but there was another awkward pause.

"I thought I saw you driving a cab the other day."

"That would have been me. One of my brother's cars. I'm doing a bit of driving while I decide what to do next."

"Where are you living?"

He gave her the address of his flat on Alfreton Road. A relationship had broken up, Sarah guessed. He'd walked out or been kicked out and was rebuilding his life.

"It'd be good to meet," she said.

"Yes. But I understand you're kind of busy for a few more days."

"You can say that again."

"I understand you're kind of busy for a few more days."

She laughed at the corny joke, one of their silly secret habits from their first days together. Nick chuckled too, but nervously. He might be intimidated by her being an MP. How could she show him she was still the person he used to know?

"I could really do with a break from the campaign. Why don't we meet sooner?"

"I don't want to . . ." His voice trailed off. She remembered the times when he couldn't be bothered to finish his sentences. He wasn't stoned, was he? At this time of day?

136

"I'll tell you what — I'm doing this debate on Tuesday. Should be over by nine. I could meet you for a meal afterwards. Or come along if you like. It's at the ICC. Might be a laugh. Remember how you used to go over every word I said at hustings when I stood for union president? The standard isn't that much higher, believe me."

"I might have to work." Nick's tone was apologetic. "I do a lot of evenings."

"I won't book a table then. If you can't come, we'll have lunch, or a drink over the weekend. Yeah?"

"Yeah. Sure."

"If you can make it Tuesday, I'll see you there. Otherwise, why don't you take my home number?" She began to explain too much, aware that she was being overeager but unable to stop. "I've rung before, you see, and not found you in . . ."

"I've just got an answering machine."

The conversation ended awkwardly. She could have mentioned seeing Andrew Saint but that might have been awkward, too. He and Nick used to be such close friends and now they weren't. Sarah wanted to know the score with the job Andrew was offering her. It was ridiculous he wouldn't tell her more until she'd signed an agreement. How could she work out the right thing to do?

In an alternative world, she and Nick had never split up. They had lived together for nearly fifteen years now, without the need for marriage or children. Nick was always there to give her counsel and support. He made sure that she had a life outside politics, keeping in touch with old friends and all the simple shit that Sarah generally forgot to do.

Sarah didn't need a man. Being with a bad one was worse than being single. But she'd held on to this idealised vision of how life might have been with Nick. She'd been so pig-headed when she was twenty-two. She'd thought that if she and Nick were right together, it was bound to work out. If things didn't work out, there were bound to be plenty more, equally interesting fish in the sea. Wrong on both counts.

CHAPTER
SIXTEEN

It was a quiet Saturday night, the quietest since Nick started doing the job. Everyone who was going out had already done so and the pubs didn't close for another two hours. Nick needed to go to Polly's. He hadn't seen her for four days, the longest gap since they got together. He wanted sex, but he wanted to see her, too. Speaking to Sarah had disturbed him. She was a ghost from the past. Polly was real. Yet he still hadn't given her his phone number. He avoided calling her from the flat — since he went inside, you could dial 1471 and check the number of whoever last called you. He didn't want Polly calling him. Joe said there was a code that withheld your number, only Nick didn't know what it was and even if he did, to use it would look underhand.

Polly would be expecting to see him tonight, but they'd made no arrangements. In the Meadows, Nick collected an Afro-Caribbean lad who said he wanted to go to the top of Radford Road in Hyson Green. This meant the Black and White cafe, although the youth didn't mention the place: it would have marked him out as a dealer or a user. A dealer, Nick reckoned — a young black guy in the Meadows wouldn't need to go across the city to score.

"Got a mobile?" he asked his fare.

"Course."

"Can I borrow it? Quick local call. I'll knock it off your fare."

"Tell me the number. I'll dial it for you. Call it your tip."

He handed Nick the phone when it began ringing. Polly took a while to answer.

"Just putting the last one to bed."

"Can I come round for an hour? I'm heading your way."

"I've got some wine in the fridge."

"Magic."

"On a promise, huh?" The fare asked, as Nick turned down Bentinck Road.

"Looks like it. Where do you want dropping?"

"My friend lives just over there. Anywhere round here will do. Nah, you're okay. Keep the change. I'm on a promise, too."

Nick waited at the lights, watched the youth head up the hill and turn into the drive of one of the big houses on the left. A lover, not a dealer.

There were wine glasses on the table, nibbles and dips in a plastic tray from Asda. Polly was wearing a short red skirt that showed off her arse to its best advantage. But this wasn't the main thing he noticed. She'd cut her hair short, almost a pageboy. It was still blonde, but more artificial looking, with pink highlights. Nick hated it.

140

"Looks like you're ready to go out."

"What do you think to my new summer cut?"

"It's great," he said. "You look five years younger, very sexy."

Both of these things were true. For the first time since he met Polly, she looked her age, years younger than him. He wanted to fuck her but he didn't fancy her any more. She looked artificial. Everything about their relationship was artificial, he realized. Who were they kidding?

"What made you change your hair?" he asked, an hour later, when they were watching *Match of the Day*. Polly assumed that, since he was a bloke, he must be interested in football, and he hadn't corrected her. It was useful fodder for cab conversation and gave them something to do.

"I used to wear it like this. No need to act older than you are."

"Right." He preferred a woman who looked more mature, but wasn't foolish enough to say this. Earlier, he had screwed her standing up, from behind, with Polly leaning over the sofa and biting on a cushion to keep herself from crying out when she came. Urgent, anonymous sex was the kind they were best at. Since they finished, she'd been quieter than normal, as though something was on her mind. Him, probably, the way he used her, only showing up when it suited him. Nick ought to offer her more. If he hadn't arranged to see Sarah, maybe he'd be ready to.

"Is there something you want to talk about . . . about us?"

She gave him a look that said she wasn't used to having this kind of conversation and Nick regretted opening his mouth.

"There isn't an *us*, is there? Maybe there would've been, if you were free to be more than a back-door man. But we agreed from the start."

If you were free to. Nick sipped his second small glass of wine, wondered how to reply. He hadn't heard the phrase *back-door man* for a long time, but knew what she meant. "Agreed what?"

"This is just for sex, comfort. We're convenient for each other."

"It's more than that," Nick said.

Polly stroked his groin. "Not a lot more. Being with you's made me realize I need someone proper. It's five years since I've felt that way."

He held her. They kissed. It was real, all right. But if anything was to come of it, Nick had to be honest. He couldn't mislead her any longer.

"There are things about me you don't know," he said.

"You're not going to tell me you're happily married?" Her voice had taken on a whinging tone he'd not heard before. "You wouldn't be working all hours, coming to me three times a week if you had everything together at home."

"I've never been married," Nick said. "But I've been in prison. I only got out two and a half months ago."

A moody silence followed. Nick had blown it. Most women, he guessed, would prefer a cheat to an ex-con.

"How long were you in?" she asked, finally.

Not what for but how long? The length of the sentence would tell her the severity of the crime. She was not a policeman's sister for nothing.

"I did five."

"How come you're driving a taxi then? Thought they had rules."

"I'm not on the books." For a moment, he nearly told her that his brother owned the firm, but he had never told Polly his surname and if he did, that would mean she could always find him through Joe.

"You're a fool. Do you want to go back inside?"

"No. I need to get a bit of money behind me, that's all."

But now he had The Saint's five grand, there was no excuse.

"You're not going to tell me what you did?"

Nick shook his head. Polly never mentioned drugs. It might freak her out. "It wasn't violent, if that worries you."

"No. You're not violent. Five years, eh? Explains why you're so horny for a used-up slapper like me."

"Don't denigrate yourself, it's not . . ."

"I don't know what *denigrate* means," Polly said. "Did an Open University degree while you were inside, did you? Terry always hated that — crims who got an education while they were doing time."

"I already had a degree," Nick told her. "I used to be a teacher."

"Interfered with kiddies, did you?" She slapped him on the face. "Why didn't you tell me?"

"I'm telling you now. It was nothing like that."

She slapped him again, harder. "What did you do?"

"I sold drugs," he told her.

"To kids?"

"No. Wholesale. Homegrown. Nobody got hurt, except me."

"Did you see *him* inside?"

"Ed? We were in the same nick for a while. I might have seen him, but I didn't know him." Nick should tell her that Ed worked for Joe, but couldn't work out how to do this tactfully. Anyway, he still held out some hope that he would persuade his brother to get rid of him.

"Why didn't you tell me? How many more secrets have you got?"

Polly had begun to hit him now. Hard. She was hurting him so he had to fend her off. Nick didn't want to hit back. He never hit women. When Polly kept coming at him, he had to push her away. She kept attacking, ignoring the concerned calls from children upstairs. He pushed her down onto the sofa, grabbing both wrists so that she couldn't hit him any more, pushing her legs down with his right knee so that she couldn't kick him. Polly stared at him, her eyes hard, resentful.

"I'll bet this gives you a hard-on," she said.

It was true.

"This isn't over," she told him. Then she gave him a full-mouthed kiss and, when he let one of her wrists go so that they could be more, comfortable, she unzipped him.

"Now it's over," Polly said, as she pulled on her knickers afterwards. Her voice was matter of fact. "I'm not having a drug dealer around these kids. We've had a good time, but I need to move on. Stay away."

CHAPTER
SEVENTEEN

It was a sparse crowd, considering that this was the only debate of the election, but events like this belonged to the past. A modern election was about phone canvassing and spinning the TV news, not engaging floating voters in a musty public hall. Sarah had been scanning the audience while the other speakers took their turn. She'd spotted Nick, two thirds of the way back. He was talking to an older bloke on the row behind but appeared to be on his own. That must mean their meal was on. Despite her excitement, she trotted out the rehearsed answers with ease. Nothing she said would affect a single vote in nine days' time.

When a blonde woman stood up, Sarah knew she knew her, but only when she spoke did Sarah take a closer look and work out where from. Polly Bolton, Terry Shanks' sister, had cut her hair since Sarah saw her last.

"I'd like to ask each candidate what they are going to do for victims of crime. Seems to me that you lot are more interested in the criminals than the innocent people who get hurt by them."

The replies started at the other end of the panel, so Sarah had plenty of time to think about her answer. Jeremy Atkinson covered compensation and counselling. The Liberal wanted more funding for victims' groups and the Green talked about better lighting and urban planning. Sarah wasn't left with much to say. She worried that Polly had an awkward supplemental saved up to throw at her. Best, therefore, to head her off before she could land a direct hit.

"I agree with most of what's been said, especially about compensation. I know — without going into details — that you and your family have been terribly affected by a serious crime where the perpetrators have not been brought to justice."

"Are you sure about that?" Polly interrupted.

"And that isn't good enough. I'll be pursuing the matter with the Chief Constable when we meet tomorrow," Sarah said, suffering a rush of blood to the head. She was due to meet the police chief for a photo op, not a pep talk on the murder of Terry Shanks. "Please don't think that I've given up your case. But we have to follow the law."

Polly tried to ask another question. The chair wouldn't let her. "We only have a few minutes left. There are several people with raised hands."

Instinctively, Sarah looked for Nick, to see how he was reacting to the one tricky encounter of the evening. He had his head turned, so his expression was hard to read. He was looking at Polly.

The debate drifted on for another twenty minutes. Sarah tried to stay focused, but it had already been a long campaign. Constituents often thought that MPs led cushy lives. When voters asked Sarah if she'd ever had to work hard, in a real job, she usually mentioned her two-year spell in the police. The reality was that most police worked set hours, during which there was plenty of downtime, whereas an MP, if she were at all conscientious, had to knock herself out every day. But that story didn't play with voters. Electoral politics was all about perception, not principle or, God forbid, the reality of being a politician trying to get things done.

The event finished just after nine. The candidates nodded at each other, mumbled acknowledgments that it had been a fair fight. Jeremy looked pleased with himself. He was no Barrett Jones, but he hadn't slipped up, so the local party would be happy with their man. This time, he might find himself with a seat in the Commons for life.

"Coming to the Peacock?" Tony Bax asked.

"No, thanks. I'm meeting an old friend for a meal. I thought I'd take the rest of the evening off politics."

"Good idea. You did very well. Bet you're glad it's out of the way."

"Thanks." Sarah was sorry not to spend time with Tony, who was radical Old Labour personified. She looked around. Winston was smiling, fending off a couple who wanted to press her about traffic calming. There was Polly Bolton. Was she going to come over? Sarah ought to speak to her if she did. But no, Polly wasn't waiting for Sarah. She was waiting for Nick. Sarah tried to interpret the look that passed between the two of them, but it was hard to make out. All she could see was Nick and Polly leaving the hall together. What the hell was that about?

When, five minutes later, her dinner date hadn't returned, she joined Tony Bax, who was in conversation with Winston.

"My friend can't make it. Guess I can have that drink after all."

Nick followed Polly out of the hall to the side of the ICC. They stood in the shadows as the last stragglers left.

"Didn't know you were so interested in politics," Polly said.

"I'm not. I had an hour to kill, thought I'd come along, that's all."

"You wanted a look at that Sarah Bone I keep slagging off."

"Something like that, yeah."

"Did you call me first, see if I was in, or I was coming?"

"No. Thing is, I'm meant to be meeting someone."

"Who? A woman?"

"An old friend." Nick was never comfortable telling a direct lie.

"The kids are at Shell's for another hour. If you gave me a lift, you could come back wi' me." She was offering him another farewell fuck.

"I'm not in the car tonight." Nick wasn't sure what to do. He didn't want to speak to Sarah while she was standing by Tony Bax. But he didn't want Sarah to think he'd deserted her. Had she seen him in the audience? Probably. There was something else. The last time he was at Polly's, before she'd finished with him, he'd meant to tell her that Ed Clark was working for his brother. Polly would want to avoid getting her taxis from Cane Cars. Now was the time.

"Before you go . . ."

Nick stepped further back into the shadows. Polly misinterpreted.

"Are you thinking what I think you're thinking? You dirty sod."

"No, I . . ." Nick paused, because he could see that the idea turned her on. And at another time, it would turn him on too, a knee-trembler down the side of a building, only yards from a busy road. Polly pushed him back towards the wall.

"You've never had better, have you? All right then. One last time."

She was right. He wanted raw, real Polly rather than the packaged, permed New Labour edition of Sarah he'd seen tonight, the Sarah he could see walking out of the ICC, accompanied by Tony Bax and a small black bloke. Sarah glanced in his direction. For a moment, Nick thought she'd noticed him. Polly stared daggers at her.

"I'll get her good, one of these days."

"You already got her," Nick said.

"What do you mean?"

Nick didn't explain. He knew what he wanted. It was over in two minutes. When he'd zipped himself back up, she ruffled his hair. "Gotta run. I like fighting with you. The sex is better."

150

He'd still not told her about Ed Clark. Maybe Ed would fail his city council test, and the problem would go away. Nick walked down Mansfield Road. He glanced through the window into the snug at the Peacock. Sarah was drinking red wine, smiling politely, not having fun. Nick could go in, take her out, and tell her about his sentence before she got it from Tony, or anybody else. But he didn't. He turned around and walked hurriedly, building up a sweat as he cut through back streets, heading for his flat on Alfreton Road. When he got in, he left a message on her answering machine, apologising.

"I met somebody who needed my help," he said, cryptically. "Sorry. You did well tonight. Catch you soon."

It was only after four drinks that Sarah worked out a way to ask Tony Bax the question. Her constituency chairman had praised the fluency of her performance and done his best to persuade Sarah that all was not lost. A stream of party members and well-wishers stopped at Sarah's table, congratulating her, urging her on. It was good for morale, but by ten to eleven, Sarah and Tony had run out of conversation. He walked her to the taxi rank outside the Victoria Centre. This was her last chance.

"I thought I saw someone I used to know in the ICC, a guy called Nick Cane. Have you come across him?"

"Nick, yes. Lovely guy. Very active in the party in the late eighties. Were you at university with him?"

"That's right." Sarah stopped herself saying more. "We were friends. I thought he might come over afterwards."

"Nick had a bit of bother with the law. Maybe he thought you'd heard about it, wouldn't want anything to do with him."

"He should know I'm not like that."

"People change," Tony said.

Did they? Sarah could never decide. People were always changing, the way she saw it, but only in superficial ways. As they got older, many relaxed into themselves, stopped pretending to be what they weren't. Others took on airs or gravitas. But they seldom seemed to change.

"What was the trouble?" she asked.

"Drugs. He probably didn't want to embarrass you, being seen with him, so close to an election."

"Yes," she said. "I expect that's right."

"Still, it was good of him to turn up. I always had a lot of time for Nick. I hope he manages to turn his life around."

They had beaten the pubs' throwing-out time, so there was no queue for a taxi. Sarah was home in five minutes. She played the message that Nick had left on her machine. Cryptic. Tony was probably right. Nick was being tactful. So he'd been busted for possession, so what? Sarah was hardly going to go all moral on him. She picked up the phone, intending to see if he was home. But that would make her seem pushy, or a pushover, Sarah wasn't sure which. It was late and she was a little drunk. She went to bed.

CHAPTER
EIGHTEEN

The morning was wet. Sarah put on a trouser suit for her meeting with the Chief Constable, then changed her mind. There would be TV and the outfit made her look too wide on camera. She didn't much like the yellow dress she replaced it with. The dress had been picked for her by a party image consultant when she fought the by-election. Evidently the colour worked well on telly. More importantly, it flattered her legs and bum, making the former seem longer and the latter smaller. It would do.

She and Eric met at police headquarters in Arnold. "The Dream Factory" was what the plods called it.

"You look wonderful," Eric announced, when she was shown into his office. He would have said that if she was wearing an anorak and combat trousers. The Chief Constable was fiftyish and not above flirtation when he judged you might be receptive to it. Sarah wasn't above flirting back.

"Let's wait for a glimpse of sunshine before we take the photos," Eric said. "Central News aren't here yet. Quick coffee?"

Sarah accepted. Her head was still a little bleary from the night before. She took the offered seat and decided to say what was on her mind, even though it might undo the good relationship she'd built up with Eric.

"Terry Shanks' sister was at the debate last night. I didn't have anything to tell her."

"That's probably because we got the right man first time around."

"The evidence against him didn't hold up," Sarah reminded Eric.

"It's possible he was innocent, I'll grant you. But everybody else with a motive was in prison at the time."

"The murder of Shanks might not have been connected to Clark and his associates," Sarah suggested. "Suppose Shanks interrupted whoever raped his wife, got shot with his own gun?"

"As I recall, Clark's lawyers used that angle in the trial but there was forensic to suggest that Shanks died up to an hour before his wife."

Their coffee arrived. Sarah waited until they were alone, gathering her thoughts before she continued.

"The prosecution tried to suggest that Ed killed Terry then hung around for the best part of an hour until Liv returned from work. But he had nothing against Liv, apart from her being married to the man who had him put away. It made no sense, him taking a risk like that."

"An evil sod like Clark doesn't have to make sense. Don't expect us to wrap the whole case up in ribbons for you. We'll never be sure what happened. We rarely are, when there are no witnesses."

"Suppose the intended victim wasn't Terry, but his wife? Ed had no motive to hang around and kill Liv."

154

"But he did," Eric said. "Liv knew what her husband had done, condoned it."

"Condoned what?"

"I've said too much. Ask Polly Bolton. We tried to keep her out of it. Biscuit?"

Sarah took a Viennese Whirl, coated at each side in plain chocolate. Before she could press him about Polly, Eric called the press officer.

"They'll be ready for us in five minutes. There was something else I wanted a brief word about. I don't want you to take it the wrong way."

"Words that usually precede an insult."

"The thing is, I do hope you get re-elected."

"Nice of you," Sarah said, irritated that he was giving her no opportunity to press him further about Ed Clark. "Me too. I appreciate your arranging this photo op."

"But your chances are, shall we say, slender?"

"So they tell me."

"Have you thought about what you'll do if you don't get back in?"

"I've had one or two offers, but nothing I'm committed to."

"You've impressed many people in the police community."

"Getting Ed Clark out on appeal? You surprise me."

"You talk hard on law and order as well as human rights. You're pragmatic about prisons. And you know the job."

"I got out of the job."

"The police aren't allowed to be politicians, for good reason. But we don't always present ourselves in the best possible light. When the new government comes in, we need a good relationship with them."

"I don't think you'll have a problem there. *Tough on crime*, we have to prove we mean that."

The phone rang and Eric answered it. The cameras were ready. "Two minutes," he said, then continued. "The Association of Police Officers is looking for a new chairman, someone who'll give the force a sharper, more modern image. A woman, ideally."

"Doesn't the chairman have to be a Chief Constable?" Sarah said. "I don't recall there being many women in that job."

"We're thinking of going outside the force, hiring someone with political experience and PR skills. Someone like you."

"I'm only thirty-five years old," Sarah said, surprised and flattered. "Aren't I at least twenty years too young for the job?"

"Youth is an extra qualification. Every time you appeared on television, especially when wearing a dress like that, you'd be a valuable recruitment tool."

"I'm not sure I want to be a tool," Sarah said, keeping her tone light, weighing up the surprising offer. "What's the salary?"

"Negotiable. Chief Constable scale, I would hazard a guess."

More than an MP earned. Quite a lot more.

"I'll certainly think about it," Sarah said.

156

"The current chairman would like to talk it over with you — after the election, obviously. We couldn't try to poach a sitting MP. But you're not entirely averse to the idea?"

"Not entirely averse," Sarah repeated. She had never considered returning to the police. Yet, as a career move, it made more sense than working for Andrew Saint. If she took the job, police rules meant she wouldn't be able to look for another parliamentary seat. That might be a relief. She didn't want to spend the next three or four years hoping to step into a dead man's shoes at another by-election. But the job would probably rule her out of the next general election, too.

"We'd better go and present these safety awards," Eric said, picking up his jacket from the hook behind Sarah, gently brushing her left breast as he did so. As they rattled along the uncarpeted corridor, Sarah made sure to ask after his wife and children.

Nick watched the local lunchtime news before going to meet his probation officer. Seeing Sarah on the telly reinforced his feeling of the night before. She inhabited a different planet from him. Sarah's smile was confident but plastic. Nick had begun the process that made her what she was today, but she had long since left him behind, reinvented herself.

The Probation service gave Nick his weekly reminder that he was only free on license. Small, dapper Dave Trapp was about Nick's age, with sandy hair brushed over a bald patch and a jutting-out chin. Had Nick made a different choice on leaving university, he could be where Dave was now. Dave was okay. He treated Nick like an equal. Their meetings so far had been short and cordial.

"Settling into the new flat?"

"It's fine. Convenient for town."

"Good of your brother to help you out with the deposit. Are you getting enough private tuition work to cover the rent?"

"Not really."

Dave started talking about benefits, but Nick had no intention of claiming. He'd signed off at the first opportunity. It was one thing, driving a taxi without a permit, another doing it while drawing the dole: they'd add time to his sentence for that.

"I get by," Nick insisted.

"You have to understand that we don't want to see you drawn back into the way you earned a living before going to prison."

"I was a school teacher for six years," Nick reminded him. "I did the other thing for less than two. It was a blip. I'm not likely to start again."

"What about when you can't afford to pay the rent?"

Nick had five grand of Andrew Saint's money, but he couldn't tell Trapp that without explaining why Saint owed him.

"It was never about money, why I started in the first place."

"What was it about then?"

It was about looking thirty in the eye and realizing that he had made nothing of himself, working himself into the ground for crap wages while money poured into the hands of flash gits who did big city jobs where the only qualifications required were greed and a lack of scruples. But this was not the whole truth. Nor was it what Dave Trapp wanted to hear. Nick had to pretend that what he'd done was wrong.

"It was about temptation," he said, "and greed. Finding those caves beneath the flat was too good an opportunity. But the flat's sold, and I'm told some very heavy people have moved into the homegrown game while I was away. I'm not that greedy, or that brave."

"Is that how you got caught?" Dave asked. "Grassed on by a competitor?"

Nick shrugged. This was new territory between them. Probation weren't supposed to be interested in his original arrest. "Why do you ask?"

"You're a bright guy. The business you were in, the clever ones usually keep a distance from their supply and get away with it. I wondered how you got caught. It's not in your notes."

Dave gave off an air of genial, low level competence but Nick suspected a hidden agenda. Did he think Nick was after revenge?

"I think one of the neighbours saw something, called the police."

Dave nodded. "Unlucky. Anyway, I'm glad things are going so well. Only one more weekly meeting to go, then we'll be down to once a fortnight. Can we move next week's appointment to Friday? I have a family thing."

"Sure." Nick made a note of the new date and time, midday on the day after the general election.

CHAPTER
NINETEEN

Nick didn't call on Wednesday. Sarah wanted to ring him, but didn't. Soon she'd be on her way: either to Surbiton or to work for his ex-best friend. Maybe she could reunite the three of them: her, Nick, Andy. But not if she worked for the Police Association. Their figurehead couldn't hang out with two notorious dopers. She remembered that time she'd saved their bacon, fifteen years ago. If Sarah had been caught then, she wouldn't have a parliamentary career now. The thought caught her up short. The last three years had been frustrating a lot of the time, but she wouldn't have missed them for anything. To work in London but not be an MP would be a kind of purgatory. She couldn't stay in Nottingham either. With the proceeds from her two flats, she could buy somewhere pretty decent, but first she'd need to decide where. Surbiton sounded anonymous. She looked it up — inside the M25 but a long way from London. It was near Esher, where one of the Beatles used to live. How did she know that? From the fund of useless knowledge she'd picked up when going out with Nick.

She was tired. The last week of the campaign was always the hardest, the most frantic. She had a busy diary, but none of it was essential any more. The voters would do what the voters decided to do. Sarah entertained a fantasy of going into a travel agent's, booking a week's cheap break somewhere, returning just in time for the count on Thursday night. The party workers could get on with it. They were a masochistic lot, who enjoyed going from door to door, irritating the apathetic, risking their fingers every time they shoved a leaflet through a letterbox. It was, she'd often thought, some kind of substitute for religion. She'd done it herself, of course, paid her dues: but that was all it was, paying dues so that she could become a candidate, and then an MP.

There were no travel agents in the Maynard Estate, the part of her constituency with the lowest turn-out. Sarah joined the doorknockers for an hour, then back to the Labour Committee Rooms. A wind was getting up. Light drizzle splashed the wheely bin by the back door. Sarah went to the loo and when she got back, the drizzle had become a downpour. Winston was talking to someone.

"Probably only last a few minutes. Hold on and have a tea before you go out."

"I don't mind getting wet," said a familiar voice.

"It's not you I'm worried about, it's the leaflets. Have you met the candidate? Sarah, this is . . . sorry, didn't catch your name."

"We've met," Sarah said. "Winston, this is an old university friend of mine. Nick Cane."

The agent left them alone. They stood awkwardly, neither embracing, nor shaking hands. Sarah's hair was windblown. Up close, she didn't look plastic. She didn't look much different from the last time they met, thirteen years before. Nick didn't know what to say.

"Sorry about the other night," he managed. "Something came up."

"Polly Bolton. I saw. How do you happen to know her?"

"You meet a lot of people, driving a cab. But it wasn't just that. There are reasons why you might not want to be seen in public with me."

Sarah put a calming hand on his upper arm, gave him a small squeeze. "I spoke to Tony Bax in the pub. He told me about your trouble, said that was probably why you were keeping your distance."

"I'm glad you know." Nick was relieved Sarah was still talking to him, even being friendly.

Sarah put on an air of forced jollity. "Are we going to catch up then? I mean, it's nice of you to come and leaflet but it's pissing down. There'll be fifty people showing up in an hour who'll be hacked off if there's nothing for them to do and, anyway, I'm going to lose. So I'd much rather go for a drink with you."

"How can I refuse?" Nick said.

"Drinks will have to be on you, though."

"I remember. Candidates aren't allowed to buy drinks for other people during an election. I'm on foot. Is there anywhere good nearby?"

"Fuck, no," Sarah said. "Let's take my car."

Seeing Sarah, walking with her, Nick wanted her, but in the same way he wanted unobtainable women on the TV. She had moved far beyond him. She was agitated,

162

he could see that, but it was to do with the election, not him. In the passenger seat of her unassuming hatchback, Nick found Sarah's proximity unnerving. The weather changed just as suddenly as it had a few minutes before, wind pushing away the cloud to create a dazzling sky.

"I don't really want a drink," Sarah said. "I've had enough to drink lately. Fancy a walk, while it's like this? University lake?"

"Great."

They turned towards the ring road and, to make conversation, he asked how the election was going.

"Labour will win big, I'll lose small. By-election gains always go back to the party that used to hold the seat."

"You've beaten their guy once, you can do it again."

"I doubt it, but thanks for your confidence. I might not have got into this lark if it hadn't been for you, all that time ago."

They reminisced about the student union election because it was safer than talking about the present. Slowly, Nick unwound. By the time they pulled up at the university, he was almost relaxed. Sarah hadn't changed, he decided. Nor had he. People didn't change: they adapted their behaviour to fit the circumstances life threw at them. Sarah was about to be unemployed, like him. They weren't so far apart.

Sarah parked at the back of the lakeside pavilion with its crumbling plaster and rowing boats for hire.

"They're planning to knock this down soon," Sarah said, as they got out of the car. "Replace it with a fancy arts pavilion — galleries, a theatre, you name it."

"Bet they don't have discos," Nick said, referring to the only event anyone used to visit the pavilion for in their day.

"Bet they don't."

Sarah took off her red rosette. "I'll stop being the candidate for a few minutes." She peeled the red sticker from Nick's *People's March For Jobs* T-shirt. "I remember you buying this. Bit tight on you now. Where did those muscles come from?"

"I don't remember the last time I was on a march," Nick said. This was a mad place to come, he decided. They had so much history here. This used to be the place they would go in order to get Sarah out of her musty Union President's office. They would come here when they needed to talk, or simply walk. Although part of the university campus, it was mainly used by townies. Children fed the ducks. Courting couples went out in the rowing boats. Family groups took constitutionals. On its right, larger side, the lake had a small island in the middle. The narrower left side ended in crossing stones and a shallow waterfall. Between the two stood a stone bridge, which led to a small patch of woodland. Nick and Sarah walked towards that.

"Until you rang, I had no idea you were still in Nottingham. Once, I saw the back of your head driving a cab but thought I was imagining it."

"I've been away too. I expect Tony told you. I've made a mess of things, Sarah. I'm only just starting to put my life back together."

164

A toddler on a tricycle was coming towards them on the path, trailed by her grandparents. Sarah was pushed towards Nick. She put her arm around his waist.

When the group had passed, Sarah left her arm where it was, and he reciprocated. "Don't be ashamed," she said. "Why don't we take a boat? Have you got time? Half an hour?"

"Why not?" Nick hadn't rowed in twelve years. His arms were stronger than they used to be. It was a chance to show off. They turned back, paid a couple of quid and clambered into the rickety craft, both grateful to be occupied by activity.

"Remember that night, after we saw The Specials?" Sarah pointed at a tree where, early in their relationship, they had made love at midnight, jeans around their ankles, with a need for each other so urgent they couldn't wait until they got back to one of their rooms.

"How about that time we took a boat out to the island and got out to explore."

"*You* got out to explore," Sarah protested. "I was shit-scared we'd lose the boat and be stuck there."

He was rowing easily now and began to ask the expected questions: family, friends, who there was in her life. Sarah was almost as bereft as him. More so, since she was an only child, while he had Joe, Caroline and a niece or nephew on the way.

"Girlfriend?" she asked.

"I was seeing someone, casually. It's over now. You?"

"There was someone, but we split up last month. It wasn't going anywhere."

"What will you do if you lose?" Nick asked. "Stay around here?"

"Doubt it. London's where the work is. I've had a couple of offers."

Nick was starting to sweat heavily. It was hot and this was the most physical exercise he'd had since getting out. "Mind if we take a breather?"

"We used to do that, didn't we? Just float."

He gazed at her, feeling good about himself, better than he had done for years. He had to tell her everything that had happened. But not yet. There was no need to spoil this moment, not when birds were singing, the sun was shining, ducks drifting by and Sarah was smiling at him.

"Do you remember why we split up?" she asked, breaking the reverie. "I've been thinking about it and I don't, not really."

"We never did officially split up, did we? We both had flings with other people, then were too proud or stubborn to call the other."

She gave a wry smile of agreement, so he took the opportunity to ask a question that had been on his mind. "How long did you stay in the police?"

"Just under three years. You were right about . . . a lot of things. I stuck it out longer than I should have done. As you said, I can be pretty stubborn."

"I kind of liked that in you," he said, and squeezed her hand.

They sat in companionable silence.

"The half hour's nearly up," she said, after a while. "I think we've played hooky for as long as we can get away with."

"Not before I do this." He leant forward and so did she. They kissed. Then they kissed again.

"You'd better stop that before we have this boat over," Sarah said.

He pulled back, smiling, and took hold of the oars. "Worried one of your constituents will see you?"

"I'm more worried about a freelance photographer with a long lens," Sarah said.

Twenty minutes later, she dropped him off outside the Committee Rooms.

"Win or lose, there's a party next Thursday night."

"I'm meant to be driving until late."

"I don't suppose I'll arrive before one. It's at the Arnold Labour Club."

"I'll try to be there," Nick told her.

She gave him her home and mobile numbers. "I'd like to see you again before then. Tomorrow?"

"I've got a family thing. But I could do Saturday." He was meant to be driving but fuck that. He ought to pack it in. If, by some miracle, he could get back with Sarah, it was too risky to do anything that would break the rules of his parole.

"I think I can free up some of Saturday night," Sarah said. "As long as you don't stand me up again."

"I promise," Nick said. They kissed again, just a peck this time, as people might be watching.

CHAPTER
TWENTY

The campaign was relentless, leaving little time to think. Easy, in these circumstances, for Sarah to compartmentalize her feelings about Nick, to put off thinking about him until Saturday afternoon. But there was one problem she had to find time for. *Ask Polly Bolton. We tried to keep her out of it.* The Chief Constable's remarks had made no sense to Sarah, but she kept replaying them in her head. There was something nuanced about the way he used the words. Sarah tried to remember their exact context. She'd been asking about Ed Clark's lack of motive for murdering Liv. She'd read the murder trial papers. Polly Bolton wasn't called as a witness. Sarah couldn't recall her even being mentioned in the trial. What was Eric getting at? He'd said something about Liv condoning what Terry had done. What had he done? Sarah couldn't go to Polly again. Whatever motive Eric was implying, it had to go back to Ed's original arrest and trial, for handling stolen goods.

Sarah phoned Brian Hicks at the *Evening Post*, explained what she was after.

"Bit late in the day, isn't it? Must be seven years ago."

"Could you photocopy me the reports from the time?"

"Certainly. Quick drink tonight?"

"Fine. I'd like that," Sarah said. It occurred to her that there would have been newspaper stories about Nick's arrest. Otherwise Tony Bax wouldn't have known about it. Nick, she realized, must have lost his job as a teacher. Sarah was curious to know more than she could comfortably ask Nick. She could phone Brian back, ask him to dig for details. But Brian would want to know why she wanted to know. Best not to go down that road. Nick would tell her the full story when he was ready.

After three hours of canvassing, she met Brian Hicks in the side bar of the Bell Inn. Brian was three quarters of the way down a pint of Shippo's, probably not his first.

"Six days to go," he said, making it sound like a death sentence.

"I'll be glad when it's over, one way or the other."

"You're looking good, in better spirits than I've seen you for ages. Think you might be closing in from behind?"

Her good spirits had nothing to do with the election. Over the last day, Sarah kept feeling suddenly happy and couldn't think why. Then she remembered seeing Nick again.

"The end's in sight, that's all. Did you dig out those cuttings for me?"

"Straight to business, as ever," Brian sighed. He handed Sarah a folder and she flicked through the contents. The *Evening Post* of 1990 hadn't covered the crime in enormous detail. There was barely any mention of Ed Clark. He was the youngest member of the gang and the police hadn't been able to prove that he was part of the robbery. He had been charged with receiving stolen goods, for which he received a year's sentence and received six months.

"It doesn't explain how they got caught," Sarah pointed out, after speed-reading a week's worth of pieces. "I reckon there's something the police are keeping back, something that won't be in the court records."

She tried to think of a way to bring Polly Bolton into it without mentioning what Eric had said. Then she noticed something that wasn't there.

"Why did Ed kill Terry Shanks rather than any of the other officers who arrested him? Terry Shanks isn't even mentioned in these reports. It doesn't sound like he can have played a big part in the arrests. He wasn't even proper CID, was he? He was only attached to them for a few months."

"You'd have to ask the sister-in-law that. Polly something. Only one left alive."

"I don't think she'll talk to me."

Brian thought for a moment. "I'll bet the husband knew the score."

"Polly's ex? Think you can find him for me?"

"I shall use the full range of my reporter's skills," Brian said, rising unsteadily from his seat, "but we will need to move to the snug. They keep my most useful tool behind the bar in there."

Sarah followed him into the bar on the right, where Brian ordered another pint for himself and a second gin and tonic for her, though she'd barely started the first.

"And can I borrow your phone book?" he asked the barmaid. He handed the directory to Sarah. "Know the guy's first name? Be your own detective."

Sarah trawled her memory. She should recall Polly's husband's name. He had left her, not long after the murder, not long after the couple were landed with two Shanks kids on top of their own two. She remembered Polly cursing him, saying he didn't keep in touch, even though he didn't live far off. MPs had to be good with names. Phil. She was pretty sure that was it.

She looked for a Philip Bolton in the Nottingham area. There were five with the initial P in the book. No Philip or Phillips. None lived in the city. One was in Arnold. Another in West Bridgford. That was nearest, so she tried it first, using her party mobile. No good. The "P" stood for Peter.

"What are you trying to find out?" Brian asked, plonking her drink in front of her, spilling a few drops onto the table as he did so.

"I'm not sure," Sarah said, punching in the Arnold number. "There's something I've not been told and, without it, I'm at a disadvantage."

"A disadvantage in what?" Brian asked, but Sarah knew better than to answer. Brian was voluble when pissed and gave an impression of oafishness, yet retained a trained reporter's memory and the curiosity that went with it. A male voice answered the phone.

"Is that Philip Bolton? I mean, Phil . . ."

171

"Speaking."

"You used to live in Basford, with your ex-wife, Polly."

"Yeah. What's this about?"

Brian was hanging on her words. Sarah decided that she couldn't do this over the phone. It was too risky, even, to reveal who she was.

"It's something I can only explain in person."

Joe's birthday meal ought to have been a treat: Caroline was a good cook, but working over a hot stove was no job for a heavily pregnant woman, so Nick volunteered to do the honours. They were having roast chicken, the Sunday dinner that was Joe's favourite meal. Nick followed Caroline's instructions on making bread sauce, but the result was lumpy and tasted too strongly of cloves. Joe tried to help with an extra dish, something complicated concerning mustard seeds and cabbage.

The roast potatoes, when they came out of the oven, were hard enough to remove prison fillings. The chicken was over-cooked. At least the gravy was all right. Nick was good at gravy.

"He passed, by the way," Joe said, as he put on the peas.

"You what?"

"Ed Clark passed his knowledge test. I've put him on the books, officially."

"I see."

"How much longer do you plan to drive for?"

"A week at most," Nick said. His resolution to stop at once had wilted.

"Probation come up with anything?"

"Silly jobs. Shelf stacking. Industrial cleaning. Applied for a couple and wasn't even called for interview. Didn't put in too convincing an application, mind. I'll find something else."

Caroline ignored the bread sauce and carefully scraped the soft part out of the hard potatoes. She was tired and conversation was strained. Nick began to describe the debate on Tuesday night.

"You used to go out with this woman?" Caroline asked.

"We lived together for two years while we were at university and just after."

"Why did you split up?"

"She joined the police," Joe pointed out. "That's what you told me."

"I don't think it was the only reason. We were — what? — twenty-two. At that age you think you know everything and there's bound to be another soul mate just round the corner."

"Only there wasn't," Caroline said.

"Nah. There was Clare. She sort of moved in with me for a few months the following year, but she wanted to settle down with someone and said I wasn't over Sarah. Then I went out with Nazia for nearly a year."

"I thought Nazia was great," Joe said, picking up his chicken leg and crunching into the skin.

"You've got a thing for Asian women," Caroline told her husband. "But you've never been out with one. Why's that?"

"I asked Nazia to marry me," Nick confessed, when Joe didn't answer. "She said yes. We knew her family wouldn't have it, not in the mid-eighties, but Mum and Dad were both alive then and I was going to take her to meet them. She bottled out at the last minute. Then she dumped me for a dentist."

"Any idea what happened to her?"

"Married the dentist, at a guess. He was from the same caste as her."

Nick wondered again if his brother was screwing Nas at the office. Did Caroline suspect, hence her jibe about Asian women? She knew Joe hadn't been entirely faithful before they were married and she'd still walked down the aisle with him. It was none of Nick's business.

"What about now?" Caroline asked, pushing round the peas on her still full plate. "Are you seeing anybody?"

She had carefully moved the conversation to this point, Nick realized. A week ago, he might have mentioned Polly, but not now.

"Not seriously," was all he said.

"What about Sarah?" Joe asked. His voice took on a schoolboy snigger. "Still interested?"

"The last thing an MP needs is to be seen chumming up with an ex-con," Nick said. "If she loses next Thursday, I'll see her."

"How gallant," Caroline said, putting down her knife and fork to signal that she had given up on the meal.

Soon Caroline went upstairs for a sleep while the two men dozed through the afternoon match on Sky. After the game, Nick borrowed Joe's bike to get home. Joe had bought the bike to "keep fit" but never used it. Nick's Canning Circus flat was only a two-mile ride,

174

but he chose a round-about route, one that took him past Polly's. He cycled slowly, still full from dinner. He'd had a couple of glasses of wine and the memory of his last visit to Polly's made him horny. But the other night was a one-off. They were over. He was going to see Polly out of friendship, to warn her about Ed, suggest she start using a different taxi firm.

Now that there was a chance of Nick getting back with Sarah, he couldn't resume the sexual relationship with Polly. He wasn't like Joe: he couldn't be with Polly one day and Sarah the next. Whatever happened, he must not sleep with Polly this afternoon. The kids wouldn't be in bed yet, so he should be spared the temptation.

It was a mild, spring evening, not yet dusk. By the time he got to Polly's, he had worked up a mild sweat. The oldest girl answered the door. Kayleigh was one of Polly's nieces. Behind her, the house was a chaos of younger kids shouting, playing, running around.

"Is she in?" he asked.

"I thought you only came when it was dark?" Kayleigh said, looking him up and down. The girl was only eleven but already had discernable breasts. Her knowing look made him uncomfortable.

"Isn't this night?" he tried to be funny, pointing at the strong evening sun that beamed through the window. "It's awfully dark outside."

"You're weird," Kayleigh said. "Polly's with her boyfriend. Upstairs."

Now she was winding him up. Nick laughed and went up the stairs. He tapped on her bedroom door. "It's me. Nick."

"Hold on." It was a long minute before Polly pulled the door half open. The girl wasn't lying. She did have someone in there.

"This isn't a good time," Polly said, her face contorted. With guilt or shame, Nick wasn't sure.

"I can see that." Nick was unsettled, but Polly was breaking no promises. She'd let him think he was her only lover, but he had never asked for, and she had never offered monogamy. Only, why was this bloke allowed in now when Nick was normally invited over only when the kids were at school or had gone to bed? At least she had the good grace to look uncomfortable.

"I had some news," he told her. "It'll only take a minute."

"Spit it out, then." Polly's dressing gown was old and her short hair was a mess, sticking up in several different directions. He didn't want to be here. After two months, Nick knew every part of Polly's body, but he had never got far inside her head.

"It's Ed Clark. He's passed his test to get a taxi permit. The firm I'm with has given him a job. Sorry, there was nothing I could do about it."

"You could have phoned," Polly said, her expression morose, inscrutable. "You're a bit late with the news anyway."

"You mean . . . ?"

"S'right," said a familiar, male voice. A large, pale, tattooed arm slid round Polly's waist, then a bald head slid into view. Ed Clark gave Nick a lascivious grin. "You see, kidder, I've already given her a ride."

CHAPTER
TWENTY-ONE

Arnold had two sides. There was a wide suburbia of dull, detached houses that spread all the way up a long hill before merging with middle-class Mapperley. Then there were the mean terraced houses off the left of the main road, a more working-class area where there were few posters for Gedling's Tory MP. It was a small Labour zone in a safe Tory seat. Sarah was pleased to note that the house she was visiting had a poster for the Labour candidate, a deputy head who at least had a job to return to in a week's time. Maybe she should get her red rosette out of the car and put it on.

The guy who opened the door was Sarah's age. Unshaven, he wore a white vest with faded blue jeans, gone at both knees, and filthy trainers. Seeing Sarah, he smiled, revealing tobacco stained teeth and a mouthful of NHS fillings. Yet Phil Bolton was handsome, in his fashion. He looked a little like Nick, with a strong jaw and dark, thick hair. Sarah could tell what Polly Shanks had seen in him. The eyes were his only weak point: slightly sunken and pale blue, giving him a haunted air.

"I'm Sarah. I phoned last night."

"I can see who you are. When you rang, I thought you might be some kind of debt collector. Nearly went out. Not that I owe anyone ought, but I wouldn't put it past Polly to buy something in my name."

"Actually, it was Polly I wanted to see you about."

Sarah stepped over old newspaper covered in oily motorbike parts. This wasn't a home that children lived in, but Phil didn't live alone. A couple of bras and a skirt hung from a laundry rack near the gas fire.

"You helped get that Ed Clark out, didn't you?" Phil said.

"Yes. Your ex wasn't too pleased about that."

"If you say so. Why do you want to see me?"

"I want to help the police find Terry and Liv's killer. I thought you might be able to help me."

"Doubt it." Phil took a copy of the *Mirror* off an uncomfortable looking armchair and waved Sarah to sit down. "Terry was always all right to me, but I wasn't around when he died."

"You were married to his sister, though . . ."

"Legally. But I'd moved out by then."

This confused Sarah. "I thought you moved out just after Terry and Elaine's kids came to live with you and Polly."

"Nah. I moved back in for a while, after the murders, to help Polly out. But the marriage was shot soon as she started having it off with Ed Clark, eighteen month before."

Sarah bit her lip to disguise her surprise, then asked Phil to repeat his last sentence.

"Claimed she hated him after, of course. Begged me to stay with her. But she doesn't know what she wants, Polly. More sides to her than an old threepenny bit.

178

Clark probably wasn't the first she played away with. I don't even know if the kids are mine. She wanted money, went through the CSA, but wouldn't let me do paternity tests. So I've stayed clear of them, too. I'm well rid."

Sarah was still having trouble taking in what he'd told her. "She was sleeping with Ed Clark before he got arrested the first time? Polly told you this?"

"Not her, no. Terry knew about it before I did. He suggested I put the bug in our bedroom. You don't know about the bug?"

"There was no bug mentioned in the trial transcripts."

"It was inadmissible evidence for the court case. Poll didn't contest the divorce, so it was never used. But that's how they caught Ed and his mates. They got the shithead on tape, in bed, boasting to Polly about how he was going to turn round all this tobacco from a warehouse job."

"Who planted the bug? CID?"

"The bloke who came round with Terry was called Slater. Jack Slater, I think. He was in plain clothes, but that doesn't mean he was CID. Terry wasn't in uniform either."

"And Polly didn't know she was being taped?"

"Not far as I know. They had to get permission from the homeowner, and that was me, but I certainly didn't tell her."

"Terry went through you to get at his sister's lover?"

"I got on better with Terry than Polly did."

"And none of this came up at the trial?"

"No. Ed must have worked it out, though. Otherwise, why would he have killed Terry and Liv?"

There was an accusation in his tone but Sarah ignored it. "Liv knew about the tape but Polly didn't?"

"Oh yeah. Terry had no secrets from her. Liv told me getting Ed sent down was one of the best things Terry had ever done."

Sarah understood why Terry Shanks' role in Ed's original arrest was kept so low-profile. He wouldn't want his adulterous sister dragged into the case, especially when she didn't know he'd recorded her in bed with her lover. In the murder trial, it would have suited both prosecution and defence not to explain how Terry Shanks had been instrumental in Ed's arrest: a role that didn't reflect well on either Shanks or Clark.

"But you don't think that, do you?" Phil said.

"What? Sorry, I was lost in thought."

"You don't think Ed killed Terry and Liv?"

"I don't know what I believe any more," Sarah confessed. "What do you think happened?"

"I reckon the police got the right man in the first place, but the evidence weren't strong enough."

"The appeal court threw out the conviction because there was reasonable doubt," Sarah said.

"Does that mean you agree with me, that Ed did it?"

"Probably," Sarah said, admitting it to herself for the first time. "I couldn't say so in public but if you asked me off the record, after what you've told me, I'd have to say yes. Yes, I think he killed them both."

★ ★ ★

It had been two days, but Nick still couldn't get his head around finding Polly with Ed Clark. Her being with him made no sense. He couldn't leave things the way they were. Late afternoon he cycled to the cab office, where Nas was alone behind the switch.

"When's Ed driving today?" he asked.

"He finishes at six," Nas replied, without looking up.

Something in her voice prevented him from hurrying off.

"Are you all right?"

When she looked up, he saw that she had been crying.

"What happened? Is it to do with you and Joe?"

"You know about that?"

He nodded, because she had just confirmed his suspicions.

"Joe told me you used to go out with a Muslim girl. You know what our men are like."

Nick was alarmed. "Your brothers? Have they hurt Joe?"

"Not Joe, no. He's on his way over, to pick me up when my shift ends. Better maybe, if you're not here."

Perturbed, Nick left. Had Nas's brothers hurt her? He wanted to do more, but she had told him to go and, whatever this was, it was Joe's mess, not his. Moreoever, Nick had to see Polly before Ed's shift finished. Less than an hour's time.

Nick still had Joe's bike, so he cycled to New Basford. There was no reply when he knocked. Polly had never given him a key, so he couldn't go in and wait. Maybe it was best to leave it, Nick decided. He'd no idea what he would have said. He cycled off.

Nick was fifty yards away when a taxi turned onto the street. Nick glanced round. It was Ed's car, with Polly in the front seat. Nick, not spoiling for a fight, swerved into the ginnel that ran between two of the terraced houses. Ed wouldn't see him. Taxi drivers never noticed cyclists. Nick waited until Ed had helped Polly get her shopping bags out and driven off. Polly let herself into the house. As soon as she was inside, Nick cycled back.

The door was still ajar, two shopping bags in the small hallway. Nick lifted his bike over the step. Polly, fag in hand, returned for the remaining bags. Seeing him, her calm demeanour changed.

"What the fuck do you want?" she spat.

"I'll only stay five minutes," Nick said. "We couldn't talk last time."

Polly was shrill. "Have you been waiting for me to come home?"

"No. I was just leaving when Ed dropped you off."

Polly's voice became high-pitched in a way he'd never heard it before. "Because if you're stalking me, God help you, I'll call him. You don't want to get on the wrong side of Ed."

Nick waited a moment before replying. This wasn't the Polly he'd built up in his mind before he found her with Ed — not the vulnerable, working-class woman who was, if anything, too good for him.

"I know what Ed's capable of," Nick said. "And I know we've finished. But I have to know: why Ed? What

182

possible reason can you have to sleep with the bloke who killed your brother, your sister-in-law?"

"You wouldn't understand," Polly said. Her voice was numb, estranged, yet contained the ghost of the woman he'd made love with. They were still standing in the hall, with Polly blocking the door to the living room. Nick tried to recall what he'd first seen in her, why he got involved. In Nick's old world, they would never have met. Yet he'd felt close to her.

"Why?" he repeated.

"Turns out Sarah Bone was right. Ed didn't do it."

"How can you be sure?" Nick asked.

"Because he told me who did."

"Who?"

"None of your fucking business."

"Okay, so you believe him," Nick said. "But I still don't see why you're sleeping with him."

"It's got nothing to do with you. You and me were going nowhere. We were only using each other for sex, right?"

Nick's feelings were more complicated than that. He didn't reply. Polly continued.

"Ed doesn't want me to see you any more."

She didn't sound at all convincing. She didn't even sound as though she had half convinced herself. Nick wanted to help, but had no idea how to. "I'm worried what you're getting into, that's all," he said.

"Don't be." Polly's voice softened. "I've known Ed for a long, long time. We had a thing, before Terry was killed, when my marriage was on the rocks. We had a misunderstanding, but it's sorted. Now please go."

CHAPTER
TWENTY-TWO

Sarah managed an hour's catch-up sleep when she got in from canvassing then freshened up with a shower before making dinner. When they lived together, Nick did all the cooking. He wouldn't expect much.

Sarah prepared lamb kebabs, one of her few fancy dishes, from a Delia Smith book, a pointed birthday present from her mother. Best end neck of lamb, minced and blended with cashews, coriander, some chilli and a little egg white to bind the mix. The only tricky bit was cooking them on a kebab, where they were liable to fall apart. Sarah got around this by shaping them into fish-finger-size rissoles, which she fried instead of grilling. She left them to firm, then went to work on a pasta salad.

Sarah found cooking dull but relaxing. It gave her time to consider what it would be like if she and Nick got together again. Her body was softer than before. Nick's looked harder. Sarah ached for Nick, ached to have again what they once had. Which was stupid. You can never go back. Everybody knew that.

She had to stop fantasizing. Sarah didn't do casual sex, no matter how much she liked someone. When you knew you weren't going to sleep with someone, it reduced the risk of giving mixed signals. No, she would not sleep with Nick tonight. She'd made Dan wait a month. Fifteen years ago, she'd made Nick wait longer. Then they'd spent a good proportion of her year as Union President in bed. It was the best year of her life. She wondered if the same went for him.

Nick arrived on the dot of seven-thirty, carrying a bunch of lilies and a bottle of Rioja. When he leant over to kiss her, his hair smelt newly washed. His lips landed softly on the side of the mouth.

"What would you like to drink?"

"What are you having?"

"A vodka and tonic."

"Sounds good."

Sarah had to fight the urge to over analyse. Most blokes, when they chose the same drink as you, were trying it on. She'd been on body language training courses, knew that mirroring someone's behaviour was a way to disarm, then seduce. But this was Nick. Sarah refreshed her drink while making his. When he wasn't looking, she wiped her brow to remove a thin layer of sweat. *Nervous Nelly*, her granddad would have said. She and Nick had gelled pretty well on Thursday, but then she'd been in MP mode. Now she was trying to be herself, but which self? The last time she'd been truly relaxed was so long ago; she no longer remembered the person she'd been. Sarah dropped ice into tumblers, splashing the stainless steel work surface, then wiped the glasses dry with a tea towel.

"Cheers."

"Cheers!" Nick took a large slurp. He was nervous too.

"Do you want to choose some music?"

"Sure." He followed her into the living room and she knew she'd screwed up. Nick was always into his music. The only new CDs she'd bought in the last five years were reissues from the sixties and seventies. She watched him flick through the pile next to the stereo.

"I haven't heard this since I was a student."

She couldn't see what he'd chosen, but when he put it on, she recognized it at once: *Al Green Explores Your Mind*. "Late night seduction music," Nick used to call it.

"Are you trying to get me into bed before we've even eaten?"

Nick grinned, the old Nick she'd been missing for thirteen years. Sarah, not sure how to react, looked away. She sat at one end of the sofa. Nick took her cue and sat at the other end of the long, matt leather settee.

"It's been too long," he said. "Neither of us know where to start."

"You're right," Sarah said. "And neither of us know where we're going. Least, I don't. I can't decide anything until next Thursday. I don't like it, not being in control of my life."

"I don't remember the last time I was in control of my life, either," Nick admitted. "But you're supposed to be running the country. Isn't that interesting?"

That got her going. She felt awkward at first. Then, seeing Nick's interest, she built up steam. Sarah explained how disorienting Parliament was. After the excitement of the by-election came the anticlimax of being an MP, at the bottom of a greasy pole she wasn't sure she had the inclination to climb. She described her loneliness in London and the pressure her job had put on her and Dan. How once she got to Parliament it was easy to forget why she'd ever wanted to be there in the first place. She talked for ten minutes or more, with him occasionally putting in a prompt or sympathetic aside.

"Sorry, I'm going on. You know, one of the things about this job is how it affects your relationships. People treat you differently. Non-political friends drift away. There aren't many people I can open up to."

"I'll try not to let the job affect the way I am with you," Nick said, then put a tentative hand on her knee. "We've both been through a lot."

"We're still the same people, aren't we? I mean, you're here because of who I am, not what I am."

"Of course."

She put her hand on his, then leant forward to accept the kiss she thought he wanted to give her. But he held back.

"Before we go any further," Nick said, "I ought to tell you about why I left teaching."

"You got busted. I heard. You had to quit. It's a shame."

"It was a bit more than that. You have to know what happened before we start anything. You might not want to take me on."

Nick began to talk rapidly. She had assumed his bust was bad luck, for which he'd suffered embarrassment, a

187

heavy fine and the loss of his job. Turned out he'd been to prison for five years after being caught growing enough skunk to get the whole city out of its tree.

"Why on earth did you did it? You weren't desperate for money, were you?"

"I was short for the mortgage, but that isn't an excuse."

"What got into you?"

"Greed, I suppose. But at first I thought it was luck."

"Oh, shit, the kebabs!"

Sarah spent the next fifteen minutes sorting out the food. Then, over dinner, Nick told her the story of how he had discovered the caves beneath the flat.

CHAPTER
TWENTY-THREE

Nick's ground-floor flat was on the Canning Circus side of the Park, the cheaper section of the private estate where Sarah now lived. Nick had always aspired to live in the Park. He and Sarah used to walk around the place, working out where they would move. Their ideal home was a stone's throw from Nottingham Castle, a five-minute walk to the city centre. In this idyll, she would be an MP and he a university lecturer.

In Thatcher's Britain, teachers found themselves earning more than university lecturers. Nick took the plunge in 1989, when he could almost afford the flat he'd always hankered after. All right, it was a tatty two-bed with no garden and he'd have to take in a lodger to meet the mortgage payments. One day, perhaps, he'd find a woman to share it with. Women always seemed to back off when Nick got serious — all but Sarah. He wished she'd never joined the police. The police were the enemy. For most people, that changed as you grew older. But not, as things turned out, for Nick.

Structurally, the flat was sound. In every other way, it was a mess. The place had been repossessed after the previous owners defaulted on the mortgage. All the

189

carpets needed replacing, but Nick couldn't afford that. He hired a sander and began to clean and varnish the floorboards, covering the worst areas with rugs from his previous, rented flat. It was a long, tedious job. He left the large hall until last, as it presented the most difficulty. The dust would get everywhere and, once he varnished, he'd have to move out of the flat until it dried. That meant staying with his younger brother, Joe, in his bachelor pad by Trent Bridge, in the heart of the city's flash-trash district. He and Joe got on, but they weren't close. Joe was six years younger, and it could prove awkward, having a younger brother who was more successful than you.

The long summer holidays were nearly over when Nick got round to taking up the hall carpet. The threadbare flooring turned out not to be tacked down at the sides, so it was easily rolled out of the way. The boards beneath were buggered beyond repair. No amount of sanding would get them into shape. Nick couldn't afford to replace them all. Several had been cut in an odd way. One even had a large hole in the middle. Tentatively, Nick put his hand through it. He was worried about splinters but the sides were smooth, as though they'd been sanded down. The gap wasn't so much a hole as a handle. Nick reached in and lifted out a large section of floor, the size of a trap door.

Below, Nick could make out the top of a ladder. Excited, he went to look for a torch, but there wasn't one. It was tempting to use a cigarette lighter, but caution prevailed. He hurried into Halfords in the

Market Square and was back twenty minutes later with a heavy-duty flashlight.

The space beneath the hall was small — not tall enough for Nick, at over six feet, to stand upright — and partially boarded, like an attic, rather than a cellar. There was a light switch, too. Once Nick switched it on, he realized that the unboarded area was another hole, one that led to another space, beneath. Beside the gap was a miner's lamp attached to a large roll of coiled electricity cable. One side of the cable came from the innards of the flat, above. Another length of heavy cable continued below.

The miner's lamp still worked, casting a dense full moon of a beam. Nick turned off his flashlight and looked for a ladder down. Nothing visible bar a couple of ridges in the sandstone. Hard to tell how deep the cave was. Nick wanted to go down straight away, but prudence got the better of him. He lowered the lamp into the hole. The cave's walls reflected light back at him. Why? The cave could be flooded, but it seemed unlikely. This was high ground. Even so, the risk of descent was too great. He might not be able to get back up. The presence of the miner's lamp, however, suggested that the previous owners had been down there. To do the same, all Nick needed was a companion above.

His brother came round the next day, after training.

"I'll tie a rope round you and hold onto it, but I'm not coming down," Joe told Nick. "Don't want to risk breaking something."

Joe was in the first team at Notts County. He tied the rope.

"You didn't know this was here?"

"Never even occurred to me."

"Think the estate agent knew?"

"Maybe. It's not in the plans. Risk of subsidence might put some people off. If she knew, I guess she'd keep quiet about it."

This city was built over caves. Pubs used them as cellars. Cave passages linked important buildings. Nottingham Castle held tours of theirs. The council were making a museum out of the caves beneath the Broadmarsh Shopping Centre, most of which had been flooded with concrete when they were laying the foundations. Nick liked caves, but at the time he bought the flat he thought all the caves in the Park were lower down the hill.

Getting down turned out to be the easy bit. The drop was only a couple of metres. Once Nick had his feet on dry sandstone, he urged his brother to follow.

"Those ridges I told you about. They're steps, cut into the side."

Gingerly, Joe climbed down. They looked around the dank cavern. It was about the size of Nick's bathroom, twenty square metres. There was a power line taped to one wall with several large electric bulbs attached to it. The sloping walls were covered with heavy, turkey-size aluminium foil. There were several large, plastic tubs, each with a little earth in them.

"Looks like you'll be getting into grow-your-own," Joe said.

"I'm not sure about that," Nick said, glancing round the makeshift dope dungeon. "Remember what happened last time?"

"No risk of anyone spotting this by accident."

Joe was referring to the story that Andy Saint had also reminded her of, when he and Nick nearly got done for growing their own. Sarah had helped him, moving the plants. No career in the police for her if she'd been caught, but that hadn't occurred to her then. Nick hadn't dabbled in homegrown since that close call. Given his job, the risk was too big. A dope conviction got you chucked out of teaching. Also, he'd never had an attic, which was what most growers used. Anyway, by the early nineties, attics were becoming dangerous. He'd heard of the police catching growers by using heat sensitive cameras in helicopters. Growing the stuff underground, in a safe dry place, was a new idea. If he got the lighting and ventilation, he could be quids in.

"Here we go," Joe said, picking up a fragment of dry leaf from the ground. He crushed it with a forefinger and thumb, then smelt his fingertips.

"Result!" he said.

"I wonder if these caves go any further back," Nick said.

Nick, lamp in hand, led the way. The sandstone caves were not picturesque, but nor were they damp. The gaps between caverns were narrow, yet not too tight. Some caves showed signs of having been widened to let people get through, but none bore any trace of recent use.

"How many of these fucking things are there?" Joe asked, as they ran out of cable for the lamp.

The caves turned out to cover half of the street, reaching back into the gardens of the big houses on Cavendish Crescent, behind. There were several spaces larger than the one beneath Nick's flat and, crucially, air was getting in from somewhere.

"I don't want you telling anybody else about this place," Nick told his brother. "Nobody at all."

For the rest of the summer, and into the new term, Nick spent many of his daylight hours, when his neighbours were out, working underground. There was plenty to do: clearing, wiring, putting fireproof matting underfoot, testing different varieties of lighting. He read books on caves and on cannabis cultivation (Mushroom, the alternative bookshop in Hockley, turned out to be a good source for them). He went on potholing expeditions to "see how he got on", then weaselled out of joining the club, blaming a bad back that was aggravated by all the twisting and turning.

After this, Nick risked extending one of the gaps at the end of the network. He knocked through a little at a time, slowly creating a passageway just wide enough to squeeze through. These caves, too, were dry, without the rank, earthy smell he'd come across when pot holing. There must be decent ventilation. The new hole led to another hole, which, as he'd hoped, led to a wide, low cave, one of many that had an entry in an overgrown garden on the Park's south slope. He disguised the enlarged hole with a foul smelling

194

oleander bush that was easily moved should he ever need another way out of the caverns. Then he began to grow weed.

It took a while to source the right strains. At first, Nick was paranoid about fires. He installed a smoke alarm, but it was unnecessary. The sandstone soaked up excess heat. Conditions were perfect. The plants grew quickly, soon acquiring bushy leaves and moist, pungent buds. As the plants thrived, Nick rethought getting a lodger. He didn't want to share his secret with anyone he couldn't completely trust. Joe pronounced the first batch of weed, dried out and ready just in time for Christmas, to be top quality.

As the plants grew, so did the mortgage rate. Nick's flat was worth less than he'd paid for it, eight months earlier, yet kept costing him more and more. Nick sold a bit of grass on, but money remained tight. He saw what he had to do, and used his credit card to buy more lighting. By spring, he'd expanded into two of the neighbouring caves.

Paranoid about the electricity board noticing an unusual pattern of high activity, he bought a small generator. It would power the lamps to heat his plants twenty-four hours a day. Now that electricity usage was no longer an issue, he brought even more of the caves in the system into his hydroponics operation. He visited organic garden centres and subscribed to arcane magazines.

It was easy to keep the equipment and literature hidden from visitors. The biggest problem was the smell. The cellar above the caves acted as a buffer but not enough of one, especially when Nick began growing new strains of skunk weed that gave a heady, dense high. The skunk also gave off a pong that combined the sweet odour of grass with the earthy, lingering stench of overcooked Brussels sprouts. Nick became so inured to this stench that he didn't notice how the flat smelt until people commented on it. He stocked up on joss sticks and air freshener. Even so, the perfumed reek would cling to him.

Selling the stuff on was a problem. It was no use saying to mates, "I bought a big bag of homegrown, cheap, do you want to take some off me while it's fresh?" The quantities were vast and the quality was rapidly increasing. Nick could have gone down Hyson Green or the Meadows and asked around. Maybe he'd hook up with a wholesaler who could do him some good. Equally likely he'd get beaten up, busted or both. Nick didn't know people who moved in those kinds of circles. But he knew somebody who did. Sarah didn't ask him to elaborate on this.

By mid-1991, Nick was turning round a new crop every month, with each cave containing plants of different varieties and ages. It was more work than he'd anticipated. This, rather than teaching, was his real career. That summer, he went onto a job-share, 0.5, telling colleagues that he was buying time to write a novel. He could easily have lived off the dope plants alone but needed a legitimate job to explain his income. Also, he did enjoy teaching English, especially now that it was only two or three days a week, which made the work much less exhausting.

What he needed most was help. The friend who gave Nick the distribution network contacts promised never to breathe a word of where the stuff came from. He gave Nick the starkest of warnings. *Trust nobody*, he said, when Nick showed him round the caves. *The business is incredibly cut-throat. Let nobody know where you grow the stuff and, if you don't get greedy, keep things around this size, you can get away with it for ever. Never have anyone with anything to do with this business round your flat. Don't give your distributors your real name. If you want, I'll show you how to set up overseas accounts. If I were you, I'd buy property. It's the best bet in the long run.*

Nick needed to start investing the money he'd made. The mortgage was paid off. He had piles of cash stacked in cardboard boxes in one of the smallest, driest cellars. Seeing them made him feel like a comic book miser. He could do with advice, but his friend was in New York (escaping, Nick suspected, from a little trouble of his own). There was only one person Nick trusted to help, the only other person who'd been into the caves with him. But Nick wasn't sure if Joe was ready.

Notts County had had an incredible beginning to the 1990s. For two consecutive seasons they had made it to the play-off finals for their division, each time winning at Wembley. This season, however, Joe had badly broken his left leg early in September. And the team were in free fall. With two months to go, their prospects of staying in the First Division were poor. Joe had hoped to be back in training, but the break was too serious. The doctors now said he would never recover sufficiently to play professional football again.

At least he was off the crutches. He had even stopped using a stick.

"I'm not going down there again," Joe said, one early April afternoon.

"You don't have to," Nick told him, and offered him the spliff he was smoking.

"Too early in the day for me. Shouldn't you be teaching?"

"One of my days off," Nick explained.

"This place stinks worse than a brothel."

"I wouldn't know," Nick said. "Never been to one."

"Believe me, this is worse. What were you after, anyway?"

"I thought you might need a job," Nick said.

Nick explained how the operation had grown. The turnover was more than adequate to support them both in style, he said, without revealing just how much style he was talking about.

"Thing is, the work's getting to be too much for one man."

"You want me to climb down those raggedy steps and become some kind of underground market gardener?" Joe said. "Forget it."

"I can handle that side of things," Nick told him. "What I need is somebody to do the driving, make deliveries, shift the stuff at night."

"You mean, the dangerous stuff?"

"It's not dangerous," Nick said. "I deliver to businessmen, not gangsters. I've never seen a gun. Come on, it's only dope. Half the people we know smoke it. You'd be getting well paid to provide a service."

"It's worth thinking about," Joe said. "But I ought to tell you that I'm starting a business of my own."

He told Nick about his plan for a taxi firm that would be based in Sherwood: Taxi firms were expanding everywhere. Even students used taxis all the time these days. Joe had been a popular footballer. With a name like his behind it, the firm would be off to a great start. He was going to buy a handful of cars, but most of his staff would be owner-drivers snatched from other firms, paying him a cut of their takings.

"Sounds like a symbiotic relationship," Nick said.

"*Sim by* what?"

"Our businesses were made for each other. If you get stopped when you're making a delivery, you're a working taxi driver. In fact, I've got an even better idea. Why don't I come in with you? We could be partners."

Joe became bashful. "I'm already taking on a partner."

"Someone I know?"

"Caroline. We're getting married."

"That's . . . you're a lucky guy." Caroline was the brightest, best looking of the many women Joe had dated over the years. He had chosen well, though Nick doubted that she had. Joe wasn't the faithful type.

"I'm going to have to think this over carefully. You know, weigh up the risks."

199

"Even if you decide not to take on the driving, I'd still like to put some money into the firm, help you out."

"Thanks for the offer, bro. I'll discuss it with Caroline and let you know."

From the guarded tone of his brother's voice, Nick could tell, without having to wait, what the answer would be.

CHAPTER
TWENTY-FOUR

Sarah listened to the story intently, punctuating it with questions. Nick left Andrew's name out of it. If Sarah guessed who "a friend" was, she didn't let on.

"How did they catch you? A neighbour? Your dodgy friend? The only other person who knew about it was . . ."

"It wasn't Joe," Nick said, with a certainty he wished he felt. "I don't know."

He told her about the night it happened. It was the evening of the last general election. Anticipating a celebration, he'd just snorted a large line of coke. Chalky flakes irritated his nose. Each bitter sniff accelerated his coke spike. The doorbell rang. Nick put down the paper and went to the window. Privacy was important to him. He didn't like people to visit the flat without phoning first. His friends knew this, though none of them knew why. Whoever was ringing the bell stood close to the door. Nick couldn't see who it was. It might be one of the political parties, knocking up their supporters. Unlikely though, as polling was nearly over.

The doorbell rang again, more insistently this time. Nick thought of hiding his living room stash. Coke paranoia. Flushing his drugs would be too extreme. He opened the flat door to do a reconnaissance. From the large, shared foyer, he could see faint figures silhouetted in the smoked glass on the top half of the door. Two people, at least.

Nick paused for a moment to gather himself.

Behind him, the bell gave a long, emphatic ring. Nick hesitated. He did a mental inventory. Tiny amounts of coke and hash. Only a fine, but in his position, it was always better to err on the side of caution. The drugs could be easily replaced, but he could lose his job, which couldn't. There was no tolerance for drug offenders in teaching. Fuck it. He went back inside, emptied the old medicine chest where he kept his stash and flushed the lot. The doorbell rang again, even longer this time. Nick decided to brazen it out.

At the door, Nick was confronted by two men a few years older than him — late thirties maybe. One had a moustache. Both wore long leather jackets which, while almost as expensive as the one Nick owned and not entirely unfashionable, nevertheless gave away exactly what they were. Nick thought quickly, but not coherently. In his current state, the only fallback position was denial.

"Nick Cane?" the moustache said.

"He's in flat one," Nick replied. "Don't think he's in."

"There's music on," the other said.

"He often does that. A lot of burglaries round here. If you don't mind, I'm on my way out."

"This is him," Moustache said, pushing his way past Nick into the foyer. He raised the photograph he held in his hand, which Nick hadn't noticed before.

"I'm on my way to a meeting," Nick said. "Whatever this is, I'm sure it can wait."

"You're a teacher, I hear," the clean-shaven one said. "Biology, is it?"

"No. English and Media Studies."

"They didn't have that in my day. I only said Biology because you've been buying a lot of equipment, it seems. You like growing things."

Nick had been careful, he thought. Now he saw that he had not been careful enough.

"Hundreds of pounds worth of high-tech gardening stuff. One odd thing — you don't have a garden, do you?"

They knew. Nick didn't respond. He had the phone number of a good lawyer, Ian Jagger, but suspected even Jagger wasn't good enough to get him out of this one.

"Perhaps he has an allotment," Moustache said.

The clean-shaven one raised a single eyebrow.

"Are you going to let us into your flat?" he asked.

"Only if you've got a search warrant," Nick said.

They produced a search warrant. Now Nick was as concerned about his coke as he was about the plants in the caves. Four grams was a lot, unless you were very well off. The police officers might accuse him of dealing, which, technically, he was, though he only ever got it for friends. But the coke was very well concealed, in one of the furthest caves. And there was nothing to say that they knew about the caves.

Once inside, the police didn't go straight to the medicine chest. They lingered in the hall. The moustachioed one began to sniff. The other one smiled. Nick figured the moustache was imitating him, letting Nick know that he knew what he had just put up his nose. But that wasn't it.

"Are you going to show us the entrance?" he asked. "Or do we have to tear this place apart?"

"Who told you?" Nick asked, in reply.

Moustache tapped his nose.

Nick nearly said a name. Only Joe and one other person knew about what he grew beneath the flat. His brother and his oldest friend. No, it must be someone or something else, something he'd done to give himself away. He'd been so careful. But if he was really careful, he wouldn't be snorting coke so early in the evening, celebrating an election victory that was by no means certain. Please God they didn't find the rest of the coke.

"I'm losing patience," Moustache said.

Nick unfurled the carpet and showed them the ladder to the caves.

"I read about there being all these caves under houses in the Park," the clean-shaven one said. "First time I've been in one."

"Reminds me of Mortimer's Hole over at the Castle," Moustache said. He clambered down behind Nick. "We'll have to give tours."

204

The drugs squad officers were impressed by the bushy plants, the elaborate lighting, the hygiene and the watering system. They made him explain everything. By the time they'd finished examining the growing operation, Nick's head had begun to clear. He no longer had any false hope. Back upstairs, the two officers formally arrested Nick, then took him to the central police station.

Later, they found the coke as well. That doubled his sentence.

Sarah muttered words of bland sympathy then poured him another drink. How else to react to a story like that?

"Those caves sound fascinating," she said. "I'd like to see them."

"I expect the oleander bush is still there. I could show you the place. I don't know what the police did to the cave system — bricked it up, I expect."

"What about getting in through your flat?"

"Had to sell it. Legal fees."

"And you've no idea how you got caught?"

"Bad luck, most likely. Someone smelt something, or the police were doing surveillance on hydroponics suppliers. Question is, now that you've heard the worst, are you still interested?"

"What do you think?" Sarah said, leaning forward again.

This time, he kissed her. The phone rang. They ignored it and the machine kicked in. Sarah heard a familiar Scots voice mumble his greetings. The Shadow

Chancellor of the Exchequer. He was hesitant, but his purpose was clear.

"In the event that you don't, but we . . . I would like you to come and work for me."

"I have to pick this up," she told Nick before grabbing the phone. She tried to sound breathless.

"Sorry, Gordon, I was in the shower." Let him imagine her naked. Gordon was easy to flirt with, but Sarah was very conscious that Nick was standing behind her. "Were you saying something about a job? You know I'm not an economist."

"I'll have my own policy unit. You could have a crucial part to play."

Sarah liked Gordon. She liked him to think that she was with him all the way. It was important to stay on the right side of him without getting on the wrong side of Tony. You couldn't flirt with Tony but Gordon was single, and liked to play the field. Sarah suspected that they were on each other's list of possibles, even though she fancied him less than she fancied Jasper March. There had been one time at a party conference when something nearly happened between them, only she'd drunk a little too much and he was too sober for the night to get naughty.

"I'd love to work with you, Gordon, but I should tell you I'm also considering an offer from the Association of Police Officers."

"You'd make an excellent representative." He knew about it already. "But accepting their offer wouldn't preclude your working with me, too."

"I'm sure that, one way or another, we'll work together," Sarah said.

They had a long chat about how the election seemed to be going.

"Was that who it sounded like?" Nick asked when she hung up. "You two sounded very friendly. He's single, isn't he?"

"There's nothing going on there."

"You two haven't ever . . .?"

Sarah decided not to mention the conference. "We've had dinner together a couple of times. Not a date, though, just a working dinner."

"Suppose you win?" he asked over dinner. "You wouldn't be able to go out with me."

"Don't be daft," Sarah told him, the insult also an old endearment.

She wasn't going to win. In the unlikely event that she did, she could still see Nick. He had served his time. While he remained on probation, she might need to keep the relationship low profile. That was manageable.

"The tabloids would love it — the MP and the ex-con. Look how they did you over with Jasper what's-his-name . . ."

"There was nothing to that," Sarah insisted. "Look, I'm on record as supporting the legalisation of dope. You and I are old friends and I have a strong reputation on penal reform. Nobody can get at me for seeing an ex-con if I choose to."

Nick looked troubled. "I'm not so sure. Ed Clark. Then me."

"Ed Clark's a different story. Let's not get into that," Sarah said. The last thing she wanted was to discuss the mistake she'd made in helping with Ed's appeal. She poured Nick a second brandy, resisting the urge to say, "Let's go to bed". His self esteem was low — it was important to let him make the move. And when he did, sod her earlier decision: she wouldn't turn him down.

Nick sipped at his brandy, not wanting to get drunk. He didn't like the way Sarah avoided talking about Ed. What was so uncomfortable about helping a man get out of prison? Unless, as Ed claimed, she had slept with him. Perhaps Sarah was more drawn to Nick because he had been in prison. It felt wrong, the way she was rushing into this. She would go to bed with him tonight, that was clear. But Nick wasn't desperate for sex. He was desperate for the kind of relationship they had before. Sleeping with her too soon might spoil any chance of that.

"I ought to go," he said at midnight. "I know how busy you are, how tired you must be."

"Don't." Sarah said. "Canvassing never starts before half ten on Sundays."

"If I stay we might do something we'd both regret."

At the door they shared a long, wet kiss good night. Nick almost changed his mind.

"You're right," she said. "No need to rush things. We've got all the time in the world."

208

CHAPTER
TWENTY-FIVE

Sarah finished canvassing at one and told the team she only had time for a quick half in the pub afterwards.

"Family stuff?" Tony Bax asked.

"Constituency business."

"It mightn't be your constituency after Thursday," Tony reminded her. He had fought this seat ten years before, got slaughtered at the polls. "Why not leave it for the other bugger?"

"I don't like loose ends," Sarah told him. "And the other bugger wouldn't touch this one with a bargepole."

"Then why are you sticking your oar in?" Tony wanted to know.

"I don't want my main legacy as an MP to be that I helped a guilty man go free."

"You've changed your mind about Ed Clark?"

"I've said enough," Sarah told her constituency chairman.

She drove to Bestwood Village, on the far side of Bestwood Park. The park was partially surrounded by one of the city's most notorious housing estates, one that, thankfully, was not in her constituency. The village itself was contrastingly smart, occupied by a combination of old money and aspirational professionals, including the ex-police officer she was here to see.

"Jack Slater?"

"You'd better come in." It had taken three phone calls to old mates for Sarah to find Slater, the one officer who had been involved in both cases against Ed Clark. He had risen to be an inspector in Traffic three years ago. Then he packed in the force and moved into home security.

"What made you leave?" Sarah asked him.

"I'd done my twenty years. Thatcher looked after us pretty well but I saw how I could be a lot better off if I took my pension. Forty-one then — young enough to start all over again. Which I have."

Sarah glanced around the knocked-through living and dining room. The furniture was IKEA and the ready-made dark blinds didn't quite fit the large windows, but Sarah could see how Jack might consider this luxury. It was too spartan for her. There would be a wife and kids somewhere else, Sarah expected. There usually were, with policemen his age, who were top of the divorce league tables.

"Why did *you* leave?" Jack asked her. "Didn't last long, from what I heard."

"Wrong career," Sarah said. "I had some cock and bull idea that the police were about justice, when they're really about crowd control. I wanted to go where the power was."

"And have you found it?"

210

"Maybe I will on Thursday. I want to talk to you about Ed Clark."

"Bit late now, isn't it? You got him out."

"And since I did, I've been discovering things I didn't know about him. Like how you and Terry Shanks bugged Terry's sister's bedroom to get the information that put Ed away."

"If an illegal bug had led to the conviction it wouldn't have stood up in court," Slater said.

"Except it wasn't needed in court. Whose idea was it?"

"Terry's."

"But CID knew about it?"

"Only when we took them the tapes. CID weren't interested in a small-time thug like Clark."

"But Terry was, and it got him murdered."

"He liked his brother-in-law, Phil Bolton. Terry hated his sister cheating on him with a shit like Clark."

"And it got him killed."

"Not according to the appeal court."

Sarah ignored this. "Ed Clark had been out of prison less than a week when Terry was murdered. What I don't understand is why he killed the wife, too."

"I heard you thought he was innocent of that. Changed your tune?"

"Humour me," Sarah said. "I know Ed. He's a sharp guy. He doesn't take unnecessary risks. His killing Liv makes no sense."

"Made no sense to me either," Jack said. "Not when I found out that she died up to an hour later. The way her body was left, we figured he'd raped the wife and made Terry watch. But the timing was wrong and there was no proof of sexual assault."

"Doesn't mean he didn't do it. She'd had sex earlier."

"Her husband had had sex recently too. The condom we found contained his sperm. Ed could be pervy enough to get off on raping the wife of a man he's just killed in front of the dead body. Doesn't sit right with me, though."

"Me neither," Sarah admitted.

They both thought for a few moments, found nothing new to say. Sarah changed tack.

"Did Ed see Polly Shanks after he got out of prison but before he murdered her brother? Were they still lovers?"

"Not according to her," Jack said. "When we spoke to her, she said she regretted ever seeing Clark, as it had cost her her marriage. Said she'd had nothing to do with him since he was sent down the first time."

"Did you believe her?"

"I believed she felt guilty about bringing Clark into her brother's life, causing so much mayhem. She wanted him put away. As to whether she saw Clark the week he got out, I don't know if she was telling the truth. It made no difference to the case against him."

"Would have shown how strongly she felt about him," Sarah said.

"Women's real feelings," Jack said, glancing around his neat bachelor home, "closed book to me. Been to see her?"

"Yes, but I think I need to go again," Sarah said.

Nick got to the cab office at four and waited for Bob to finish. On Friday, he'd told Joe that he would only drive for another week, taking him up to election day. Now he was, potentially at least, back with Sarah, five days was too big a risk.

"Bob's on an airport run," Nas told Nick. "He'll be a while."

She made a personal call. Nick tried to settle in to the *News of the World*, not taking in the stories, trying not to listen to Nas's call. He was very curious about what was going on with her, her brothers and Joe. Maybe he should go home. He'd told Sarah he was working today, but she might be happy to see him later. The latest polls showed Labour comfortably ahead, but not enough to give Sarah a fighting chance of holding on to her seat. Nick could see how much she loved the job, how frustrated she'd be when she was forced to leave office as Labour took power. There was nothing he could do to help except pick up the pieces. A depressing way to start a relationship. He could take her on holiday. He still had most of the money from Andrew Saint. He could afford to treat her.

Where to go? He had no idea where she'd been abroad. Their one foreign holiday had been two weeks island-hopping around Greece. Did people still do that? He'd heard Caroline go on about the time she and Joe went to the Seychelles. Nick didn't know where the Seychelles were, though they sounded like they were outside his price range. They shouldn't go on a holiday where Sarah would have lots of time to brood. They should be on the move, keeping occupied. Maybe Eastern Europe.

Joe came in. He usually showed his face on Sundays.

"Could you mind the switch for a few minutes? I need a word with Nas."

Nick frowned at his brother. "Bob could be here any minute, Joe."

"This really won't take long."

Joe and Nas went outside. Nick wondered if Joe was giving her the push. Then he heard Joe's car drive off.

Nas returned twenty minutes later, her long hair down and clothes crumpled.

"Thanks," she said to Nick. "I appreciate it."

"S'alright. Joe gone?"

"Back to his very pregnant wife, yes."

"The other day, when I found you crying, what happened? Did your husband find out what was going on with you and Joe?"

Nas shook her head. "Satnam wouldn't mind. He's been giving it to my fifteen-year-old nephew, Prakesh. My sister's husband caught them at it."

"Ouch. You knew he was gay?"

"I'd worked out he wasn't straight, after three years of marriage and not much chance of getting pregnant."

"What did your brother-in-law do?"

"Took Prakesh to Pakistan, but only after putting Satnam in the Queen's with three broken ribs and a severely bruised groin. I'm visiting him when I finish my shift."

"Getting a divorce?"

"If Satnam lives long enough." She gave Nick a cheerful smile, the smile of a woman who'd just had sex and didn't mind him knowing it. "Is it true you're seeing Sarah Bone, the MP?"

"We're just good friends," Nick said, winking.

"Old friends?"

"We lived together at uni, yeah."

"You're a dark horse," she said, and grinned. He wondered what on earth she saw in his younger brother, the lucky sod.

"Does Joe know that I know?"

"Sure. Why do you think I rang and asked him to come over?"

That was how Joe worked, sharing a secret with Nick but not actually acknowledging it. Nick couldn't understand why women stuck with Joe after they found out that he was feckless and unfaithful. Even Caroline, who was cleverer than Joe's other girlfriends. Caroline, with whom Nick shared the one secret that Joe knew nothing about.

Their mother was still alive when Joe met Caroline. He brought her home to Sunday dinner and, for the first time, Nick envied his brother for one of his girlfriends. She was a teacher, like Nick, and a couple of years older than Joe. A beauty, too. Back then, Joe was still playing. Caroline was a County supporter, but a far cry from the groupies he used to see. Even so, he treated her like shit, and they soon parted.

Nick thought Caroline's feelings for Joe were as casual as Joe's for her, otherwise he would never have made a play for her. He invited her out for a drink. At first, it went badly. All she wanted to talk about was Joe. Then, after drowning her sorrows with Nick, she spent the night at his flat. The morning after she let him seduce her, she made Nick promise not to tell.

"I thought your split with Joe was mutual," he'd said.

"Is that what he told you? No, I finished with him. I didn't want to share him. But I don't want to hurt him."

Then, as if to show that the deception was nothing personal, she made love with him again before breakfast. Back then, Nick and Joe had very similar bodies. During their fling, a total of six or seven nights spread over as many weeks, Nick sometimes suspected that Caroline was sleeping with him because of his physical resemblance to Joe.

Their affair lasted until Joe persuaded Caroline to go out with him again. She'd told Joe that she was seeing someone else, but not whom. Later, in prison, Nick developed a theory that Caroline went out with him in order to find out more about Joe, to get the knowledge that would allow her to get inside his head, learn how to lure him back and keep him. Nick was a means to an end. But Nick had had a lot of paranoid thoughts in prison, many of them unfounded. Caroline was lonely. Nick was available. They had teaching in common, and got on, without any grand passion on either side. To Caroline, Nick was a casual conquest. Joe was her prize.

Every woman he'd slept with had chucked him, that was another thing Nick often reflected on inside. He could add Polly to that list. The only one who hadn't chucked him was Sarah. Instead she'd taken a job that made it impossible for Nick to stay with her.

Prison did strange things to you. For a while, he'd convinced himself that Joe found about the affair with Caroline and, thinking it was still going on, had betrayed him to the police to get Nick out of the way. Joe was the only person in Nottingham who knew about the skunk operation. He'd been right to turn down Nick's offer of a partnership. If Joe had taken Nick's money for the cab firm, Cane Cars might have gone down with him. Instead, six years later, Caroline was having Joe's baby and the cab company was the city's third biggest. Joe had chosen wisely. So had Caroline. Back then, when Joe persuaded Caroline to start seeing him again, Nick had lost it. He'd begged her to stay with him instead. Caroline said she loved Joe. Nick, foolishly, slagged his brother off. He warned Caroline that Joe would never be faithful to her.

"We'll see," was all she'd said.

"Why? Why him, not me?" he kept asking, until she snapped.

"Because he's younger and better looking than you, if you really have to have a reason. And better in bed. Because I love him. Is that enough reasons?"

"That's enough."

"He must never know. I don't want us to come between him and you. You're his only brother. So this stays our secret, right?"

"Right," Nick had said, and he had kept the secret from Joe. Now he was keeping a secret from Caroline.

Or maybe she knew about Nas. Caroline was the sort of woman who knew a lot more than she let on.

Halfway through his shift he rang Sarah but only got the machine. He didn't know what kind of message to leave and hung up. He realized it was time to make a decision. He worked through the night until he had thought it through.

"I'm packing this in," he told Bob when he returned his taxi early on Monday morning. "Today."

"Going back to the teaching?"

"Something like that. I've been taking too big a risk."

"Aye, well, I can't say the extra money's not been useful but it was always a short-term thing." He glanced outside. "Your cab's here."

It was five in the morning, so the car didn't sound its horn. Nick left Bob to his breakfast. He'd been lucky to get a ride this early. He'd thought he might have to hang around in Wollaton until Bob went on shift. When he got outside, he wished he'd waited.

"A'right, kidder? Had a long night?"

"You're usually off by now," Nick commented, getting into the front passenger door.

"You're my last call. Been waiting for you, as it happens."

Nick wasn't slow to spot the menace in Ed Clark's voice. But what was the point of running? Sooner or later, they had to have it out. He fastened his seat belt.

"Wasn't expecting to see you on Friday," Nick said as they hit the ring road.

"Sounded like it."

A responsible driver, Ed didn't turn round when he talked. Nick, too, stared straight ahead, not wanting to see the expression on Ed's face.

"Maybe I got the wrong end of the stick, but I was under the impression that Polly wouldn't want to go anywhere near you."

"Understandable mistake," Ed said. "But things have changed. That's why I wanted to see you."

"To warn me off?" Nick asked, keeping his voice light, tentative.

"You've had your fun. That's all it was, is what she tells me. Bit of fun, like me giving that MP a poke. Nothing serious. But Poll's wi'me now. Understood?"

"No," Nick said. "I don't understand why . . ." He stopped himself.

Ed knew full well what Nick couldn't understand, yet he didn't fill the silence. He turned onto Alfreton Road. They were nearly at Nick's place. Nick spat it out.

"How can she be with you if she thinks you killed her brother?"

"She doesn't think that," Ed said. "I won my appeal, remember?"

"Sure, but . . ."

"But nothing," Ed interrupted. "This is you."

Nick got out of the car, dragged himself up the steps to his flat. Throughout the conversation, Ed had been firm but friendly. Had Nick got him wrong? He needed to think. A smoke would help, but when you got home in daylight, smoking a joint felt out of whack. He made himself a mug of hot chocolate and went to bed. He was knackered, but it took a long time for him to drift off. Even if Ed was innocent of murder, the taxi driver should still be the last person Polly would want a relationship with. How could someone who wanted Nick also like being with Ed? And why did Ed keep going on about Sarah? The thought that he might have swapped girlfriends with Ed kept Nick awake for hours, then crept into his shallow, restless dreams.

CHAPTER
TWENTY-SIX

Sarah found a free hour to see Nick for lunch on Tuesday. They met in the Indian social centre at the back end of Forest Fields, a venue where Sarah liked to be seen.

"I don't know this place," Nick said, wiping a thin line of sweat from his glowing forehead. Sarah couldn't get over how healthy and well built he was these days.

"I thought it was your kind of thing," Sarah said, hoping he wouldn't read too much into her words. The centre served a very cheap vegetarian lunch, mainly to Asian OAPs, in a cavernous former church hall. They queued up for their food, which was served in stainless steel airline-style trays, then got one of the long tables to themselves.

"This is good," Nick said, dipping one of his chapatis into the thin dal, which was accompanied by rice, vegetable curry, yoghurt, chutney and a sickly-sweet barfi. "A big lunch that's within my means."

"You're not that badly off, are you?"

"I am now I've packed in the driving. It was too big a risk."

"I'm glad you've done that. You'll find something else."

"I will, given time."

Sarah tried to meet his eyes with a sympathetic look, but they darted from side to side, a trait she remembered.

"There's something on your mind. What is it?"

Nick gave a facial grimace that she also remembered, but hadn't seen for a long time — a sign of embarrassment. He used to do it when he'd broken something, or had bad news for her.

"This probably isn't the time."

"What? I want to know."

Nick looked around as if to see who could hear them. A couple of white, social worker types had just been served but showed no sign of bringing their trays to Nick and Sarah's table.

"Don't tease me, Nick."

"It's probably a case of somebody teasing me. One of the other taxi drivers, he claims that — I mean, it's none of my business, only I guess I want to know . . ."

"What?"

"He claims that, since he got out of prison, about the same time that I did, he's been having a thing with you."

Sarah closed her eyes for a moment. "Ed Clark."

Nick leant forward. "Yes. You didn't want to talk about him when I was round yours the other night. Were you and him . . .?"

"No!" Sarah said. "Something happened — I can't talk about it here."

Ed fucking Clark. She got more disheartened when she was thinking about him than she did when fretting about losing the election. Nick still looked suspicious.

As Sarah tried to find a form of words to reassure him, Ranjit, the centre manager, came over.

"It's so good to see you again, Miss Bone. You still like our food?"

"Very much," Sarah said. "Best value in Nottingham."

Ranjit began a long, involved monologue about how the proposals to install a tram network across the city were likely to impact on Forest Fields. Sarah didn't have anything to say. She doubted that the tram project would go ahead: too expensive. By the time Ranjit took his leave, Nick had finished eating.

"Sorry about that," Sarah said. "I've had enough to eat. Want to get out before we're interrupted again?"

"Okay."

"Are you in a car?" she asked, when they were outside.

"I walked."

"I've still got twenty minutes," Sarah told Nick. "Can I give you a lift?"

Her car was parked by a small, deserted playground up a hill.

"I'm okay."

She didn't push it. Possibly he didn't want her to see where he was living.

"Let's talk in here."

He followed her into the playground. By unspoken agreement, she sat on the bright red merry-go-round. Nick started it going, then jumped on. Sarah figured that her in MP mode had been putting him off, so began to reminisce about the one time she'd taken acid, with him. The pair of them had sat on a Lenton merry-go-round for hours, talking, occasionally remembering to spin the carousel again. Then they would watch the world whirl and distort before it froze back into dull dusk.

"I remember," Nick said. He didn't add to her reminiscence, or fill the silence that followed it. The merry-go-round began to slow down.

"Nothing happened between me and Ed Clark," Sarah said. "I had no interest in him, except . . ." she watched his frown and chose her words carefully. "The night of his release, there was a party and he tried it on. I turned him down nicely but firmly. Later — I was a bit pissed or I wouldn't have got myself into this situation: he pulled me into his room and tried to . . . force himself on me."

Nick put his foot down. The sole of his shoe squeaked on warm tarmac. He brought the merry-go-round to a halt. "He tried to rape you?"

"He didn't get that far. He was off his face on coke, speed, crystal meth . . . something. He knocked me over. I fought him off, sort of — I kneed him in the balls. But he could have raped me if he'd wanted to. Instead, he humiliated me."

Nick got out a tissue. Only when he handed it to her did Sarah realize that she was crying. "It sounds like he did more than humiliate you. Did you report it to anyone? What did you do?"

"You don't understand," Sarah said. "He humiliated me by telling me that I'd made a fool of myself: that he really did kill Terry Shanks, then raped and murdered his wife."

224

CHAPTER
TWENTY-SEVEN

It was ten past nine the next morning before Nick made up his mind how to play it. This was a quiet time of day. Ed Clark would have just finished his school runs. A few drivers often had a late breakfast at the greasy spoon on Rawson Street, near the Indian social centre. Nick sometimes used the place himself. He could walk there in fifteen minutes. Nick did a lot of his best thinking while walking. Maybe by the time he got to the caff, he'd have worked out what to do and say.

Thin drizzle spattered the shabby cobbles. Apart from the café, Rawson Street was all light industry — a garage, a warehouse, a fizzy-pop company. There was no reason for Ed to be in the caff. He was more likely to go to Polly's for his breakfast and the rest once the kids had gone to school. All yesterday evening, Nick had been tempted to go round to Polly's, have it out with Ed. But he didn't know if Ed was living with Polly. Nor did he know if, in a fair fight, Ed could have him. Nick might have muscled up inside, but he hadn't got into fights. He didn't really know how to fight, and it felt too late to learn. He was tempted to pick up some broken brick, shove it into the wide, inside pocket of the denim jacket he was wearing. Suppose he were stopped? Would a brick count as carrying a concealed weapon, revoke his probation? If Nick was going to risk that, he might as well carry a knife. No, make that a dagger, or a rope, or a piece of lead piping . . .

It was nearly ten by the time he got to the caff. Ed wasn't there, but Bob was, tucking into a full English with chips.

"Missing me already?" he asked Nick.

"Just hungry." Nick ordered a sausage sandwich and a pint mug of tea, then sat down. "Seen Ed today?"

Bob shook his head. "But I've only been here five minutes. Get on with him, do you? S'pose you knew each other inside."

Nick didn't answer. Bob was reading the *Sun* which, to Nick's amazement, seemed to be supporting Labour. The sandwich arrived and he smothered the contents with brown sauce before disposing of it in half a dozen rapid mouthfuls. Nick was only halfway down his mug of tea when Bob declared that he was leaving.

"Mind if I come out with you?" Nick asked. "Use your radio."

"Be my guest," Bob said, handing him the keys. "Need a slash first."

Bob's car was parked opposite the caff. Nick got in and turned the radio on. He was about to call Nas, see if he could find out where Ed was, when Clark's car pulled up alongside him. Ed wound down the window and Nick did the same.

"I heard you'd stopped driving."

"That's why I'm in the passenger seat," Nick said. "I need a word with you."

226

Ed grinned. "I'm on the way to Polly's. Meet me there. Never know your luck, she might be in the mood for a threesome. And if she isn't in the mood, you might get lucky wi' me instead." His laugh was obnoxious yet ingratiating, as though he and Nick were mates.

Ed drove off. Bob came out a minute later and Nick asked to be dropped down the road in Basford.

"You found him then?"

"Yeah, I found him. But I dunno what I'm going to do with him."

"You talk like you're up for a fight, youth."

"It may come to that."

"Ed's a hard lad. He'll have you, unless you're kitted up, like. Want this?"

Bob pulled out the flick knife that he kept beneath his seat.

"I might be tempted to do something stupid," Nick said.

"And Ed might be tempted to kill you," Bob said, then showed him how the catch worked. The knife was small enough for Ed not to know Nick was carrying. It was insurance, that was all. Nick was good at keeping his temper, always had been, but if Ed came at him with a blade, Nick needed to be able to strike first. Prison had taught him that.

"Okay, mate. I'll take it. Appreciated."

Bob gave him a wry smile. "Want me to wait for you?"

"I don't know how long I'll be."

"I'll stick at the end of the road for a few mins."

It wasn't as though they were friends, or Bob was in Nick's debt, but if this were prison, what Bob was doing would make him Nick's mate for life. Bob drove three doors down and parked. Polly answered the door.

"Can't keep away, can you?" she said. Her manner mingled mockery and affection. It annoyed him, because she was right, he still wanted her. Her short, blonde hair was mussed like she'd just got out of bed. Until a few days ago, this woman had let him do every dirty thing his imprisoned mind had imagined. And more.

"Can I come in?"

"I suppose. You're expected," Polly said. She looked at him as if he was a wounded animal that one of the kids had brought in. "Are you sure about this?"

Without answering, he followed her into the living room, where Polly resumed ironing one of the kids' grey polo shirts for school.

"Where is he?"

"Ed's on the loo. He'll be down in a minute." She finished the shirt and put down the iron. "What do you want, Nick?"

"I want to know why you're with him."

Polly shook her head, then reached over to touch Nick's face. She stroked his cheeks and felt under his chin. He couldn't tell whether she meant this to resemble a doctor's examination or a caress.

"You're filling out," she said. "I didn't notice at first. Thought you looked the way you always do. Then, when I found out you'd been inside, it made sense. Guys inside, they don't eat well, but they work out a lot. They get these hollow faces, dark lines below the eyes, like ghosts. Ed was like that the first time he came out. This time, too. And he's hardly put the weight in his face back on. But you, you're a softboy, aren't cha? Mister university graduate who used to go out with an MP."

"Who told you that?" Nick asked.

"I did," Ed said, doing up his flies as he walked in. "Got the word at the cab office. Still in touch with her, are you?"

Nick didn't reply.

"I'll bet you are. One or two looks you gave me when I talked about her, they make a bit of sense now. Jealous of what you'd lost, eh? Still, she were nought in't sack compared to our Poll, was she?"

Polly gave them both a strained look.

"Ne'er mind that threesome we talked about, let's go the whole hog, get Sarah round for a foursome — cocks and cunt all over t'shop. What do you say?"

Bob's knife felt heavy in Nick's pocket. He didn't know if Ed's exaggeration of his Nottingham accent was deliberate or unconscious. Either way, Nick ought to get out. Yet he owed something to Polly, and to Sarah.

"Listen," he said to Polly, "there are things you need to know."

"Oh yeah? And you know them, do you?"

He ignored her hostility. "I spoke to Sarah Bone about Ed. She told me about the night of the party, when he was released. Has Ed told you about that?"

Polly was silent. So was Ed. Maybe Nick had him worried.

"He made a pass at Sarah and she brushed it off. No big deal, she thought. Only later, when she was about to leave, he grabbed her and dragged her into his hotel room."

"Really?" Polly didn't do sarcasm well, but he recognised the attempt.

"Really. He tried to rape her, but she fought him off."

"You seen the size of her, and me?" Ed said. "If I'd wanted to rape her, I would've done."

Nick tried to remember the detail of what Sarah had told him and continued talking to Polly.

"He knocked her over. She managed to knee him in the groin. So he couldn't perform. He settled for scaring her, instead. And he told her a story, something I'm going to tell you now. Then I'll go. Ed told Sarah she'd made a fool of herself. He did kill your brother, and your sister-in-law, both of them. And this is the man that you're seeing instead of me."

Polly stared at him for a moment. He thought he saw shock, then disdain, then disgust. But he had never been good at reading her.

"Are you back with her?" she asked, finally.

"I'm not with anyone," Nick said.

She spoke to her boyfriend. "I can't deal with this."

Nick turned to Ed, ready to respond if the bigger man thumped him. Ed merely pointed to the front of the house. Nick followed him out.

"You believe that crap?" Ed asked, in the same matey tone he'd used earlier, but with less menace. "I mean, which is more likely, Nickyboy — that I murdered two people and got away with it thanks to Sarah Bone, or that I was grateful, so I fucked her, then chucked her when I got bored."

"You're the one talking crap," Nick said, and immediately regretted sinking to his level.

"Oh aye? You're lucky I'm treating you so nice, pretty boy. Polly says you treated her right, near enough. So you and me, we're not enemies — not mates, either. Before you get out of here, I'm going to give you a word to the wise."

"Go on, then," Nick said.

"When you were with our Sarah, fifteen year ago or whenever — did you keep the lights on?"

"What are you on about?"

"Eyesight good, is it? Dunt matter. I'll bet you went down on her."

"Where is this heading?" Nick asked, trying to sneer but sounding like a teacher, even to himself.

"Remember the little purple birth mark she's got, right hand side, just where her pubes end, couple of inches from the belly button. Shape of Ireland, size of a new fivepenny piece. Do you remember that?"

When Nick didn't answer, Ed gave him a wide grin.

"Thought you would," he said.

CHAPTER
TWENTY-EIGHT

Before going to bed, Sarah set the answering machine to activate rather than let the phone ring. When she got up and checked the machine, there were already seven messages waiting. She left them for later. The next call came when she was getting out of the shower. Sarah stood in her bedroom, still dripping, as she answered it. The view from her window was obscured by a huge elm tree which protected her privacy. Through the branches she could see that it was a beautiful, sunny day.

"Sarah, it's Andrew. I called to wish you good luck."

"Nice of you, if just a tad hypocritical."

Andrew laughed. "Either way, will you be in town on Saturday?"

By "town" he meant London. "I should think so," Sarah said.

"Then why don't we have dinner rather than lunch this time," Andrew suggested. "The Sugar Club?"

"I haven't eaten there yet," Sarah admitted. "Okay, see if you can get a table. Dinner's on me if I win."

"I'll keep you to that. Good luck."

Sarah dusted herself with talcum powder, rolled on deodorant. Today would be a long day and looked like being a hot one, too. She checked her messages then returned some calls. Nick hadn't rung, as he'd promised to. He wasn't a busy man. If he hadn't called there would be a reason. She left her mobile turned on. If he didn't call by lunch, she would ring to make sure he was coming to the party tonight.

It was a perfect first of May. Cherry blossoms bloomed. The sun sparkled on the roofs of expensive cars. Change was in the air. Sarah drove past last-minute leafleters delivering ballot-card-shaped reminders. They were all working for her side. At campaign headquarters optimism was rife. However, the smiles were being worn because everybody expected a Labour victory, not a Bone victory. Sarah wished she could share their exhilaration. She began to practise her good loser demeanour.

"You said you'd give me until the election."

"I changed my mind," Nick explained to his brother. "I decided to bring my retirement forward, on your advice. I'm mad to risk going back inside."

"You are. But it's an election night and I've told Caroline I'm going to the Labour party do. Nas's told her hubby the same thing."

"I thought you'd told her it was over."

Joe shrugged, indicating the hopelessness of denying his sexual impulses. "Stuart's covering the phones. You can use his car. One last time, please. Otherwise, I'll have to drive myself and Nas will give me hell. God knows how many chances we'll get once the baby's born."

Loads, if Nick knew anything about his brother. But he relented, promising Joe that he would turn up at the office later. The risk of being caught was negligible, especially since he had Joe's ID. Sarah had invited him to the party, but he wasn't comfortable about going, and didn't fancy watching the TV election coverage on his own. If he pulled a long shift, he could follow it all on the radio as it happened. Nick meant to stay up until he found out how Sarah did.

He'd not returned her call yesterday. He didn't understand why she'd lied to him about Ed. Sarah had slept with Ed and he had slept with Polly, a sad synchronicity. Nick must learn to live with both the women he wanted fancying a psychotic slaphead as much as or more than they did him. Ed had an animal force, a brutish intelligence that must be a total contrast to the wimpy-sounding social worker Sarah was with before. Ed was also an expert manipulator. Nick could just about see how Sarah might have given him a sympathy fuck as soon as he was released, then kicked him into touch, leading Ed to exaggerate the rest. If Sarah lost, Nick would forgive her for lying about Ed and take her off on that holiday, see if they could start things up again. And if, by some chance, she won, it would be over. He would finish his GCSE tuitions then make a new start somewhere else.

"I'll be back in at six," he told Joe.

"Start earlier if you want."

"Better not," Nick said, then fed his brother a credible fib to cover up the absurdity of what he was

234

about to do. "I've got an appointment with my probation officer."

The appointment wasn't until tomorrow, but it was a plausible lie. The best lies were the ones that stuck closest to the truth.

Election days can be very slow. The worst job was standing outside a polling station and taking numbers from voters to check against the electoral register. Sarah, as the candidate, wasn't allowed to do this. Soon, canvassers would call on friendly voters to remind them that they hadn't voted yet. This was called "knocking up" and didn't really start until late afternoon. To remind people earlier could be counterproductive. Voting numbers would be checked against the electoral register and the party's record of voting intentions, so that only Labour homes would be visited.

If you were the candidate, time ought to pass more quickly. There were plenty of legitimate things to do, even if it was only saluting the volunteers as they went out to deliver the day-of-poll leaflet. But every ten minutes felt like an hour. Sarah travelled to and from each set of committee rooms, smiling all the time, trying to project an optimism she didn't feel or expect party workers to share. She'd like to catch a nap but knew that she was too wound up to sleep. So she stopped at the main committee rooms for another mug of tea and prepared to rally the troops.

In a good committee room, time never hangs heavily. Nobody sticks around. The organiser gets workers in and out quickly and the candidate can be a hindrance. After a few minutes of bland conversation, Sarah went for a pee and came back to find an empty front room.

"Sent out the first lot knocking up," Barry Griffiths, who was running the show, told her. He turned to a new arrival. "You've just missed 'em", he said. "But if you hurry down the road . . ."

"Sorry," said a familiar voice. "I have to go to work in a few minutes. I did all those leaflets you sent me out with. Thought I'd bring you back the spares."

"Good lad," Barry said. "Say hello to the candidate before you go. Sarah, this is . . . I'm sorry, I don't know your name."

"Nick," Sarah said, smiling awkwardly. "I'll walk you out."

Once they were outside, she asked Nick. "Time for a quick drink?"

"I can make time if you can."

She took him to the pub round the corner, where Sarah was a familiar sight and nobody bothered her. Sarah sat at a table while Nick bought a tomato juice for her and a half of bitter for himself.

"You didn't need to come out today," she said.

"I haven't missed helping out in an election since I've been old enough to vote. I figured you needed more help than the other buggers."

"Thanks," Sarah sipped her drink. It was insipid without Worcester sauce, but she didn't want to interrupt the conversation by asking for some. "I was expecting you to call."

"I meant to but . . . things on my mind."

"Did I hear you say you were going to work?"

"Joe persuaded me to do one last day. The election's got us busy."

"I hope you'll come to the party tonight."

"Oh, I don't know," Nick said. "My membership's been lapsed for five years and most people there would know why."

"Time to start rehabilitating yourself, maybe."

He looked away and she reached out to him, squeezing his left wrist with her right hand. "Nick, this is me. Tell me what's on your mind."

"This isn't the place. I said I'd start a shift at six. I ought to ring for a cab."

"I'll take you," Sarah said. "I'm a spare part today anyway."

They left their drinks unfinished. Cane Cars was only five minutes' drive at this time of day, so Sarah went as slowly as she could. "Please talk to me, Nick. There's something wrong. What is it?"

"I went to see Ed Clark yesterday."

"Oh." Whatever this was, she knew it would be bad. "And?"

"Ed said you were lovers. Described the purple birth mark on your groin."

Sarah shivered, then exhaled. "I didn't tell you the whole thing. It was too . . ." She wanted to say *upsetting* but that wasn't the right word. "Degrading."

"It's your business, not mine."

Behind her, somebody sounded their horn. Sarah was forced to drive on. "I'm just going to pull over for a minute."

They were on the edge of some playing fields, half of which had been replaced with ugly, new Housing Association builds.

"He ripped my knickers off, Nick. He had my dress up round my waist. The room was brightly lit, so he got a good look, yeah. Then I kneed him in the groin. How could you think that I'd give myself to a neanderthal like him?"

Although she'd stopped driving, Nick still stared ahead. "You knocked yourself out to get him out of prison."

"Because I thought he was innocent!"

Her mobile rang. Sarah snapped a "hello", then recognised her party leader's voice. Taken aback, she stumbled out an apology for her abruptness. Tony pooh-poohed this in his most earnest, blokey manner. He told her how much he appreciated the work Sarah had done over the last two years. "I admire you sticking with your seat. It was the right thing to do, but I know you were given . . . options. If things work out for us tonight and they don't work out for you, I want you to know this: we'll find you a role. A good one."

She didn't need to tell Nick who she'd been talking to. When the call ended, he sounded impressed.

"Call you often, does he?"

Sarah shook her head. "First time ever. Do you believe me about Ed?"

She turned to face him and they looked each other straight in the eye, only a few inches apart. "How can I not believe you?" he said.

This was not the moment to kiss him, though Sarah wanted to. But it was their most intimate moment since they stopped being lovers.

"Suppose I'd better drive you back," she said.

Nick only spoke again when she was almost at the cab firm.

"Something I haven't told you. Something important."

"Wait a mo." She didn't want to end the conversation but the road outside Cane Cars was double yellowed and busy. Sarah turned into the cab firm car park, where there was one space, which she took. At least they couldn't be seen here. Words tumbled out of Nick.

"The woman I was seeing until recently . . . it wasn't serious, but you know her. I picked her up in the cab from one of your surgeries."

Sarah could feel it coming, knew at once who her rival was.

"It was entirely physical. You can't imagine what it's like, not having any for five years. Anyway, it was Polly. Polly Bolton."

"You were screwing *that?*" Sarah shook her head in disbelief.

"That's not all of it. I went round to see her the other day. I wanted to warn her that Ed's driving a taxi for my brother. Only, she already knew. Thing is, and this is hard to believe, she's seeing Ed."

"Polly's got back with Ed? That's beyond bizarre."

"You knew that they were together before?"

"I only just found out. How close are they, have you any idea?"

"They're living together, as far as I can tell. She's a hard case, Polly. I told her what you'd told me about Ed. She didn't give a shit. She says he didn't do it. She says he told her who did."

"If he knew that," Sarah said, "he'd have told me. Or at the very least he'd have told his solicitor."

"I'd better go," Nick said, awkwardly leaning over and putting an arm around her. "Do you want me to ring you later?"

"Please. I ought to be at the count by ten. Until then, whatever I do is displacement activity."

He kissed her on the cheek, then got out of the car. Sarah began to back out of her space, distracted. What could a man like Nick see in a woman like Polly? Had prison coarsened Nick so much? No wonder he'd believed it when he heard that Sarah had been with Ed Clark.

A cab was waiting in the narrow driveway. Sarah held up her hand to indicate that she was on her way out and pulled down the sun visor to keep off the glare. The cab pulled alongside Sarah and she manoeuvred carefully around it to make her way out, not once looking at the driver.

"What was Sarah Bone doing in the car park?" Ed Clark asked.

"No idea," Nas said, as Nick put down the paper, which was predicting a comfortable Labour win.

"Thought you'd stopped working here, duck," Ed said to Nick.

240

"I'm not working," Nick said, and Nas didn't contradict him.

"You and Sarah. Back together again, are you?"

"She gave me a lift, that's all."

"I'd have thought she had better things to do on a day like today," Ed said. "But she has strong needs, Sarah, dun't she?"

Nick couldn't stop himself. He hit Ed in the face, hard, sideswiping his nose. The other driver didn't go down. Without waiting to recover, he lunged at Nick. Before Ed had time to get in a good punch, Nick kneed him in the groin, hard.

"From what I hear," he said, as Ed keeled over, "you're used to being hit there."

Nas threw Nick the keys to Stuart's cab. "Get out of here before he can stand up."

CHAPTER
TWENTY-NINE

Best to be straight with her. Sarah couldn't pretend to be at Polly's house by accident. Suppose Ed was there? His taxi wasn't outside but maybe, like Nick, he shared one. Meeting Ed was a risk she would have to take. Sarah knocked on the door, then took deep breaths, inflating the anger she needed before she was able to tackle Polly.

"You again."

"We need to talk. Now. Away from the kids."

Sarah's demeanour was stern enough for Polly to step aside and let her in. She yelled into the front room.

"I've got a visitor, so watch the telly quietly. No interruptions."

She ushered Sarah into the back room, which was messier than on Sarah's last visit. There was a leather jacket hanging from the cellar door. It was the one Ed had been wearing on the night of his release. Sarah pointed at it.

"How could you, Polly? You were so convinced he killed your brother, your sister-in-law."

"Nick told you, did he? Ed said you used to know him but I found that hard to credit. The MP and the

242

jailbird. We're not so different, are we? Both go for blokes who've been inside."

"Nick's crime was a lot less serious than Ed's."

"Except for one thing," Polly said, looking at the stairway. "Ed didn't do it."

"You've changed your tune. I don't get it, Polly. How could you let that . . ." — she was going to say "sociopath" but doubted Polly would know what the word meant — "that creep near enough to you to convince you he's innocent, never mind let him into your bed?"

"Ed gets what he wants," Polly sneered. "But then, you'd know that, wouldn't you?"

"If you're saying . . ."

"It bothers you, dunnit, that I've had the same men you've had. Nick, he's the one who likes it rough. Did he learn to be like that from you? Ed, he's a gent compared to Nick. Don't look at me that way. You're not going to pretend Ed forced you, are you? I know what you told Nick. But I know what you're like."

"You know nothing," Sarah said. "Ed Clark tried to attack me and if I hadn't hurt him, he would have raped me. I went out with Nick fourteen years ago and how he could have stooped to sleep with the likes of you, I can't fathom."

"*Stoop? Sleep? Fathom?* Listen to her. Your Nick never slept here. He came to fuck me when he felt like it and didn't give a shit if the kids heard a thing or not. Ed sleeps here. He's good to those kids. And if he offered you a jump and you turned him down, you missed out."

"I think Ed murdered your brother," Sarah said.

"You're wrong."

"How can you be so sure, so suddenly?"

"I am sure. I know who done it."

"Who?"

"Think I'd tell you, way you've treated me?"

"I treated you with nothing but respect. And I helped get Ed out of prison. You've suddenly decided I did the right thing, but I'm not so sure any more."

"The evidence against Ed was rubbish. He only got put away because they needed someone for killing a cop. He'd have got out without you."

"Convince me," Sarah pleaded. "Tell me what Ed told you. Who killed Terry and Liv Shanks? Why did they do it?"

The front door opened and closed. Ed charged into the room. His nose was red and there was blood on his shirt.

"Get out," Polly told Sarah. "Ed, what happened?"

Sarah stood with her back to the door. Ed glared at her.

"Who attacked you, Ed?" Sarah asked, allowing no sympathy in her voice.

"You know who did."

"Nick hit you?"

"Then ran off, 'sright. But I'll catch up with him, don't you worry."

Sarah felt a warm buzz of affection for Nick.

"Look how smug she is," Polly said, as Ed took off his shirt.

"How did you do it, Ed?" Sarah asked. "How did you convince Polly you didn't attack me? The same way you made her believe you didn't kill her brother?"

"She dun't need convincing of ought. Poll knows what happened to Terry, and to Liv. And she knows what's going to happen to you." Ed lowered his voice and reached over Sarah. His sweaty chest crushed her breasts, while his right hand jammed the door closed. "There were no witnesses, were there? There's only me and you know how hard I fucked you, how you told me it were the best shag you'd had your whole life. But this afternoon, Poll's a witness. What do you say, Poll? A'right wi' you if I give her seconds?"

Sarah couldn't tell if Ed was serious. She reached for her phone. It wasn't in her pocket. She'd left it in the car. She looked over Ed's shoulder for help, assurance that they were winding her up. Polly's face was a blank, unreadable.

"Let's finish what we started," Ed said.

It was Nick's last shift and one of his first jobs was to pick up his brother.

"How is she?"

"Don't reckon it'll be long now," Joe said. "Thanks for agreeing to do a shift."

"You're not going to the Labour bash?"

"I'll be there late on, I expect. Nas has to get home sometime."

"Nas's brothers," Nick said. "Do they know about you?"

"You must be joking."

"You lead a risky life," Nick said.

"There's no fun without risk," Joe said. "You told me that once, when I warned you about the skunk operation."

"I don't remember it being all that much fun. Profitable, yes, but half of it went up my nose. It was certainly a risk."

"You were bound to get caught sometime."

"Most people don't," Nick said. "I was unlucky."

"You make your own luck. If I'd come in with you, like you wanted, I wouldn't have any of . . . this."

"No need to rub it in," Nick said. His brother had never been good at tact. It was one reason he always got what he wanted. Joe changed the subject.

"Someone said they saw that Andrew Saint in town the other day. You still in touch with him?"

"Not really."

"I tried to call him, like you asked me to, when you got busted. He never returned my calls."

"He was in the States, I think. Doesn't matter. He couldn't have done much."

"No? Not much is still better than nothing."

Nick let Joe out at the Cane Cars office, where Nas was bound to tell him about his fight with Ed. It shouldn't matter to Joe, not with Nick leaving. The two men operated on a "need to know" basis. This was, Nick decided, the safest way. He could never completely rule out the thought that Joe had betrayed him to the police as some kind of retaliation for his affair with Caroline, to get him out of the way. But Joe still didn't seem to suspect they'd had a fling and Nick was no longer so paranoid. They might not be as close as some, but Joe was his brother. He wouldn't give him up. Whereas Andrew Saint was merely an old friend, one he'd drifted apart from. And Andrew had warned him when he began the skunk operation: in the drugs business, there were no real friendships, only alliances.

Since getting out, Nick had slowly come to the conclusion that the Saint must have betrayed him. He knew about the caves, had given Nick the contacts to sell the stuff on. He took a small commission at first, then told Nick not to bother. He didn't want any of his income traceable to a criminal enterprise. At the time, Nick thought this was generous, an act of friendship. Now he wasn't so sure. Andrew had been overgenerous since Nick got out, too. Two grand would have been enough. The extra three, the home visit, these things smelt of guilt more than kind-heartedness.

But the betrayal? That puzzled Nick. Andrew was either out of the country already, or had fled shortly after Nick's arrest. Had he given Nick to the police as a bargaining chip to get himself off some lesser charge? Or was Nick still being paranoid and the whole debacle was what the police claimed, a combination of police work and luck?

Inside, Nick never allowed himself to dream that he might rekindle something with Sarah. He still doubted it. Some people used a long stretch to study. He'd had time to get an MA, a PhD even. Instead, he'd slacked the days away, becoming a cruder, less complicated person than he was on the out. That was how you got through. Nick knew he'd live to regret hitting Ed. Inside, he'd not got into fights. He'd hit back a couple times when he had to, but never struck out in blind rage, the way he had with Ed, today. Violence should always be calculated to have the maximum effect, that was what the smart cons said. What effect did hitting Ed have? He'd probably go home and take it out on Polly.

And maybe Polly liked being hit. When they were together, Nick had been surprised by how rough she wanted him to be. Polly brought out a side of Nick he hadn't been aware of.

What if Ed decided to take it out on Sarah? This was her big day. The last thing she needed was big Ed turning up while she was campaigning, throwing a spanner in the works. He ought to warn her.

She answered on the second ring. There was something wrong with her voice.

"I know," she said, when he told her about Ed.

"How?"

"I've seen him."

"Already? I don't understand . . ."

"I went to see Polly. He came back . . ." She began to cry.

"Where are you?" he asked. "I'm coming."

"I'm sitting in my car." She told him where.

Nick was with Sarah within five minutes.

"I'll kill him," he vowed. "I'll take a brick to the bastard and . . ."

"Stop, stop. You know it wouldn't do any good. Ed can control himself. You have to learn the same or you'll end up back in prison."

"The bastard assaulted you."

"He brushed his hand against my breasts. He scared me so much I wet myself. He didn't physically hurt me. He made it clear that he could rape me and get away with it, that his girlfriend would hold me down."

"Polly helped?"

"She didn't do anything to stop him. She didn't help him either. She's in Ed's power. She acts hard, but she's terrified of him, I'm sure of it. If I went to the police, she'd swear I suggested a threesome. Only Ed isn't stupid enough to go that far. He enjoys power but he's too clever to take unnecessary risks."

"Then why did he get caught killing Polly's brother?"

"I don't know. Maybe Polly's telling the truth about that and Ed is innocent. Whatever happens tonight, I have to find out what really happened. I don't know how, but I will. Until then, stay away from him."

"In case he takes his revenge through you?"

"He won't get near me again," Sarah said. "Once I go back to the committee rooms, there'll be people with me every minute of the day. But he knows where to find you. Be careful. And hold me, please."

Awkwardly, he put his arm around her shoulders, then nuzzled his head against hers. He began to kiss her hair, then her neck. Sarah's mobile rang. She answered it. Winston.

"I'll be on my way in a minute. Oh, I'll have fish and chips with everyone else, it's a campaign tradition, isn't it? No, I'm fine. It's just a bad line. See you in five."

She looked at Nick. "Promise me you won't get into any more trouble today. And that you'll come to the party. I want you to take me home tonight."

"Yes, please," he said, and kissed her again, a long, full-throated kiss.

"Oh, and I know you don't live in my constituency, but don't forget to vote."

Nick replied with a regretful smile. Of course, he'd been in prison too recently to have registered. He didn't have a vote.

CHAPTER
THIRTY

At the count, boxes were opened and ballot slips sorted. All four Nottingham constituencies were being counted in the same hall. Old hands like Sarah could quickly tell where the election was heading. Within an hour, she would know the result to the nearest thousand votes. Her majority in the by-election had been five thousand, but that was on a huge anti-government swing. Previous Tory majorities had been in five figures.

Winston gave Sarah his hipflask and sent her to sit in the TV room.

"Long night ahead."

Exit polls showed New Labour on course for a comfortable victory. There was a brief piece on how the face of the House Of Commons would change if Labour won big. The place would be younger, with far more women: an exciting prospect, if you were going to be there. With so many women on board, Tony was bound to promote a few. Sarah might have had a chance of joining the government. Nothing flashy, but something responsible: pensions, perhaps, or a junior Health minister.

"Looking good, eh?" Tony Bax said, winking at her. "Do they need us out there yet?"

"In a few minutes," Sarah said.

There were too many people in the TV room, so Sarah wandered through the dingy sports hall until she found the ladies'. When she returned to the hall, she stood at the back, watching the watchers. Easier to do this than gawp at TV and have to discuss what she saw. The counters began to empty the ballot boxes.

"Have you seen the exit polls?" One of the volunteer scrutineers whispered. "They're predicting a majority of eighty to ninety."

Sarah nodded unenthusiastically.

"What do you reckon?" Winston asked.

The votes were being put into piles for each party.

"Not sure," she said, unwilling to believe the evidence of her own eyes. "We haven't seen anywhere near enough yet."

Winston stared at the growing piles, counting votes the way a professional gambler counted cards. "West's too close to call," he told her. "If the vote's like this everywhere, we're talking about a landslide."

Nick had the radio on. The first results weren't far away. He'd taken a couple of councillors he knew from way back to the Labour workers' party at Trent University's student union building. Neither of them had recognised him. Nick had fallen through the invisible net that separated the connected from the unconnected. He'd felt this way when he was sixteen. Then he'd gone to university and become someone.

Could he reinvent himself? Joe had managed it. Andrew too. Nick could start again, but it would have to be somewhere new. The decision was beginning to harden in his mind.

He was being called on the radio.

"Nick?" Stuart's voice was agitated. "Know where Joe is?"

"At the Labour Party do. Probably plastered by now."

"Right, I'll send someone to try and find him."

"Don't you want me to . . .?"

"No. Get over to his house. Caroline's gone into labour. You'd better run her to the hospital, pronto."

Nick accelerated. When he got to Sherwood, Caroline was in the hall, leaning on the end of the banister. Her waters had broken.

"I don't want to mess up Stuart's cab," Caroline groaned, holding out an old beach towel. "Spread this across the back."

Nick took the towel then helped her into the car. The hospital was only a two-minute drive.

"Where's Joe?" she asked, once she was settled in. "His mobile's off."

"On his way," Nick said, though that was presuming Joe really was at the election do and not still in bed with Nas. Caroline moaned. Nick drove fast.

"Over there."

They entered City Hospital and turned towards the maternity unit. Nick sounded his horn. Caroline had already rung them. She was expected.

"You'll be all right now," he said.

"Nick? Stay until Joe arrives, please?"

"Of course I will," Nick said, though being in on the birth was the last thing he felt like doing. He spoke into the radio. "Where's Joe? Was he at the do?"

"If he's there, they haven't found him yet. We'll keep looking."

Nick swore. Behind him, he heard a siren. Why would they need sirens inside a hospital? He parked and opened the door for Caroline, had to help her out. When someone tapped his shoulder, he thought it would be a nurse. It wasn't.

"Is this your cab, sir?" the officer asked.

"Not now," Caroline moaned.

Two porters were coming. The policeman was reaching over the driver's seat, peering at the ID tag hung beneath the rear-view mirror. Luckily, Nick had replaced Stuart's tag with Joe's when he took the car.

"You're Joseph Cane?"

The nurse spoke at the same time. "Is that the father?"

"No," Caroline moaned. "It's my brother-in-law."

"Are you Joseph Cane?" The officer repeated.

Had the policeman heard Caroline? Nick didn't know what to say. He didn't have time for this, but it began to dawn on him that he could be in trouble. Even a small infringement of the law could break his parole and send him back to prison. He must stay cool. When in doubt, Nick had long since figured out, it was always best to tell the truth.

"No. I'm his brother. Joe isn't around and his wife's in labour. That's why . . ."

Caroline was being wheeled away and couldn't confirm or deny any story he told.

"So you're driving this cab illegally?"

"I wasn't charging her, for Christ's sake! Look, she might drop the little bugger at any minute, so if you don't mind leaving it for now . . ."

The officer smiled firmly. "You did just break the speed limit. So, a couple more questions, if you don't mind. You say that you haven't been driving this cab for hire?"

"No."

"So who was observed driving it earlier this evening, outside Trent Students' Union and later on Gregory Boulevard?"

Nick began to sweat. "That would be my brother."

"When did you take over from him?"

"I gave him a lift then brought the car back to his at about eleven."

"So you dropped him at an election party then went home to look after his wife? Have I got that straight?"

"Sort of."

"Your brother wears glasses, I see, unlike you."

Nick hadn't had time to get the clear-lensed pair from home, which was probably a good thing. He would only get in deeper. This was worse than he'd feared. They knew that he'd been driving a cab for hire. He'd definitely broken the terms of his probation. Once they found out who he was, he'd be back inside.

"Look," he said, "can't this wait? I promised Caroline that I'd stay with her."

"I'm afraid not," the officer said. "You are under arrest. You do not have to say anything, but if you do not mention now something which you later use in your defence the court may decide that your failure to mention it now strengthens the case against you . . ."

Sarah couldn't concentrate on the counts. She kept losing track and didn't want to discuss the numbers with any of the other scrutineers. Her colleagues were each watching one of the counters: local government workers on overtime. The result would be closer than anybody could have predicted. Impossible to say how close.

What if she won? Superstitiously, Sarah hadn't planned a speech. It was down to the winner to thank the police and the returning officers but the rest was a blank. Winston was walking over. He had just completed the most contentious part of the evening, when the candidates or their representatives checked the spoiled ballots and marginally unclear votes. The returning officer had the final say over which ones were valid and which weren't, but the parties could have their say, too. If there was a recount, every decision had the potential to be crucial. But Sarah had never been involved in a recount. She thought of them as a kind of urban myth. Before Winston got to her, Sarah's mobile rang.

"Is that Sarah Bone, the MP?"

"Yes."

"I'm the custody sergeant at Canning Circus police station. We've got a gentleman under arrest who insisted on making his mandatory phone call to you."

"Is it one of my constituents?"

"I don't think so, ma'am."

Sarah wasn't a member of the royal family, but sometimes the police got their knickers in a twist over rank and titles. Sarah let the *ma'am* work in her favour.

"What's his name?"

"Nicholas Cane."

"And what's he done?"

"Driving a taxi cab without the appropriate license."

"And you've got him in custody for that?"

"He's on probation, ma'am."

Probation. Of course he was.

"Even so, it's hardly a hanging offence, is it? He's supposed to be collecting me later on. He's my driver for the evening."

"He doesn't have a taxi permit."

"I don't think he was going to charge me. From what he told me earlier, he was borrowing the cab from his brother to help out with my campaign today."

This was a fib but, if the last thing she did as an MP was getting an ex-boyfriend released from custody, it wouldn't be a bad night's work.

"Do you want me to put him on, ma'am?"

"I do. And when I've finished talking to him, if you haven't changed your mind, I'm going to track down Eric and get him over to sort you out. I think he's coming to my party later. Possibly Mr Cane would be driving him home, too."

The Chief Constable wasn't invited to the party, but using his first name seemed to have an effect.

"I see, ma'am. I'll have a word with the arresting officer."

There was a long, tense, infuriating delay during which Sarah had to wave away several supporters. It was nearly one when a sheepish Nick appeared on the phone. "Sarah, I'm so sorry. Yours was the only mobile number I had. They caught me speeding, taking my sister-in-law to hospital. She's having a baby as we speak. But evidently the police were already watching me. I've got a solicitor, Ian Jagger, but I haven't seen him since I got out and I don't have his number."

"Ian's probably at the party," Sarah said, "I can get his number for you, but it might not be necessary."

"The custody sergeant wants a word," Nick said, sheepishly.

The sergeant came back on. "We're prepared to let him go tonight," he said. "Seeing as you say he was helping you out earlier and not charging anybody. But earlier today we had a tip off that he's been working for his brother for weeks."

Sarah was aware that this was true. Somebody had it in for Nick Cane. She knew exactly who it was.

"Sounds like a malicious call to me, sergeant. I know Nick's done some silly things in the past, but I'll vouch for him now."

"Fair enough, ma'am. We'll send him to you." He put Nick back on just as Winston began signalling to her. "I've got to go," she said. "They're about to announce the result."

"Do you want me to come and collect you from the count?" Nick asked, as she walked into the hall, still talking on the mobile, not the image she wanted to present to the watching TV cameras.

"No, meet me at the party after you've checked on your sister-in-law. And, Nick, leave the car. After what you've been through, I expect you could do with a drink."

The other candidates were already lined up on the stage. In the end, it hadn't been close enough to require a recount. Sarah climbed the shallow stairs, prepared to meet her fate.

CHAPTER
THIRTY-ONE

Nick raced into the delivery room. It was less than an hour since he'd taken Caroline in.

"Here's the father," said a breezy nurse. "Better late than never."

Caroline gave her a tired but brave smile. Seeing Nick, her expression returned to that of the perpetually pissed-off school teacher.

"Not the father. His brother. Again. Where is he, Nick?"

"Not sure. Stuart said he'd call the party. I've come straight from the police."

"How did you go on?" Caroline said. "Sort it out?"

"I think so," Nick said, leaning over his tiny, new, wrinkled niece. The thought of going back to prison for three years scared the fuck out of him. But he couldn't allow himself to focus on that, not here. Not now.

"She's beautiful."

"Thank you," Caroline said. "And thank you for earlier. I'm sorry if it caused you grief."

He kissed her on the cheek. "How do you feel?"

"I'm good, now it's over. Aching, but good. Where the fuck's Joe?"

"I'll go and call him," Nick said.

The nurse directed him to a phone down a corridor. Stuart answered.

"Caroline wants to know where Joe is. Any ideas?"

"None at all. I asked for an announcement to be made over the PA at that party, but it sounded pretty noisy there. I've been trying his mobile every ten minutes, left a message each time. Has she had it yet?"

"Little girl. Mother and baby fine. Have you got a mobile number for Nas?"

"Afraid not," Stuart said, awkwardly. Nick wished he hadn't asked.

"I guess I'll head over to the party."

He explained to Caroline that the party was very loud and the message might not have got through. "I'll go and see if I can find him."

"Thanks. Oh, your ex-girlfriend . . . did she win?"

"I don't know yet."

They were alone. Caroline looked exhausted but happy. Nick wanted to get away before she quizzed him about Joe's whereabouts again. He wanted to find out Sarah's result. But he couldn't just leave. So he squeezed his sister-in-law's hand. She burst into tears.

"I'm so sorry."

"What about?" He thought she realized how likely he was to end up back in prison. Or maybe she was emotional about Joe's absence.

"You've been so nice to me since you got out. You never once dropped a hint to Joe that we were once, you know . . ."

"He still doesn't know?" Nick asked.

"He never suspected a thing. But you must have worked out what happened. I don't know how you found it in your heart to forgive me."

"I've been dumped before," Nick said, then he saw from the way her face was contorting that this wasn't what Caroline was talking about.

"It was you, wasn't it, who called the police?"

Caroline nodded. "Joe told me, so proudly, how you grew the stuff, how you were making a fortune, but he wouldn't get involved. He was impressed with you. I thought he might change his mind. I was angry that you'd asked him, that you'd let your younger brother get involved in something so dangerous."

"He was only just starting the cab firm then," Nick told her. "He — you two — could have used the money. I thought the risk was pretty low. And I needed someone I could really trust."

"I was angry with you, Nick. I wanted you out of the way. I'm so sorry."

She was crying again when the nurse came back in, holding his as-yet-unnamed niece. The nurse gave Nick a patient smile.

"Her first, isn't it?" She said, producing tissues. "Mothers do get emotional at these times."

"She'll be fine," Nick said. "Can you give us another minute alone?"

When she was gone, he leant over Caroline and the baby, who smelt of everything that was real, and fresh, and new. The past was gone. The next generation had begun. He said what he had to say.

"I'm glad you told me, but it's water under the bridge now. We're family. We stick together no matter how much we hurt each other."

Caroline kissed him on the mouth. "You're treating me better than I deserve. Unlike your brother. Go on, get going to your MP. You must be desperate to find out how she did."

In the car, Nick tuned into a local station. Radio Nottingham was covering the announcement in Nottingham South, an easy Labour win. This was the second Labour win in the city tonight, the commentator said, but that meant nothing — North and East were also safe Labour seats.

He knew he was mad, driving again after what had happened earlier. If the police caught him, Nick would be locked up for sure, in front of a judge in the morning, back in nick by midnight. Three more years. It didn't bear thinking about. But Joe might well need the cab and Nick was already in deep shit. The students' union was only a ten-minute drive. He took the risk.

Where did Joe take Nas for sex? Nick had no idea. Joe had never asked for a spare key to his flat, and Nick wasn't sure if he would have offered it if he had. Maybe he sprang for a cheap hotel room.

The bar was heaving with excited party members. A big screen TV was predicting a Labour majority of over a hundred. Every time a victory flashed up on the red bar at the bottom of the screen, there was a loud cheer. Nick looked around, picking out faces, failing to put names to most of them. No Joe. Most partygoers were glued to the TV.

"Get ready everybody," a voice said over the PA. "She's here!"

Both of the hall doors opened at once. A scrum of people pushed their way through. It took a moment for Nick to see who they were carrying. He had never heard a football crowd give as hearty a roar as the one that greeted Sarah, her legs akimbo, face beaming. Waving both arms in the air, the triumphant MP was carried to the small stage at the front of the hall, where the scrum set her down.

Sarah wobbled to her feet. Her hair was messed up and the grey suit she was wearing had become dishevelled. She pushed her hair back before giving the crowd an enormous smile. That set them off cheering again.

"Comrades," she said. "Friends. I can't believe we did it. If we've won in West — not narrowly either, but by nearly *two thousand votes* — it means that we're about to see the biggest Labour victory since 1945. Possibly the biggest Labour victory ever!"

The cheers resounded. Nick joined in. She had won, as he had wanted her to win. She might have saved his bacon tonight, too. Sarah deserved the best the world could give her. But now he'd never get together with her again. Looking at her on the stage he saw the same woman he'd stood beside at her first victory, fifteen years ago. He realized how much he still wanted her. He ought to be by her side now.

264

"I want to thank you, all of you, for working so hard and to say that I won't let you down."

"You've never let us down!" someone yelled.

"I'd prepared this plucky little good-loser speech and now I have no idea what to say except, this is wonderful and we all really deserve it. Let's enjoy tonight because, tomorrow, the real work begins."

She left the stage to a tuneless but gusto filled rendition of "For She's a Jolly Good Fellow". Champagne corks popped. Nick took a glass.

"Nick! You made it! Come and have a drink!"

Sarah threw her arms around him and planted a wet kiss on his cheek. She smelt of sweat and expensive perfume.

"How's your sister-in-law?"

"Fine. Lovely baby girl. Seven pounds two ounces."

"Brilliant."

Nick felt conspicuous. The half glass of warm champagne did little to help. He needed to sink two or three pints before he could relax around Sarah, who was now accepting a kiss from his younger brother. When did Joe arrive?

"It's marvellous news," he was saying. "You won't remember me, but . . ."

"Of course I recognise you," Sarah shouted. "Nick's brother. Congratulations on your news, too. A little girl. You must be so thrilled."

Seeing Joe's dumbfounded expression, Sarah hesitated. As somebody else came to congratulate her, Nick tapped his brother on the shoulder.

"Been trying to get you all evening. Where the fuck have you been?"

"Incommunicado. Sarah's got the wrong end of the stick, yeah?"

Nick shook his head. "I left Caroline twenty minutes ago. Tell her you were at the party but didn't get the message and your mobile's malfunctioning. She might just buy it." He handed his brother the key to Stuart's car, adding where it was parked.

"She's okay? The baby's okay?"

"They're fine. Congratulations. Now get the fuck out of here."

"I owe you one. Here, take this. I never drive with it. Cheers, bro."

His brother handed Nick his tobacco pouch then pushed his way out of the crowded hall. Nick stood near Sarah, watching her accept congratulatory hugs from friend and foe alike. Everybody wanted to be part of her success. Tony Bax came over, his eyes watering. Seeing Nick, he raised a fist.

"All four seats Labour. We didn't even get that in 'forty-five. It's wonderful."

On the TV screen, big Tory names were falling fast. Rifkind was gone. Jasper March, they were saying, was in trouble. Michael Howard, the Home Secretary, might lose to the Liberals. Gill Temperley's seat was no longer safe. Even Michael Portillo was considered to be in danger. The Labour leader was boarding a plane to London. The TV kept showing a crowd of familiar, famous faces at the Royal Festival Hall.

266

Time accelerated. At three or so, Nick checked his brother's tobacco pouch and found, as he'd expected, some skunk in a separate bag at the bottom. He sat on the loo and skinned up a couple of small spliffs, then went outside for a smoke. He could hear the radio playing through an open window. The results had taken on a surreal flavour. Portillo — the Defence Minister who most expected to be the next Conservative leader — had lost his "safe" seat. Jasper March was in a recount. Optimists began saying that the Tories were finished, gone for good.

The mild night was starting to become a little chill. The results were slowing down. Nick could hear a few people leaving. One set of footsteps approached him.

"I thought you might have left," a familiar voice said. Sarah.

"Wouldn't have gone without saying goodbye," he told her, hiding the joint by cupping it in his hand.

"I remember that guilty look," she said, amusement in her voice. "Are you smoking what I think you're smoking? You must be mad. What if the police had found it on you?"

"I didn't have it earlier," Nick explained. "Joe got me to hold it for him when he drove to the hospital. Want some?"

"I hardly touch the stuff these days," Sarah said. Nevertheless, she took the spliff and had a couple of small hits before passing it back to him. "I'd better not be seen doing this."

"You'd better not," Nick agreed, and stubbed the spliff out on the wall.

Sarah giggled. "I feel twenty-one again."

"You look great," Nick told her. "Better than ever."

"So do you." When he didn't try to kiss her straight away, Sarah took a step towards him. "Give us a smokey kiss, then."

He did as he was told. The kiss lasted a long time. Nick held Sarah tightly, until he heard someone behind them and broke away. It was one of the youngest campaign workers. Oblivious to Sarah and Nick, he threw up into a bush. Sarah got out her mobile and handed it to Nick.

"Call us one of your taxis. Take me home."

"I don't want to take advantage," he said.

"I'm not that drunk," she said, her voice slurring slightly. "I'm celebrating. So let me take advantage of you. Please."

He made the call. "Five minutes. I said you'd be waiting at the front."

"I'll go and take my leave. I'd rather you didn't . . ."

"I understand. I'll wait for you at the end of the road."

Fifteen minutes later, they were in a cab.

"Where to?" The driver asked.

Nick, instead of doing up his seat belt, slid an arm round Sarah's shoulder, the hand carelessly brushing her right breast.

She gave him the address. Dawn was only an hour away. Nick wanted to kiss Sarah but she'd flinched slightly when he put his arm round her and he sensed that was because they weren't alone. Nick didn't know the driver, Rodney. A request to be discreet might have the opposite effect, so he kept quiet. Then the silence began to feel awkward, so he talked to Sarah in a low murmur, up close, the way he used to talk to her in bed.

"I can't believe you're still single."

"I've always been choosy, you should know that."

He chuckled. "I should never have let you go."

"As I recall, I didn't give you a lot of choice." She squeezed his thigh.

"Here we are," said Rodney.

Sarah tried to insist on paying, but Nick wouldn't let her. Rodney nodded when Nick told him to keep the change. He didn't acknowledge that he recognised Nick or knew who Sarah was. He'd keep schtum, Nick reckoned. Sarah stumbled out of the car and Nick helped her to the door. Inside the well-lit hall, she fumbled with the burglar alarm, taking two goes to turn it off. When she'd succeeded, he kissed her, propping her up with his arms as he did so. She was done in.

"Let's get you to bed," he said.

"Bed," she repeated after him. "Yes, please."

"Which way?"

"Follow me," she said, and began to sing, to the tune of a hit from when they were both toddlers, "Chirpy Chirpy Cheep Cheep": "One thousand, nine hundred and eighty-nine votes, tha-aa-at's the size of my majority. One thousand, nine hundred and eighty-nine votes . . ."

She let go of his hand to open the bedroom door, turned on the light and, as soon as they were inside, began to tear off her crumpled clothes, not stopping at the underwear.

"C'mere." Naked, her figure was fuller than before, which only made her all the more alluring. Sarah's long hair fell across her chest, setting off her taut, perfect breasts. Nick found himself staring at the small purple birthmark above her cleft of pubic hair, then stopped himself. He had forgotten the way one of her knees seemed to point away from the other. First love, best love. This might be the last time he slept with a woman for three years. He wanted to remember every moment.

"Do I have to undress you, too?" she asked, reaching to unbutton his fly.

"No. Get into bed. I'm going to find us both a glass of water."

"Hurry," she said, obeying his instructions. "I've been dreaming about this for as long as I can remember. I want you inside me, now."

When he returned from the kitchen, two minutes later, she was fast asleep.

CHAPTER
THIRTY-TWO

Nick got out of the shower and returned to the bedroom with a large towel wrapped around his waist. Sarah lay in the bed where he had slept, chastely, alongside her. Hearing Nick, she blinked awake.

"You're in good shape," she said, as he removed the towel.

"I got a lot of exercise, the last few years."

"What happened last night?"

"You fell asleep as soon as your head hit the pillow."

"And before that?"

"You won an election."

"I did, didn't I?"

He let the towel drop and came over, kissed her on the forehead.

"Congratulations again. Why don't I make you some tea?"

"That'd be nice." Sarah got out of bed and rattled open the blinds. It was a glorious, sunny day.

"New Labour, new weather," she observed. "I think I'll take a shower myself."

Nick made tea and considered making breakfast, too, but could only find two slices of bread that were at least three days old. No eggs or butter, just marge, half an inch of Old English marmalade and a small jar of Marmite. At least she had milk, skimmed. He checked the hall but she didn't have a paper delivered.

When he returned to the bedroom, Sarah was still in the shower. He got back into bed and turned on her portable radio. Labour's majority was 179. Sarah would be one of 419 Labour MPs. John Major had resigned the Tory party leadership. He summed up these details when Sarah returned from the shower, wearing a white towelling dressing gown.

"This is like old times." She hadn't washed her hair but it was damp at the edges so looked shorter. Sarah swigged her tea, then reached into her night table and put on a pair of glasses with round lenses, like the ones she always used to wear.

"You look even better now that I can see you properly."

Sarah lifted up the bed sheets and kissed his flaccid penis, which uncurled at her touch. There was a clicking noise from the hall.

"What's that?" he asked.

"Just the answering machine. I set it to 'no rings'. There'll be a ton of messages. But I'm still in bed." She kissed him on the lips.

"How's the head?" he asked, sliding his hand up between her thighs, which were still a little clammy from the shower.

"I took a couple of paracetamols. I'll be fine." She kissed him again. "Now let's do what we didn't get round to last night."

There was a knock on the front door.

Nick waited in the bedroom until the journalist had gone. Then he got dressed. The day was too busy for sex. Sarah toasted stale bread and made coffee. Radio Four announced the appointment of the new Home Secretary.

"Will you get any kind of job?" Nick asked, feeling grubby in his clothes from the night before.

"Me? I'm just one of the masses. I wasn't expected to get back in, so I won't figure in anybody's calculations."

"When will you go back to London?"

"Monday. I was expecting to have to clear my office in a hurry. No need now." She cursed. "Forgot. I was meant to be meeting this guy for dinner tomorrow — about a job — I'll get out of it."

Before Nick could ask who the someone was, the doorbell rang. Sarah returned with a huge bunch of lilies. She read the card.

"That's sweet of him. I'll get a vase."

While she was gone, Nick couldn't resist reading the card. *Seems you won't be needing that job after all. Couldn't be happier for you. Well done. AS.* The message had been written by the florist yet Sarah seemed to know who AS was.

When she returned, before Nick could ask about the flowers, Sarah underwent a personality change.

"I'm going to have to go into work mode for a while," she said.

"I'll get out of your way," Nick said, awkwardly.

"I don't want to kick you out. You've not got anywhere you have to be?"

"No. I do a bit of English GCSE tuition, but I don't have a lesson until Sunday. I'd like to make myself useful. Is there anything you need?"

"I could really use an *Evening Post*."

"Why don't I go and get one?" Nick felt awkward, unsure what to say to her next, and was glad to have an excuse to get out of the flat. "I could pick up some food while I'm out."

"Would you? That'd be fantastic."

She was already opening a notebook, arranging it on the table by the phone. The answering machine's red LED indicated that Sarah had forty-three messages waiting. Nick tried to remember how much money he had on him. He didn't want to ask Sarah for any. Enough, he reckoned, even after paying for the taxi last night.

"Don't be too long," Sarah called. "I'm starving."

"An hour at most," he shouted. Outside, he marvelled at the cherry blossom cascading onto the Park's wide, sun-drenched streets, covering the paving stones in a shower of pink snow. He began the brief walk into town, a spring in his step, filled with thoughts of Sarah.

He was back at the flat an hour later, festooned with Marks and Sparks bags. Nick gave Sarah a smile as wide as the Trent when she opened the door. He watched Sarah try to mirror the smile back. She failed.

"You look like you've been at that table since I left," he told her.

"I only just got through my messages," she said. "Listen to this one."

274

She played him one from a bloke with a nasal, educated voice.

"Eric here. Delighted you got back in. I understand you'll be swamped but I need to discuss something with you. It concerns a taxi driver you vouched for last night, an ex-con called Nicholas Cane. I wanted to check what you know about Cane before we decide whether to go ahead with the case against him."

"Who's Eric?" Nick asked.

"The Chief Constable. I need to decide how to reply to Eric, see if I can stop them putting you back inside."

"I'd appreciate that," Nick mumbled, the old dread settling on him. Sarah picked up the phone.

"I'll put him on speaker so you can hear, but keep quiet."

All the affection had left her voice. He was part of her caseload now. She had the Chief Constable on speed dial, Nick noted. At times like this, he wished he was a praying man. If this call went badly Nick would be within spitting distance of forty before he got out of the big house. "Eric" answered on the second ring. Sarah accepted fulsome congratulations.

"We're expecting big things of you now that you're in government," the Chief Constable said. "Very big things indeed. What can I do for you?"

"Two things," Sarah said. "I think they're connected. The taxi driver I vouched for last night: do you know who reported him?"

"An anonymous tip, I think. There's not enough evidence for a prosecution, but since he's out on license, we can take him back in for any infringement. Do you still want to vouch for him?"

"He's an old friend who's trying to turn his life around," Sarah said. "He was taking his sister-in-law to have her first baby. I'd appreciate it if this could go away."

"Done. What was the other thing?"

"I think I know who had it in for Nick Cane — my bad penny, the one that keeps showing up: Ed Clark."

"What's the connection. A prison feud?"

"No. Something that happened since then. Trouble over a woman."

"Trouble usually is," the Chief Constable said, in his thin voice, which managed to be both obsequious and authoritative at the same time. Surely senior police weren't usually this cosy with local MPs. But Sarah used to be a police officer. Maybe that made a difference.

"When we spoke last week you said you'd look into the Shanks case again."

"I spoke to the officers involved. The evidence against him wasn't strong enough for the appeal court, but we're still sure Clark did it. Looking for somebody else would be a waste of time."

"So he got away with murder?"

The Chief Constable didn't attempt to conceal his impatience.

"What else did you expect when you campaigned for his release?"

"I thought a retrial would get to the bottom of the matter."

276

"If you don't mind me saying, that's a very naïve point of view."

"Ed wrote to me. So did a couple of other people who were convinced that he was innocent. I thought they were right and that's why I started the campaign. There was no real evidence against him."

"Nothing concrete enough for a conviction, but there's plenty of proof, if you know where to look. There was a lot of tenuous stuff that never made it into court. Most of it pointed in his direction, too."

"Terry Shanks wasn't the only police officer responsible for Ed being sent down."

"That's right. But he was the only officer whose sister was having it away with Ed."

"I wish you'd told me that before," Sarah said. "Polly Bolton played me for a fool."

"We kept her name out of the robbery trial, at her brother's insistence. Bolton wasn't relevant to Clark's first or second case — involving her would have muddied the waters."

"What would you say if I told you that Polly's going out with Ed Clark again?"

"I'd say pull the other one."

"I'm pulling hard," Sarah said. "He's been seeing her for at least a couple of weeks."

There was a long pause before the Chief Constable responded. "Clark managed to convince you he was innocent," he said. "Maybe he pulled the same stunt on her. But I'll pass that information on. Tell your taxi driver we might have a few questions for him, but he's off the hook."

"I will, Eric. Appreciated. Thanks."

She hung up. Nick wanted to hug her, to thank her, to go to bed with her.

"Thanks," he said.

"It was nothing." Sarah's face was serious, glum. She was already focused on Ed. Nick's problem was in the past. He had to help her in the present.

"Perhaps Ed really is innocent," Nick said. "If he convinced Polly . . ."

"It would be much better all round if he were innocent," Sarah said. "But I think he killed those people. I think I made a terrible mistake."

Nick had no reply. Sarah got up and put the kettle on. While she was waiting for it to boil, she looked at the papers.

The *Guardian* talked about a late swing to the Tories not being enough to prevent a Labour victory. The local paper had OUT OUT OUT in a red strip below its masthead. Next to each word was the photograph of a defeated Tory MP. The main headline was LABOUR ROMP IN. A list of local results showed Five Labour gains. The only East Midlands seat the Tories had managed to hang on to was across the Trent in rich, middle-class West Bridgford, where the Tory Chancellor of the Exchequer had held on to his seat with a much reduced majority. On page five was a picture of an ecstatic-looking Sarah with the caption: BONE BREAKS BY-ELECTION JINX. The paper reminded its readers that, according to statisticians, seats lost in by-elections always reverted to the losing party. Not anymore.

Sarah made coffee. They sat together, reading papers, like the cosy couple they had once been. At five, Sarah put on the news, listened to the latest cabinet appointments. The new parliamentary term started on Tuesday. Nick would lose Sarah then, if not before. He didn't know what to say to her.

As afternoon became evening, she kept answering the phone, turning down invitations to drinks, parties, meals, earnestly discussing the make-up of the new government. Every so often someone asked about her prospects of a government job.

"Not a chance, but I have to stay near a phone just in case," was her standard reply. "Me and every other bugger who got re-elected."

Nick phoned the hospital. Caroline had already been sent home. In Sherwood, his brother answered the phone.

"It's mad here," he said. "When are you coming round?"

"Tomorrow, I guess. I'm with somebody."

"You pulled last night? Lucky bugger."

"Did you straighten things out with Caroline?"

"In a manner of speaking. I've had to agree to let Nas go. Turns out she's known about it for months."

"She doesn't miss much, Caroline."

"Baby's crying. Come to lunch tomorrow. Gotta run."

Perhaps fatherhood would make a new man of Joe, though Nick doubted it. While Sarah made more calls, Nick prepared her dinner: cold chicken with potato salad, vine tomatoes and crusty French bread, washed down with Sauvignon Blanc. They ate with gusto.

"What am I going to do with you?" Sarah asked, as she finished her meal and poured each of them a third glass of wine. "I can't be seen with you here. Everybody knows you're fresh out of prison."

"Take me to London with you," Nick suggested.

"And find you a job, with a serious criminal record? Not easy."

"I could be a house-husband," Nick said, not entirely joking, "taking care of your every need."

"I've got a tiny one-bedroom flat in London. There's barely room for one, never mind two. And you're hardly the house-husband type. Even if you were, we can't go leaping into that kind of a relationship."

"I could," Nick said.

"You've got less to lose than I have," Sarah said, softly, apologetically.

"I've got nothing to lose," Nick told her.

"Except your freedom. Again."

"Oh. That."

CHAPTER
THIRTY-THREE

Somehow it got to be midnight on the second of May and Nick was still there. Sarah knew he expected to spend the night with her, as he had the one before. When the phone calls finally fizzled out, and the TV coverage finished, Sarah found herself exhausted. The campaign had caught up with her. She would prefer to sleep alone, but couldn't throw Nick out. He'd think it was a rejection. Easier to make love to him.

Yet they couldn't stay together. The papers would have a field day — RISING BACKBENCHER DATES CONVICTED DRUG DEALER. For Sarah to be with Nick, she'd have to steer clear of law and order issues, or the media would attribute her liberal leanings on penal policy to her relationship rather than her principles. Nick must realize this.

As she stared at the weather forecast, he got out his brother's tobacco pouch.

"A smoke to help you sleep?" he offered.

"I don't think I'll need much help. But don't let me stop you."

He put it away. "Do you want me to go?" he asked, tenderly.

"No. Yes. I don't know."

"Glad I've got such a decisive MP." Nick stood up. "I'd best leave."

Sarah reached over and squeezed his hand. "It's just that I don't know whether I should sleep with you."

"Has something changed since last night?"

"I'm sober. I won an election I wasn't expecting to win. I know I said I could see you if I won, but I was fooling myself."

"I could be your back-door man," Nick argued, trying to inject some humour into his voice. "Your secret bit of stuff in the constituency. In time, I'll become more respectable. I'm not quite sure how, but I will."

"I'm sure you will," Sarah said. "But that doesn't change now. The tabloids would tear me apart."

"I shouldn't be here," Nick said. "I'll go home."

"Not like this."

"There are no journalists camped outside."

"We can't leave it like this," Sarah said. "And there's still something we both want to work out."

"Is there? I'm nearly past caring who killed Terry and Liv Shanks."

"Can we talk it through one more time?" she asked.

"Okay," Nick told her. "Maybe I will have that joint after all. Weed helps me think."

Maybe a joint would help her think, too. They smoked on the balcony of her flat, overlooking the gardens of the Park and, beyond, the outskirts of the city: County Hall, Colwick Park, the football grounds.

"Suppose," Sarah said, "Polly was playing an elaborate bluff. She was with Ed all along and only came protesting to me because she felt it would look bad if she didn't?"

"If she was with Ed all along, why did she start seeing me?" Nick asked.

"Because you're irresistible," Sarah said, stroking his face. "What bothers me is why you started seeing her."

"An attractive woman was offering commitment-free sex," Nick said, adding, "at the time, she was the best I could do."

"I find that hard to believe. What's she like in bed?" Sarah asked.

"You what?" Nick said. "You must be stoned, to ask me that."

He was right. This stuff was much stronger than the hash they used to smoke together. Nick answered regardless.

"We didn't do it much in bed. Carpet, sofa, standing up, leant over the cooker, you name it. She likes to be treated rough. She scratches, and hits, and kisses like a vacuum cleaner. It never lasts long."

He paused, as though realizing that he was using the present tense.

Nick's description of the relationship was the same as the one Polly had given her, albeit with changed nuance. Polly might be over Nick, but he still had some feelings for her. He was even jealous of Ed. Sarah stubbed the joint out on the terrace railing then threw the roach onto the soil below. Smoking dope had always made her randy, never more so than tonight. The stuff made her brain rush too.

"I can't believe Polly was acting when she protested about Ed, when she started seeing you. Something happened to change her mind. Ed must have given Polly a really compelling reason to stop seeing you and take up with him again. She wouldn't explain it to me, beyond saying that Ed had told her who really killed Terry and it wasn't him."

"I thought that everybody else who had a motive for revenge was inside at the time?"

"Contract killing?" Sarah suggested.

"If so, why wait until Ed was released?"

"Maybe . . .?" Sarah was on the verge of grasping something, then a wave of tiredness overcame her. "I think I'd better go to bed."

"You look exhausted," Nick said. "I'll go. Can I see you tomorrow?"

"Yes, please."

He kissed her on the cheek, then left, like the gentleman he had always been.

CHAPTER
THIRTY-FOUR

There was a message on Nick's answering machine. His probation officer. He'd missed a meeting. Tough. Sarah hadn't said anything about having plans for Saturday evening. Nick decided to cook. Maybe they could rent a video. There were tons of films from the last five years that he hadn't seen and he'd bet an MP didn't get to the movies often. He and Sarah used to go to the cinema each week. They'd spend ages discussing the latest Lynch or Altman in the pub afterwards. There was a place that rented videos just off the top end of the Park, on Derby Road, a shop that used to be an off-license. He and Sarah used it often when they were students.

First, food. In the old days, he'd have checked a recipe, but most of his cookery books had been given away when he was sent down. There was a limit on how much stuff you could ask your brother to look after for you. Nick decided to take the simplest option. He bought two sirloin steaks, an onion, mushrooms and baking potatoes.

He rang her a couple of times before setting off. Engaged. He decided to risk Sarah having made other plans and go straight round. If Sarah wanted to go out tonight, the ingredients would keep until tomorrow. She didn't have to be in London until Monday at the earliest. Maybe by then he would have persuaded her to give their relationship another chance, on whatever basis she chose.

He stopped at the video shop on the way over, but they wouldn't let him join because he didn't have the requisite credit card or multiple proofs of address to establish his identity. If he'd given an address in the Park, rather than scruffy Alfreton Road, they'd most likely have treated him differently. Never mind. Sarah probably belonged. They could go later, if she fancied it.

It was ten past six when he got to her flat, a bottle of wine in each hand. The car was still outside, so she hadn't gone anywhere. When he rang the bell, however, she took a while to answer. The door opened on the chain. Sarah was dressed smartly, fully made up, about to go out.

"I thought I'd cook you dinner," he said, giving her his broadest smile. "But if you've got other plans . . ."

"Nick, you should have phoned first. I have to go out this evening, a celebration meal with the constituency officers."

"Maybe I can leave this stuff here and we can have it tomorrow."

"Sounds good."

She took the chain off and he stepped into the hall. He reminded her where his flat was.

"If you want to call by on your way back, I'll be in. Or if you need company. It's not far."

He saw from the look on her face that he was being overeager.

"I could do with a little space, Nick. It's been a huge few days."

"No bother." He turned to go, not even pushing his luck for a kiss.

"Wait."

For a moment, he thought she'd changed her mind.

"There's something I need your help with. Do you think you could find out what shift Ed Clark's working on Monday?"

"Sure," Nick said. "No problem. But how does it fit with what we discussed last night?"

"I'll tell you later," Sarah promised, then gave him a kiss, followed by a small hug. "I'm not pushing you away, Nick. I need a little space, time to take things in."

"I understand." He returned to his flat, disappointed but not dejected. In her situation, he'd need space, too. And, since he wasn't seeing her tonight, he could get a few cans, smoke some weed, get wasted and watch TV. Not too wasted. He had to do two hours' teaching before he cooked Sarah her dinner tomorrow. Why did Sarah want to know Ed's schedule? Nick rang the Cane Cars switchboard and got Nas, which meant that Joe hadn't sacked her yet.

"Ed's on tomorrow from two till eight, then he's on holiday for three weeks. His compensation came through. Why you wanna know?"

"A friend of mine needs to see him," Nick said. "But do me a favour, don't tell him I asked."

"I don't talk to that baldy-head fascist unless I have to," Nas said. "I'm sorry you don't work here any more, Nick. I won't be around much longer myself. Let's have a drink soon, yeah?"

"Yeah." Nick's reply sounded unconvincing, even to himself, so he added, "That'd be nice."

"You know where to find me."

Nick hung up. Nas was about to be sacked. She would be vulnerable and she was into him. He liked her too, but wasn't going to see another of his brother's cast-offs, not even if Sarah blew him out. Nick reminded himself that he might be reading too much into the offer of a drink. After so many years without female company, he saw sexual nuance in everything. If Sarah could read his mind, she'd run a mile.

He went out onto the fire escape and listened to the city: cars, conversation, wailing sirens and snatches of song. The endless clatter of everyday life blended into an exhilarating hum. When he was sure nobody was looking, Nick removed a brick from the wall, pulled out the tin containing his stash, and went back inside to skin up.

CHAPTER
THIRTY-FIVE

Sarah phoned Andrew Saint mid-afternoon on Sunday. He answered his mobile on the third ring.

"Sarah! Well done."

"Thanks for the flowers. I appreciated them."

"Called to invite me to dinner?"

"Afraid not. I'm still in Nottingham. But we'll meet up soon, I promise. In the meantime, I have a favour to ask you."

"Anything."

She had deliberated all day over whether to do this. "It's for a mutual friend."

"Intriguing. What mutual friend would this be?"

"Nick Cane. I . . . happened to run into him this week and we've been catching up. I don't know if you're aware, but he's had some serious bother."

"I was aware," Andrew said, in a different, more formal voice. "But I didn't want you getting drawn into it. You and Nick are ancient history."

"Maybe so, but I still care about him. And he used to be your best friend."

"What's the favour?" Andrew asked, tersely.

"He needs to get out of Nottingham, make a fresh start. London, ideally. I wondered if you could find him some sort of job."

There was a long pause. "Did he tell you he'd been to see me?"

"No. We haven't discussed you . . . there's not been time."

"He came to see me almost as soon as he got out, hit me up for a few grand. So I feel like I've discharged my obligations to him. In my business, Sarah, clients have to depend on your integrity. Nick's blown his. There are a lot of police checks. I'm not sure I could have him on my books. This is probably making you think badly of me and I'm sorry, but I have to be straight with you."

"That's all right. Like I said, Nick doesn't know I'm calling you. Let's pretend this conversation never took place."

"Agreed. I'd keep your distance from Nick if I were you. He got involved in some heavy stuff. Remember, you can't change your family, but you can change your friends. You're not bound together unless you choose to be."

"That's good advice, Andrew, thanks. I'll see you soon."

Sarah hung up. She shouldn't have called Andrew without first asking Nick how things stood between the two of them. It didn't sound like Nick, pressuring his old friend for money. But people changed. Prison must change people. Parliament had changed her. Sarah had become more ruthless and, according to Dan when they split, she had steadily become less playful, less take-people-as-they-are. She wanted to be relaxed, but a necessary uptightness went with the life. Last night, despite the exhilaration from the victory, none of the constituency officers really let go, even after a few drinks. They wanted to gossip, and made sure they remained sober enough to remember what was said the next morning.

Afterwards, it would have been wonderful to have a lover to come home to. She had walked back from town, looked up at what she presumed was Nick's flat and nearly rung the doorbell. But that would have been so, so weak. Instead, unwilling to walk through the Park's badly lit streets so late, she had hailed a cab for the three-minute ride home. Having talked to Andrew, Sarah was relieved she hadn't succumbed to temptation. It was only just beginning to sink in. She was still an MP. For the last few weeks, she'd had the wobbles — certain of losing, obsessed with the Ed Clark affair which, when put in perspective, was just one out of hundreds of cases she had on her plate. She couldn't get them all right, no matter how hard she tried.

Sarah made her weekly phone call to her mother, who, true to form, had failed to call and congratulate her on being re-elected. Mum had been angry with Sarah for taking a year out to become Union President and had supported none of her career choices since. All Mum wanted was to be a grandmother. Sarah was her only, fast-fading chance. They stuttered through a few minutes of strained conversation.

"Guess who showed up at my post-election party?" Sarah said, before she was forced to return to discussing the unseasonably warm weather. "Nick Cane."

"I always liked Nick. Is he still in Nottingham?"

"He's just moved back."

"I suppose he's married now, with lots of children."

"No, same old Nick. A little heavier, not much more mature. Single."

"Just like you, then. You ought to snap him up."

"I've been thinking about it," Sarah confessed. Was still thinking about it, despite what Andrew had said earlier. "He's cooking dinner for me tonight."

"Did he stay in teaching?" Mum asked.

"I think so. We haven't really discussed work." Nick had said something about private tuition, Sarah remembered. He was working this afternoon, so he wasn't a complete no-hoper. One could even argue that he was a good project for rehabilitation.

"Take my advice. Make your move. Second chances don't come often."

"I'll bear that in mind, Mum." She brought the call to a close, feeling foolish that she'd brought up Nick to keep her mother interested. Then the doorbell rang and Nick was there. It was a little after five. Early to be cooking her dinner.

"I thought you'd want to know," he said. "Ed Clark's compensation came through. He's off on holiday for three weeks from tomorrow."

"With Polly?"

"I presume so. He's working until eight tonight. So, if you want to see her, the next couple of hours may be your only chance."

"Will you come with me?"

Nick winced. "I'd have thought my presence would make the meeting even more awkward. Polly's no threat on her own. Why don't I stay here, cook you that dinner?"

Sarah saw the sense in that. She showed Nick where things were in the kitchen then drove to New Basford alone. How to play this? As a copper, like most coppers, she'd had aspirations to join CID. But she'd barely got beyond her probationary period, and her interrogation training had been minimal. She was cleverer than Polly, or at least, more educated. Their last conversation had been interrupted by Ed's return. Sarah needed to dig deeper into Polly's motives. She ought to be able to catch her out.

"I wondered when you'd show your face again," Polly said, letting Sarah in. "How did you know he'd be out?"

"Nick checked his shift."

"You and him, back on, is it?" Polly said, her back to Sarah, voice almost cracking. "Ed told me you used to shack up together."

"We're old friends, that's all," Sarah said, not wanting to stir up any latent jealousy.

"That's why he went home with you t'other night, is it? Rodney told Ed and Ed told me. You won, I hear."

"Yeah, I won. Nick saw me home."

"And you'll be taking him to London with you."

"I don't think so," Sarah said. "I hear you're off to the Caribbean with Ed."

"Do you see any bags packed?"

Sarah looked around. The place was the usual mess. A copy of *Hello* lay open on the ironing board. Dirty mugs and sweet-wrappers were strewn around the carpet. But there were no summer clothes waiting to be ironed, no suitcases.

"He's not taking you?"

"If it'd been just me, he might have done. Sex on tap for three weeks. I'd have had to get a passport first, mind. But me and four kids? Ed's far too selfish."

"You said he got on well with the kids."

"I lied. I'm good at lying. Maybe I should be in your job."

"Is he coming back?" Sarah asked.

"Tonight? Doubt it. He's got an early flight. From holiday? Your guess is as good as mine. Why are you here, anyhow? To show off that you've got Nick back and I'm on my tod again?"

"No, I . . ." Sarah tried to remember the argument. "Since I'm going back to Parliament, I needed to know about your case. I've spent three years trying to get Ed out, get the case reopened. Do you want me to carry on, to push the police to find the real killer or killers?"

"I don't know what I want."

"You told me that Ed convinced you he didn't do it. But if Ed didn't kill them, somebody else did. Have you any idea who?"

"I'm not going to do the police's job for them, or yours," Polly said. "I just want this to go away. I want Ed to stay away too."

"If he went back to prison . . ."

"Oh, fuck off, will you!" Polly raised her voice for the first time. "You and me, we're both frightened of Ed. We've both done things we shouldn't have done, 'cos of him. I hope he never comes back. I've got nothing. You've got Nick. You've got your job back. You've got it all."

"I want to help."

"*Help*? You're the one got Ed out of prison."

"The appeal court did that. The evidence against him wasn't safe. Look, Polly, if you know who did it, then you owe it to your brother to see them prosecuted. Don't you?"

"You want to know who was really responsible for Terry's death?" Polly spat. "It was his own fault."

"His?"

"If it weren't for Terry, nothing would've happened."

"What do you . . .?"

"Just fuck off, will you?"

When Sarah got in, Nick told her that the phone had been ringing.

"Your mobile too. I let the machine take it, like you asked. How did you find her?"

"Different." Sarah summed up the conversation, including the thing Polly said about her brother.

"You think she's split up with Ed?"

"I don't know. I don't know if she knows. The way she talked, Ed might not be coming back. What got to me, though, was the way she talked about Terry being responsible for the murders. I mean, if she thought that before, why did she protest so hard about Ed's release?"

"Ed must have told her something that convinced her."

"Anyway, that's it. Over. We'll never know what really happened."

"That doesn't sound like you," Nick told her.

"Call it *realpolitik*. How's dinner coming along?"

"I can put the steak on whenever you want. Then it'll be ten minutes or so."

"Make it soon. I'm starving."

While Nick cooked, she went to the machine. She had eleven messages waiting, but before she could check them, the phone rang.

"Sarah, I find you in at last." It was the Chief Whip.

"Sorry, I was out on constituency business, case work."

"That's what local councillors are for. You'd better find some tame, reliable ones quickly, you'll be needing them. I'm calling on behalf of the Prime Minister. He wants to offer you a job."

Sarah was to be a Junior Minister. That was a huge deal. As soon as she'd put down the phone, and told him, Nick knew their chances of being together were over.

He congratulated her. "That's an incredibly responsible job. You were made to do it."

"There were hints I'd get something, but I was so sure that I'd lose my seat, I didn't let myself think about them." She told him how the job fitted with the areas she'd concentrated on in the Commons. She felt vindicated for campaigning to stop the spread of HIV in prisons. "I guess even the Ed Clark thing helped."

"I suppose." He had to say something, so chose his words carefully. "That's it for us, isn't it? I'm too big a risk. The quicker I go, the better."

She squeezed his hand. "At least nothing really happened between us," she said. "It wouldn't have worked, Nick. You can't go back. We were kidding ourselves."

"Sure." He smiled ruefully and she went back to talking about her new job. Soon afterwards, he left. It was the dignified way to behave. The future was out of their hands. He couldn't blame himself for the thing with Sarah going wrong. *At least nothing really happened between us*, she'd said, forgetting the kisses, the promises made prior to her passing out on election night. The absence of sex made it easier for Sarah to move on. Women were like that. For men, it was the other way round. If he'd made love to her one last time, it would be easier to put this behind him. The more time he'd spent with Sarah this last fortnight, the more he'd wanted her in bed. One night could, at the very least, have satisfied some of his curiosity about how it would be between them. As it was, he knew he would obsess about her for months.

CHAPTER
THIRTY-SIX

When Nick got home on Sunday evening, he rang the Cane Cars office.

"Has Ed Clark booked a cab to take him to the airport tomorrow?"

"Yeah. Four-thirty a.m. pick-up to get him to Birmingham. Why?"

"I need to do the job."

"Didn't you get stopped by the police for driving without a permit?" Nas asked.

"I won't charge him," Nick said. "I'll use my sister-in-law's car, rather than a cab. Just don't give anyone else the job."

"What's your game? You going to stop Ed having a holiday?"

"I need a chat with him, that's all. What's the address?"

He cycled over to Joe's, made an excuse and collected Caroline's car. Then he went to bed and set the alarm. Impossible to sleep, but he mustn't drink any more. He needed to be sharp when he picked up Ed.

Ed wasn't leaving from Polly's place. The address he'd given Nas was a road on the Bestwood Estate, where it was notoriously easy to get lost. Ed's secret base turned out to be in one of the nicer parts of the estate, near the country park that sat incongruously at its edge. The semi had net curtains and a neat front garden. As Ed came out, with his bags, a sixtyish woman appeared at the door next to him. She kissed him on the lips and Ed hugged her. Only then did Ed turn and call out to Nick.

"You going to help me wi' these, then?"

It was dark and the streetlights were sparse. Ed didn't recognise Nick until he got out of the car and opened the boot. Nick had been worried about this moment, but the presence of Ed's mother removed all risk of violence.

"Nice of you to get up early for me, Nicholas," Ed said, as he placed the first huge suitcase in the car. "T'other one's too big for this boot. Reckon we'll put it on the back seat."

He joined Nick in the front of the car. Ed's mother, in her dressing gown, waved the two men goodbye. Nick negotiated his way out of the estate. Ed grinned when they drove past Oxclose Lane police station.

"Whose car is this?"

"A friend's."

"Didn't want to risk being seen in a cab? You're in trouble, a little bird tells me."

"I'm not in any trouble," Nick said.

"Your girlfriend got you off, did she?"

"She's not my girlfriend," Nick said. "Just an old friend."

"You can't be friends with a good-looking woman you're not related to," Ed said. "Not without thinking about sticking it to her all the time."

He was right, so Nick shut up. With the roads empty, the journey to the airport only took forty-five minutes, less if you didn't stick to the speed limit. Nick didn't want to spend that time talking about Ed's philosophy of sex. He wanted to talk about murder. But it had to be Ed who brought the subject up.

"What time's your plane?"

"Seven-thirty. Plenty of time for check-in."

"And you're going to . . .?"

"Far, far fucking away. The land of five-star fuck-and-suck with constant sunshine and warm seas on tap."

"Not taking Polly?"

Ed didn't reply.

"I suppose her and her kids would cramp your style."

"What the fuck is it to you?" Ed asked. "You want her back?"

"Why, have you finished with her?"

"I won't be using her for the next three weeks anyways. You offering to keep her in training for me?"

"We were okay until you showed," Nick said, keeping his eye on the road ahead.

Ed laughed. "Look on your face, when you walked in on me and her. You had no idea, did you?"

"Why should I? Did you think she'd have told me?"

"Told you what? That she were kicking you into touch, or that she were fucking me before I got sent down the first time?"

This was the opening Nick needed to seize on, but his brain was slow at this time of the morning, whereas Ed seemed his usual self: bold, teasing, arrogant. He chose his words carefully.

"What about when you got out the first time. Were you fucking her then, too?"

"What do you think?"

"The way Sarah tells it, you were arrested for the murders within two weeks. And wasn't there a working girl in the story too? Doesn't give you much time to see Polly."

"Her husband had gone by then, just her at home wi' the two kids. She had all the time in the world for me."

"Was it then she told you Terry Shanks had been recording you?"

Ed turned to look at him but Nick kept his eyes on the road. "Where'd you hear that?"

"Sarah. She said that was how you got caught."

Ed was silent. Nick glanced round to see his reaction. Blank. He took a right turn at the roundabout by Nottingham University. The Derby Road was only a single carriageway, with the university on one side and Wollaton Park on the other, but it was wide enough for him to easily overtake a milk float.

"I could tell you it all," Ed said as they bypassed Beeston.

"Go on."

"But then, after we got to the airport, I'd have to kill you."

Nick laughed unconvincingly. "It's Polly I'm interested in," he said, "not getting you to confess what you did or didn't do."

"Good thing," Ed said, "'cos I've got the money now, free and clear. And if you think I'm coming back to this shithole, you've got another thing coming. There's enough in the kitty for me to start up again anywhere. Offshore account. No tax, high interest. What've you got to show for your five years inside?"

"Fuck all. You mean it? You're not coming back?"

"What's it to you?"

"You work for my brother."

"That's not it. You want to get back together with Poll. I'll bet she's the best you ever had."

Nick played along. "We seemed to be getting close, for a while."

"You don't get close to Poll," Ed says. "She keeps it all in."

For a moment, Ed seemed to have stopped boasting. Nick had to be careful not to force it. "I thought she needed me," he mumbled.

"She pulled the old hard-done-by routine on you, did she?"

"You could say that."

"Aye, me too. I was a real sucker for her. All that time inside, thinking about when I got out, knowing she were on her own, waiting. Then, when I go to see her, she's not interested."

"What do you expect when she thought you'd killed her brother and sister-in-law?" Nick said, taking the exit for Long Eaton and the M1.

"I didn't mean the second time," Ed muttered.

Nick considered what he was saying. Polly had given Ed the cold shoulder when he got out of prison after doing six months for theft. Was that a motive for murder? Ed killed Terry and Liv to get back at Polly? It didn't add up.

"I don't understand," he said.

"I'll tell you what," Ed said, "your life's so fucked up, maybe you deserve a bit of advice."

"Go ahead," Nick said, adrenaline making him accelerate to ninety, before he remembered that he needed to make this journey last as long as possible.

"If Sarah's not interested, don't go after Polly. She might have you, but she'll lie to you, use you, take what she can, fuck you up and spit you out. She can't help herself."

"Thanks for the warning," Nick said.

"I'm tired of talking. Put radio on."

Ed didn't say another word during the journey. When they got to the part of the news where Sarah's appointment was announced, he turned to Nick.

"You knew about that?"

Nick nodded. Ed laughed long and hard.

Fifteen minutes later, Nick pulled up outside Departures at Birmingham Airport. They'd made good time. He would be back in Nottingham by six, when the sun rose.

"You're really not coming back?"

"To Nottingham? Never. Police there'll do me for the smallest thing, first chance they get. I'll see what I find.

I hear word Cuba's opening up. My money'll go a long way over there. I might get into tourism."

"There's still one thing I don't get," Nick said.

"Only one?" Ed asked, getting out of the car.

Nick put the hazard lights on and helped Ed unload his heavy bags. "Killing Terry makes sense. Revenge for putting you inside. But waiting around to kill the wife was such a big risk. It screwed your alibi. The kids could have been with her."

"Is that why you drove me here?" Ed asked. "You thought you'd talk me into some kind of confession?"

"They can't try you again," Nick pointed out.

"But they can try the real killer," Ed said. "It weren't me killed Terry, all right? I'll tell you one thing about Liv. The photos in the paper didn't do her justice. She were right fit." He lowered his voice. "I like it best when they're frightened."

Ed loaded his stuff onto a baggage trolley.

"I can manage from here," he said. "Hold on. I owe you something."

Ed reached into his pocket.

"I don't want . . ."

"Did you think I'd forgotten?" Ed interrupted, as Nick stood, unguarded, in front of him.

He kicked Nick in the balls, hard. When Nick fell to the ground, in agony. Ed leant over him.

"You're lucky I'm only wearing trainers," he said. "If I'd known you were driving, I wouldn't have packed me boots."

CHAPTER
THIRTY-SEVEN

Sarah took the 8.03 train to St Pancras. At least travelling first-class gave her a measure of privacy and peace. She needed quiet after sleeping badly, her mind alternating between excitement at her new job and sadness at being forced to dump Nick so soon after starting things up again. She'd had no choice and he'd understood. That didn't stop her feeling bad about it.

"Mind if I join you for a few minutes?"

"You mean until they come and inspect the tickets?" Sarah waved Brian Hicks into one of the free seats opposite her.

"I did a nice piece about you for today's paper."

"I'll look forward to it." The *Evening Post* had just gone to press. Her constituency office would fax her any important local stories by midday.

"One story that isn't in the paper today, I thought you'd want to know. Ed Clark."

"What about him?"

"Got his compensation through. A quarter of a million he settled for. Could have held out for more, given the strong implications that the police fitted him up for killing one of their own, but he was in a hurry for the money, evidently. I'm surprised he didn't call to thank you."

"Maybe he left a message at my office," Sarah said, not revealing she already knew about Ed's ill-gotten gains. "Unlike you, he doesn't have my home number."

"Word is, he's gone to the Caribbean," Brian told her. "In the air now. I spoke to his mother just before I left the office. She says he bought a one-way ticket, doesn't know when he's coming back."

"Was he on his own?"

"That's what I heard."

Sarah wondered if Polly knew about the one-way ticket. But she'd exhausted her sympathy for the bereaved sister.

"I rang the police after I heard about the compo, asked if they'd reopened the case."

"Don't tell me," Sarah said. "You were given the usual *we are not pursuing any other suspects.*"

"No, even they realized that was a bit tactless in the circumstances. They said, off the record, that we'd never know if Liv Shanks killed her husband, or not."

"They never proved that those were her fingerprints on the gun," Sarah pointed out, angry and a little bored that the police were trotting out a theory she had always avoided as being in bad taste.

"The fingerprints on the gun were smeared, but a close match nevertheless. She could have shot him, then shot herself."

"With the best part of an hour between the shootings? It still doesn't make sense."

306

"There was a blow to the head before the shooting. Maybe Liv knocked Terry out, then went hunting for the gun. It took her a while to find it, to work up the courage to finish him off."

"And the motive? Marital rape?"

"That we'll never know," Brian said. "But it makes as much sense as Ed Clark having hung around to kill Liv. I thought you'd like to know what the police were saying, so you could put it behind you. Congratulations on the job. You'll be in the cabinet before you know it."

"Thanks, Brian. I appreciate your support."

"You'd have beaten Barrett Jones easily even without my help. You know that?"

"Probably," Sarah said, aware that Brian was none-too-subtly reminding her she owed him a favour. "Water under the bridge. Anyway, if there are any stories I can put your way, I will."

"Appreciated," Brian said. "I'll let you get back to your work."

He left for second class. Sarah opened her copy of the *Guardian* but didn't read. She thought about Ed in the air. He was gone for good, with any luck. She could put that behind her now. There was work to do.

Nick managed to catch a couple of hours' sleep before seeing his probation officer. He apologised profusely for missing his meeting of the week before.

"No problem," said Dave Trapp. "I expect you were ill."

Dave liked to treat Nick as an equal. They were two guys with degrees and careers, only Nick had taken a wrong turning: that was Dave's approach, one that Nick found easy to go along with. He was about to tell the truth when he remembered that failure to provide a legitimate excuse resulted in a warning, three of which would put you back inside.

"I came down with some kind of fever, lost track of time."

"Been to the doctor?"

"No. I was too ill to go out. When I felt better, it was the weekend so the doctor wasn't open. Didn't seem much point in going today. I had a lie-in, but I seem to be on the mend."

"You don't look too bad now," Dave said. "But, next time, do yourself a favour, get a doctor's note."

"Will do," Nick said. He was being treated with respect but still felt humiliated, a naughty schoolboy forced to sustain a trivial lie.

"Any work?" the probation officer asked.

"Just the two private tutees I told you about."

"No problems there?" They had discussed at their last meeting whether Nick was required to disclose his convictions to the parents. He'd have to disclose them were he applying to work in a school. Dave had reached the conclusion that this wasn't necessary, so long as Nick didn't lie if asked. Probation wanted him to work. Statistically, Nick was much more likely to reoffend if he was unemployed.

"None at all."

"All this free time isn't giving the devil work for idle hands?"

At least he hadn't asked the awkward question he'd asked in their first few meetings: *Keeping off the wacky baccy?* Smoking it wasn't the same as growing it. According to Dave, Probation Services assessed Nick's biggest risk factor as a return to some kind of drug dealing.

"My sister-in-law just had a baby. I've been round there a lot."

"Good to hear. Have you thought about doing some voluntary work? It's a good way of getting recent references for a job you like. In the long run, with someone of your experience and intelligence, it could lead to a full-time job. Drug counselling, for instance."

"That's a thought," Nick said.

"I'll give you some leaflets. Think it over. That's it, then. Another couple of weeks and you'll be down to once-a-fortnight interviews."

After that it would be once a month, until Nick reached what would have been the three-quarters point in his sentence: six years. Beyond that, he would no longer be on license. He could still be recalled to prison if he was convicted of another crime — but only if a punitive judge decided to embellish his sentence with the unused time from his previous sentence. It would be two and a half years before Nick was completely clear. Even then, as he'd served more than five years, the law said that he would always have to declare his conviction on application forms, no matter how inconsequential the job.

"Anything I can help you with? Courses, references, whatever . . ."

"No, I'm fine."

Despite the missed appointment, Nick's interview had taken less than ten minutes, as usual. He walked back through the city, thinking about the love of a good woman. He'd nearly had that with Sarah. Deep down, though, he'd always known Sarah was too good for him, even in the days when they were living together. Maybe that was why he'd not fought harder to keep her when she joined the police.

He bought a first edition of the *Evening Post* from a paper stand by the Council House. LOCAL MP JOINS GOVERNMENT the headline said, with the story that Nick had heard on the early morning news. Sarah Bone, after her surprise re-election, was joining the home office as a junior minister. For prisons.

CHAPTER
THIRTY-EIGHT

"So he took it well, you dumping him?"

"I didn't give him much choice. Nick's still on probation. He's liable to be recalled if he commits another crime, no matter how minor. I've already got him out of hot water once."

"What for?"

"The police were threatening to do him for perverting the course of justice, pretending to be his brother when he drove a cab. Not serious, but enough to put him back inside if they prosecuted. I care about Nick, a lot. But I couldn't turn down the job. Think I was too hard on him?"

"No. If you'd known what he'd done, you wouldn't have started things up with him again."

It wasn't as simple as that, but Sarah wasn't going to show Andrew how guilty she felt. It was a relief to find somebody she could talk this over with, someone who knew Nick nearly as well as she did. They had both dumped him. That was how friendship worked when you were older — you stuck with someone while you could be of use to each other, then let go when the wind changed. Maybe it had always worked that way.

"If I'd known . . ." She shook her head and looked around her. "I still can't believe I'm back here."

They were drinking tea on the wide terrace of the House of Commons. New MPs were avidly admiring the view over the river. They looked like teenagers dazed on ecstasy. All had just heard their leader tell them they were here "not to enjoy the trappings of power but to do a job and uphold the highest standards in public life". There were so many Labour MPs that there was no room big enough to hold them in the Palace of Westminster. They'd had to go down the road to Church House to listen to the sermon.

"It's an exciting time," Andrew said.

Sarah described the meeting the previous day, when the fledgling Home Secretary had outlined her new duties. Then she tried to engage Andrew in conversation about the independence of the Bank of England. She quickly gathered that Andrew had no interest in politics, not even fiscal policy, except where it affected how much tax he paid on his profits from property development.

"How does it feel to be one of *Blair's babes*?" he asked.

"I'm hardly a babe," Sarah said.

"I think you are," Andrew assured her.

Sarah accepted the compliment. There had been a photoshoot that morning with all of the new female MPs. Their wide-eyed optimism reminded Sarah of herself, two years previously. An MP's job quickly became mundane. Doable, even satisfying at times, but never glamorous. Sarah had missed out by arriving halfway through the government's term, long after all the committees had been doled out and alliances between new MPs had been forged. The thrill of her by-election victory soon faded. The most exciting part of being an MP was campaigning to get the job. As this election drew closer, she'd helped prepare policies for the near-certainty of power. Her excitement had been dampened by the conviction that she would not be re-elected.

Yet here she was. Was there any feeling better than getting something you'd long since given up on? She couldn't explain to Andrew how exhilarating this job was, how it made sense of everything she'd done up to this point in her life, how she was living in every moment and couldn't wait to get out of bed in the morning. She spotted the Prime Minister's Press Secretary.

"Would you like me to introduce you to Alastair?"

Sarah watched her guest gladhanding, greasing. It was funny, she reflected, that in all of their conversations, neither she nor Nick had once mentioned Andy . . . she meant *Andrew*.

Her new office would be ready tomorrow. The Home Secretary had assured Sarah that her concerns about penal reform were shared at cabinet level. Her appointment had created little waves of approval in the liberal press and drew barbed comments about needle exchanges in prisons from *The Times* and *Telegraph*. But prisons were low-profile and Sarah was young. She was not being touted as a high-flyer, yet. Even if she did the job well, she couldn't expect to get into the top team before the next general election. When she was more than likely to lose her seat.

At least the media no longer had her tagged as Jasper March's totty. Jasper, having lost to a Liberal Democrat, was one of yesterday's men. He would have to bugger a dozen blokes on Brighton Beach in broad daylight before he saw his name in the tabloids again.

"So you'll be spending the next few months slogging round Her Majesty's high-security hotels, eh?" Andrew said. "Not my idea of fun."

"As long as I don't run into any more old boyfriends," Sarah said.

"Alastair said something about a party for donors at Number Ten."

"Are you a donor?" Sarah asked, surprised. At university, Andrew was always known for being tight with his money.

"No, but he assumed I was, since you were giving me tea on the terrace. How much would I have to give to get the big invites?"

"Ten grand is the smallest sum that would get their attention. You'd have to hint it was a down payment while you waited to see if the new government delivers on its promise. But do you like all that rubbing shoulders stuff? I run a mile from fundraising events."

"Business is business. Liking's got nothing to do with it."

Sarah had a meeting to go to. Visitors weren't allowed to walk around the Commons unescorted, so she saw Andrew out of the building.

"Let's do dinner next time," he suggested.

"As long as you don't mind eating late. Lots of legislating to do. By the way, what job were you going to offer me, had I not won? I'm curious."

"It hardly matters now," Andrew replied. "I never worked out a title. Head of Public Relations might have done it."

"I don't know anything about PR," Sarah protested.

"Don't underestimate yourself. I suspect you can do anything you turn your mind to. And thanks for giving me Gill Temperley's number."

"Did you get on with her?"

"I did. She's weighing up offers, but reckons she'll have a lot of time on her hands now her party's out of power. She might be able to give me a couple of days a week to do the job I wanted you to do."

The glint in Andrew's eyes indicated that he hoped for more than work from Gill. Sarah wondered if the Tory MP was interested. Gill had scraped back into office, but had already made it clear that she wouldn't be seeking a shadow cabinet post. Like most members of the last government, she would want to make money, catch up on the opportunities missed during eighteen years of power.

Sarah and Andrew exchanged pecks on the cheek. Andrew hailed a taxi. Sarah went back inside to meet a prospective secretary. Replacing Clare was her top priority. Sarah used to share her with her Nottingham East counterpart, but Clare had managed to get herself elected in what had hitherto been a safe Tory seat. Now that she was a junior minister, Sarah needed somebody full time. She would have to delegate nearly all of her constituency case work. The person she was about to see had short, blonde hair, blue eyes and a weak chin. He came highly recommended by his former boss, who had lost his seat.

"I'm not a Tory," was the first thing Hugh Race told her.

"So your reference says."

"And I'm not gay."

"I wouldn't mind if you were. It might even be an advantage."

"I only say that because I know you're aware of my previous employer's . . . predilections, and I didn't want you to think I got the job because there was anything going on."

"You want to follow a career path in Parliament because you're more interested in government than you are in party politics. That's fine. My last secretary was a candidate and she hardly got any work done in the last eight weeks. So there's a big backlog and I need somebody who can catch up quickly, who can make minor decisions independently. According to Jasper, you're very good at that."

"Mr March was a very good employer. He made my duties clear. I'd never take on anything that was properly a member's remit."

Sarah wondered whether Hugh would take charge of her, rather than the other way round. Good secretaries were hard to find, especially now, with all the new MPs sloshing about the house. Hugh was easy on the eye, too, good looking in a pale, effete way. He could be one of Gill Temperley's "researchers".

316

"Okay," she said. "I'll put you on the same salary scale you were on with Jasper. Three months' probation and no hard feelings if either of us wants to back out at the end of it. How does that sound?"

"Excellent," Hugh said. "When do you want me start?"

Sarah pointed at the two bin bags full of mail waiting for attention.

"Now."

She collected an inch-thick pile of faxes that had arrived during her absence. Near the top, she saw that the BMA foundation for AIDS was about to publish its survey on the availability of condoms in state prisons. That was something she ought to be able to move on quickly; it probably wasn't "sexy" enough to be one of the hundred projects in a hundred days to be announced over the next three months. But things might change.

There was no need for the new government to be as cautious as the party had had to be until now. The size of their majority had shocked everyone. After a landslide, people expected large changes. Prisons didn't work and they were her responsibility. If she got everyone who didn't belong in prison out, the government would make a huge financial saving. The biggest cut, she liked to say at meetings, would be in human misery. That was what she had come into politics to do, the kind of achievement it was worth making sacrifices for. Nick knew that. He would understand.

She had waited all of her life for this.

Epilogue

Autumn 1997

The meeting took several weeks to set up. Sarah had not forgotten the favour Eric did for Nick Cane on her behalf. The Chief Constable would want something in return. Men always did. But first, he reminded Sarah of an offer he had made before the election.

"In four years time, you'll be even better qualified to run the association. So if you don't hold on to your seat . . ."

"That's awfully nice of you, Eric, but I'm not looking to pack a parachute just yet. And I may not be so popular with your colleagues once they've seen what I do when I actually have some power."

"Power, in my experience, is largely an illusion. While you have it, you're most conscious of what you lack, and of how little you can affect the things that matter to you. Only when it's gone do you realize what you had."

The coffee arrived. Both of them took it black.

"How are the kids?" Sarah asked, delaying the question she'd invited him over to answer.

"Youngest started at university this week. Strange feeling, the empty nest. Makes you wonder why you go home at the end of the day."

That was enough small talk. They only had ten minutes before her next appointment.

"I wanted to clear up a loose end or two."

"Of course," Eric said. "I looked into that matter for you. I checked out your friend as well, Nicholas Cane."

"I didn't ask you to . . ."

Eric shrugged. "I put my neck on the line where he was concerned. I wanted to make sure I hadn't left either of us open to embarrassment. But he's living an exemplary life, as far as we can tell. Volunteers at a drugs rehabilitation drop-in centre, keeps his probation appointments, hasn't done any more illicit cab driving."

"I'm glad to hear it," Sarah said. "We've not spoken."

"Who knows, in time, you might be able to use him as a consultant," Eric said. Seeing that he'd got her attention, he went on. "I hear rumours. Downgrading cannabis from Class B to Class C, virtually decriminalising the stuff. Any truth in that?"

"Not my department," Sarah said.

"Be a good thing, if you want my opinion. The laws at the moment, we make outlaws out of the middle-class punters we need on our side, make youngsters think that if we've got cannabis wrong, we're probably wrong about the hard drugs, too. And we're not."

"I agree."

"Cane, he wasn't just growing the stuff, you know. He was a cocaine dealer."

"Really?" Sarah thought it best to affect ignorance, even though Nick had told her about the coke.

"Not big-time, but it made his sentence a lot heavier."

"How did you catch him?" Sarah asked, remembering the bitter hints that Nick had given. He even suspected his own brother. "Nosy neighbour smelt something?"

Eric shook his head. "Same as the way we caught him driving illegally. Anonymous tip-off."

"How anonymous?" Sarah asked, her heartbeat accelerating.

"Not very. We traced the call to his brother's home."

"His brother told you about the dope growing?"

"No, it was a woman's voice on the phone. Some kind of family trouble, it's often the way. You rarely get to the bottom of it."

Sarah had never met Nick's sister-in-law, a teacher with a little baby. She wondered why the woman had it in for him.

"That's interesting to know," she told Eric. "What about the thing I asked you to check for me: Ed Clark. Has he resurfaced yet?"

"No, but he's on an Interpol watch-list. I've talked to them. Clark's bought a place in St Lucia, is setting up some kind of property business there. Nineteen-year-old girlfriend, place on the beach. Sounds like paradise to me. How did we end up in such mundane jobs?"

Sarah didn't answer this. She liked, no, *loved* her job. Whereas Eric was brushing fifty. In the police, that was retirement age. No wonder he was jaded.

"We'll never find out, will we, what really happened that afternoon?"

320

"Probably not. You get used to that in my line of work. But if anything does crop up, I'll let you know."

"Thanks."

"Want me to keep tabs on Cane, too, update you as and when . . . ?"

"I don't think so, Eric. He's entitled to a private life."

Sarah stood up and Eric followed suit.

"Talking of private lives," he said, "there's a weekend get-together coming up — the police committee and one or two interested parties. Hambleton Hall, do you know it? Lovely hotel on the edge of Rutland Water. Michelin Star chef. We could really use your input on a couple of matters. Not too heavy an agenda, mind. Plenty of time for relaxation."

There it was, the *quid pro quo*.

"I should be able to manage it," Sarah said. "Fax me the details and I'll run it past my diary secretary."

Eric gave her his most suave smile and kissed her on the cheek. When he was gone, Sarah poured herself a glass of water and tried to collect her thoughts. She was about to meet the press officer of the Prison Governors' Association to coordinate her tour of the UK's most improved jails, but she had other things on her mind. She couldn't, she decided, betray Caroline Cane. Telling Nick would solve a mystery for him, but it would poison his relations with his sister-in-law. And Sarah was still Nick's friend. Friends didn't get involved with each other's family feuds, not if they wanted to stay friends. As for Ed Clark, the guilty went free all the time. So, he was living a life of luxury. So what? Get over it.

The phone rang, announcing the arrival of her next appointment.

Nick didn't see Polly for five months. Then, one October night, he happened upon her in the Lion. She had more slap on than she used to. The mate she was with had pulled and Polly was adrift. It would have been churlish of Nick not to buy her a drink. Polly looked wary, but accepted the offer. She bought the second. After two more rounds she let him walk her home. Nick figured she'd already drunk enough to talk openly, but he produced a quarter-bottle of scotch anyway.

"Have you heard from him?" Nick asked, when she'd sent the babysitter home.

"Ed? Not even a card. He got what he wanted from me."

"How do you mean?"

"He wanted to prove he could get me back, after being inside. Me being with him stopped people thinking he was guilty, saying he only got out on a technicality. He was always going to piss off when the compensation came through."

"But you dumped me for him."

"I didn't dump you," Polly reminded him. "I tried to, but I couldn't. Then you walked in on me with him so I couldn't stay with you."

"You mean you'd have kept seeing me if I hadn't found out?" Nick asked this gently, without recrimination in his voice.

"Ed didn't know about you at first. I wanted you, not him." She gave a hard frown. "Turned out you were knocking about with Sarah Bone anyroad."

"Sarah wasn't after me," Nick said. "Not really."

"Happen she wanted to prove she could still have you, same as Ed with me. If Ed sets his mind on something, he gets it. Is she the same?"

"I suppose so," Nick said.

He'd glimpsed Sarah in town one day, heading past the Royal Concert Hall to the Labour Party offices on Talbot Street. Despite the summer heat, she wore a tailored trouser suit. She'd had her hair restyled, cut a little shorter. He saw then that nothing could resume between them. Sarah lived on a different planet from him. He'd been chasing the ghost of a relationship.

Polly kissed him and he kissed her back.

"It was always you I wanted," she told him. "Why don't you get in bed while I check on the kids?"

He'd not meant to sleep with her, but would do whatever it took to get what he wanted. And the sex, ten minutes later, was good. Sex with Polly was always good. Over too quickly, but that was because it was so intense, for both of them: a visceral, animal pleasure. Afterwards, she found it easier to talk. That was what he was banking on. They cuddled.

"Why couldn't you say no to Ed? Would he have hurt you?"

"Not in the way you mean."

"Explain."

"Listen to him: *explain*. There's always the schoolteacher in you."

"Sorry." He waited for her to explain anyway.

"I did a stupid thing and Ed knew about it. He could have got me into trouble."

"What was it?"

"You don't want to know."

"I think I've guessed already."

"You can't have," she muttered, head turned away from him.

"You want to tell me," he insisted. "You have to tell someone. It can't be right that only Ed knows. It gives him too much power over you."

If he was wrong about what had happened, she would ask him what he meant. But she didn't. Nick waited, nuzzling her chest, listening to her heartbeat speed up and slow down. When she began, her voice was little more than a whisper.

"Me and Ed, it started out as a bit of fun. I'd married Phil too young, never been with another bloke and there I was all of a sudden, stuck at home with two kids. Ed chased me, spent money on me. I was flattered, but it weren't meant to go anywhere. We'd have finished in a month or two if Ed hadn't got arrested. Then, when Ed got out of prison, first time, he came round, wanted to start up again. I didn't want to know. Until Ed told me how Terry had bugged my bedroom. That was how he got caught."

She paused, collecting herself. When she started again, her voice was louder, colder. "I had no idea. That my own brother could . . . I went straight round there. Terry didn't deny it. He said we both got what we deserved: Ed in prison, me — separated, halfway to being divorced. That's when I hit him. Terry hit me back."

"It was self-defence."

"Yeah. Terry were too strong for me. He pushed me away, would have hit me again if I'd given him chance. I picked up the nearest thing I could reach. A golf trophy. The base were made of slate."

Polly stopped, leaving him to fill in the blanks. She had killed her own brother. How did you deal with that? On the drive to the airport, Ed had warned him, only Nick had lacked the imagination to understand. It had taken him months to figure out what Ed was getting at.

"How many times did you hit him?" he asked.

"Once was enough. When he fell, I could tell how bad it was. An ambulance would've done no good. And he weren't just my brother, he were a policeman. I should've called the ambulance anyway, but I was terrified. I did the only thing I could think of. I called Ed. And he sorted it. Said he'd throw the golf trophy in the Trent for me, then told me to go home, make sure I wasn't seen. I thought he were going to make it look like a robbery gone wrong. I didn't know Terry had a gun. It was unregistered, hidden under the bed. Police reckon he bought it in case of a revenge attack. I told Ed what time Liv got home from work so he'd be gone by then. I had no idea what he was going to do to her. He found the gun while he was waiting."

Nick could guess the rest, but she kept talking.

"Ed decided to make it look like she'd shot him, then herself. He shot Terry where I'd hit his head, which confused the police. Only when Liv came in, Ed must have liked what he saw. He couldn't resist raping her first. And that made him careless. He left traces. When he rang up, he boasted that what he'd done made me even safer. I was so ashamed. He was far worse than I thought he was. But he was right. The police didn't suspect me at all, didn't even check I really was at home with the kids when it happened. They wanted Ed. And the alibi he'd set up for himself had holes in it."

"The police knew you'd had an affair with him?"

"Far as they were concerned, that was long over. And I didn't have any more contact with Ed after the shooting. One call from a box, that were it. He didn't bring me into his story at trial. He'd have got as bad a sentence for one murder as two, so there were no point. But he knew he owned me. I thought that was all right, because he was safely inside. I played the grieved sister, wanting to make sure he stayed there. It weren't an act. I hated him."

She went quiet.

"Only then his appeal was successful," Nick prompted.

"Once he were out, I shouted all the louder about him being released. I thought it'd help keep Ed away from me. I didn't realize he was worried about not getting his compensation, the money he wanted to start a new life with. So he turned up one day, told me I had to play happy families or he'd land me in it. I had no alibi for the murder. The police never thought I was a suspect, but once Ed testified, they could have me. Especially if he still had the trophy I killed Terry with.

326

According to him, he never threw it away. It was well hid. He could've cleared himself any time."

"Except that he raped and killed Liv."

"Once he was freed, that didn't matter. He'd already been tried. They couldn't do him again. But they could do me. When he turned up, made his threats, I had to sleep with him, to stop him telling. When you found out, I had to let you think . . . what you thought. I didn't want to. I wanted him gone. And now he is."

Nick let his head slip from her breast. She didn't seem to notice. He lay staring at the dark ceiling.

"It's a relief to say it out loud," she said, nuzzling him, then added, in a whisper, "You won't tell, will you?"

"I won't tell," Nick said.

She went quiet. He'd got what he'd come for. Time to go.

"I'm sorry you've had to live with that," he said, preparing his exit. "No one to share it with. Beating yourself up."

No reply. She was already asleep, her chest rising and falling against his. Nick couldn't get out of bed without waking her.

He waited for her to shift in her sleep. He was anxious to find a phone, tell Sarah the truth. Only what would be the point? The truth wouldn't change anything. He'd be betraying a confidence in order to satisfy Sarah's curiosity. Maybe truth was never the point. Most days he thought there was no point to anything.

Beside him, Polly snored softly. She always slept heavily, no matter what was going on. He must get her to teach him the trick. It never ceased to surprise Nick, the things some people could learn to live with.

And without.

Also available in ISIS Large Print:

Blitz

Ken Bruen

Detective Sergeant Brant is tough and uncompromising, as sleazy and ruthless as the villains he's out to get. His violent methods may be questionable, but he always gets results.

A psychopath has started a killing spree across London. Calling himself "The Blitz", his weapon of choice is a workman's hammer. And his victims are all cops.

The police squad are desperate to catch the killer before he catches up with them. And Brant is top of his list . . .

ISBN 978-0-7531-8916-0 (hb)
ISBN 978-0-7531-8917-7 (pb)

The Hanging Shed

Gordon Ferris

Glasgow 1946. The last time Brodie came home he was a proud young man in uniform. Now Brodie's back in Scotland to try and save childhood friend Shug Donovan from the gallows. Everyone thought Donovan was dead, shot down in the war. The man who eventually returns is horribly burned, only venturing out for heroin to deaden his pain. When a local boy is found raped and murdered, there is only one suspect, but Donovan claims he's innocent.

Ex-policeman Brodie feels compelled to help him. Working with advocate Samantha Campbell, Brodie finds an unholy alliance of troublesome priests, corrupt coppers and Glasgow's deadliest razor gang. As time runs out for Donovan, the murder tally of innocents starts to climb. When Sam Campbell disappears, it's the last straw for Brodie . . .

ISBN 978-0-7531-8902-3 (hb)
ISBN 978-0-7531-8903-0 (pb)